THE SINGING STONES

Dolores Ashcroft-Nowicki

Twin Eagles Publishing
2009

Library and Archives Canada Cataloguing in Publication

Ashcroft-Nowicki, Dolores
  The singing stones / Dolores Ashcroft-Nowicki

ISBN 978-1-896238-08-1

   1. Title.

PR6101.S53S54 2009 823'.92   C2009-903550-2

TWIN EAGLES PUBLISHING

Box 2031
Sechelt BC
V0N 3A0
pblakey@telus.net
604 885 7503

www.twineaglespublishing.webs.com

ACKNOWLEDGEMENTS

My thanks first go to my grandson Thomas William Ashcroft-Nowicki, whose suggestion that I write a book for him began the whole adventure.

Herbie and Jackie Brennan whose encouragement, enthusiasm, and energy have spurred me on.

My husband Michael, who never complains when I 'disappear' to write a book.

Peter Bengtson who wrote the music that opens the King's Chamber and was able to write down the tune for the School Hymn after I had sent him a very badly sung tape of what I wanted. Thank you Peter.

Debbie Chapnick without whose expertise my haphazard manuscript would never have seen the light of day.

Paul Blakey of Twin Eagles Publishing who has made my dream of writing fiction come true.

Tony Clark for his exquisite illustrations that have so enhanced the whole book and for his patience when I kept sending them back and asking for changes.

lyonedes@hotmail.co.uk

To Willie Rowbotham and Odyssey, Adventures in Archaeology, for permission to use the stunning cover photo.

www.odysseyadventures.ca

Lastly my thanks go to the characters themselves who told me the whole story, corrected me when I went off track and celebrated with me at the end by asking when I was going to begin writing the sequel!!

DEDICATION

This book is for my grandson
Thomas William Ashcroft-Nowicki,
who was, and is, the prototype
Thomas Greystone.

With all my love
Babciu.

Jersey, 2004 - 2009

THE BOOK SPELL

Earth and water, fire and air
this I do and this I dare.
Through these words I offer you
A window clear to gaze into.
A world of dreams surrounds us all.
But will you dare to heed its call?
For Magic is a simple thing
a word, a thought, a golden ring.
Within this world and by my power
You may spend a magic hour.
Read and listen, memorize.
Open wide your human eyes.
You will see the past appear.
Long forgotten, always near.
If I can give you power to see
then as I will so mote it be.

ONE

Thomas *screamed, and the woman's long black hair whipped around her head as she raised the spear. His heart pounded as he threw up his hands in a useless gesture of defense, his body already reacting to the pain of the imagined thrust. Suddenly a coal black horse broke through the melee and reared skywards, its hooves slashing at the air within inches of his head. Then a black shield emblazoned with a snarling bear's head curved over him and he heard the thud of the spearhead as it hit the tempered metal. Around him he could hear the noise of battle and the screams of horses and men as they fought with a strength born of desperation. But over it all he heard the voice of the owner of the shield.*

"Beware young Thomas, my mother has a long memory and you have thwarted her once too often." His saviour, clothed from head to foot in black armour grinned down at him from the saddle, then wheeled his horse back into the thick of the fighting. Crouching down amid the mud, blood and bodies of both horses

and men Thomas tried to make sense of what was happening.

He knew it was a dream, it was always the same dream and always the same man in black armour was there. He knew him in a dreamlike way, but then again, he didn't. It was as if he was remembering something that had happened a long time ago. But at the same time it was something that was always happening, or maybe it was going to happen. He had to get out of the dream, he had to get out, now!

"Get out, I must get out, let me out … please …! I must wake up, must wake…!"

"Thomas, Tom, wake up, wake up, it's alright, I'm here lad, dad's here, everything going to be alright." There were arms around him, strong safe arms, and a soothing voice in his ear. Slowly Thomas opened his eyes and looked up at his father sitting on the side of his bed his arms locked around the shaking boy.

"There, that's better, just take some deep breaths Tombo, you're perfectly safe. Here's mum with some hot milk and an aspirin, drink it down lad." Still bemused Thomas sat up and took the milk and the aspirin. He looked at his father over the rim of the glass.

"It was the same dream dad, it's always the same and I know the man, I just can't remember his name, or why he's helping me. I just know I have to wake up. It's getting closer somehow, as if it's already happened but it's going to happen again, I know it is."

"Sounds like the plot of one of my books." His father smiled and ruffled his hair. "Now do you think you can get to sleep again. Or would you like me to stay with you for a while?" Thomas shook his head.

"No, it never comes twice on the same night, I'll be alright dad, I'm sorry I woke you. You too mum, I know you have to be up real early tomorrow." He turned his pillow over and banged it hard a few times to hide the fact that he felt a little teary.

"I just wish you didn't have to go to LA for such a long time that's all." He huddled down under the duvet. "I guess I'll get over it, 'cos I know it's important for you dad and I'm really proud of you."

His father bent over him and stroked a rebellious lock of dark blond hair back from his face. "I'm proud of you too Tom, for being so brave about it all. One day I promise you, we'll all go together, but this time it's just not possible." He paused by the door. "Sleep well lad, I love you."

Lying in the warm darkness Thomas went over the dream in his thoughts. If only he could remember the name of the man on the black horse, if only there was more to it than those few short moments. On the other hand it was scary enough without wishing for more of the same. Tomorrow his parents were leaving for America and he would be left with just Mrs. Jackson and her husband Frank for company.

Wearily he closed his eyes and slept, this time dreamlessly.

Far away in a different time and a different place a man with a long grey beard raised his eyes from the crystal ball he was studying and sighed. "As he gets closer to his fourteenth birthday the power in him becomes stronger." He looked up at the tall regal figure beside him. "The time is right Arthur. I pray that this boy will prove worthy of his ancestry, for all our sakes."

Thomas woke with a vague feeling of having been talking to someone about something important, but couldn't remember what it was. Then he remembered something else, this was the day his parents were leaving for America. He got out of bed and went over to the window.

It was raining again. Thomas sighed, it had been raining on and off the whole holiday and it was boring having to stay inside. Holidays were not supposed to be boring, they were not supposed to be rainy either.

He sighed again and headed for the bathroom. As he brushed his teeth, he saw a very ordinary boy looking back from the mirror. Dark blond hair with lighter streaks here and there, deep blue eyes, ordinary nose, and ears that stuck out just a very little bit. There was nothing at all in that reflection to suggest that within a short time his whole life would change ... forever.

He finished washing, dressed and ran downstairs to the kitchen where the smell of eggs, bacon and mushrooms filled the air. His parents were already halfway through their breakfast and Mrs. Jackson was just dishing up Thomas's when he came in.

"Mornin' Tom," she said, "Do you want a piece of fried bread with this."

"Yes please Mrs. Jackson, and some tomatoes if you have any." Betty Jackson beamed. "Coming up right away."

Stephen Greystone finished off the last of his coffee and stood up. "I'll bring the cases down," he said casting an anxious look at Thomas who bent over his breakfast and avoided his glance. "Don't hurry Thomas, we still have a bit of time and we certainly won't go without saying goodbye."

Thomas nodded and concentrated hard on not being a wimp. His mother waited until his father had gone, then leaned over to him.

"Darling, I know it's a big disappointment for you, but you can't miss school for so long, it would set you back such a long way. The time will go by quickly you'll see, we'll be back before you know it. Mrs. Jackson will look after you well and Frank will run you into school and pick you up each day. You'll be fine." She smiled and ruffled his hair, though she knew he hated it. "I'll bring you back something really nice. What would you like?"

Suddenly it was too much to bear, the parting for several months, the battle dream last night, the new school that was still strange after several terms, Thomas scowled and pushed his plate away half eaten.

"I don't want anything, I have too many things already. I just want you and dad at home and not always running off to other places. I want things to be like they were before. I wish dad had never sold that darned book."

Nora Greystone drew in a sharp breath. "Thomas, you don't mean that."

"Yes I do! I do! We were really happy before. We joked about what we'd do when it happened, but when it did, it wasn't like it was supposed to be. You're never here, dad is never home, I hate this new school and I miss ... I miss grandma. We don't seem to be a family anymore." He turned and ran out of the kitchen up the stairs and into his room and slammed the door. It made a good 'I don't care,' kind of noise.

He sat on the bed and looked around his room. It was

much larger than the little box room he'd had in Manchester. He even had his own bathroom with a shower. The colours were bright and there were posters on the wall of Stonehenge, and Callanish Circle and a couple of posters signed by film stars, that his dad had brought back from his last trip to America. He had a desk with a real office chair like his dads.

He had a TV he could watch from his bed and a computer that was the envy of all his friends, his dad had given him his old Apple Mac when he got his new one. Everything he had dreamed about having was here, so why wasn't he happy?

He got up and went to the window. Outside it was foggy, cold, and wet and the roads gleamed in the headlights of passing cars. Having what you want was not as wonderful as he had thought it would be.

Maybe it was because he wanted the wrong things, if so what did he really want? Staring out of the window he thought about it.

He wanted to sit in front of the fire on a Friday night and watch a creepy film with Mum and Dad on either side of him. He wanted to go to the cinema on Dodd Street on Saturday afternoon and watch old cowboy films. He wanted to sit in the musty reference room of the library and pore over books on ancient times, reading about Merlin and Arthur and Raleigh and Drake. To come home to tea and toasted crumpets loaded with butter and strawberry jam. That's what he wanted, what he felt was confused, lonely and let down by the whole world. And it had all begun with his dad's book.

Two years ago they had lived in a top floor flat in Manchester and he had gone to a school just down the road. His mum worked in a bank and his dad wrote books. He didn't sell very many, but mum always said that one day he would write a really great book and they would go to live in a big house in the country. It was a dream they all shared. Dad would have a study looking out on to the garden, mum would give up work and Thomas would have a big bedroom with a computer and his own television. Oh, and a mountain bike, so he could do what he really liked doing, exploring old ruins, houses, ancient woods, and stone circles. They used to talk about it all the time telling each other all the things that would happen when dad wrote THE BOOK. But they didn't really believe it would happen. Then, one day it did.

Suddenly money wasn't a problem any more. Dad came home with a brand new car; he threw out his scruffy jeans and bought suits and handmade shirts. He was interviewed on television and had write ups in the Sunday magazines, with his face on the covers. Important people kept saying what a wonderful writer he was and presenting him with prizes, which were usually cheques for large amounts. Mum bought lots of new clothes and had her hair dyed. Thomas got the promised computer and a TV for his bedroom and they moved to a house in the Derbyshire Dales in the village where his grandma had lived when she was young. Then the book was made into a film and won an Oscar and things really went crazy. The Dream had come true with a vengeance.

His father's voice broke in to his reverie. "Thomas, come on lad, it's time for us to go."

"Coming, I'm coming." He ran down the stairs and flung himself into his father's arms holding him tight. Stephen held his son close and tried to find words of comfort. But they stayed unspoken and Thomas went to his mother and hugged her.

"I hope … I really hope you have a nice time, and don't worry about me I'm going to explore while you're away. See all those places Grandma talked about and I'll try to do really well at school and make you proud of me." Steven bent down to give him a final hug.

"I'm always proud of you Tom lad, no matter what happens, you know that." Thomas nodded, willing back the sissy tears that threatened and smiled broadly. "I expect a letter every single week dad, promise?"

"Promise."

They hurried into the waiting taxi and waved goodbye, but Thomas had already gone back into the house, unwilling to watch them out of sight. Mrs. Jackson and her husband followed slowly.

"'E's takin' it bad old girl, he be a lot closer to his dad than his mum." Frank didn't say a lot, but he noticed things and he was fond of Thomas. His wife was more practical.

"He'll be alright once he gets back to school, besides there's a lot going on in the village at the moment…" She stopped suddenly giving her husband a sidelong glance, but he was back with his paper again. She tightened her lips and shook her head and went back to clearing away the breakfast things.

Upstairs Thomas tried to shake off his gloom, it was half term and he'd hoped to do some exploring while his parents were away, but so far it had done nothing but rain. He wandered over to the window, it was still dull outside, but a small ray of sunshine was struggling to make it through the clouds. He looked at it hopefully. Maybe he could go out on his new bike after all. It had been delivered a few days ago and had lots of gears and attachments including a place for a water bottle on the handlebars and he was eager to try it out on the country roads. With a new burst of energy he began to get things ready.

He unearthed an old backpack and set about filling it with things he'd need, binoculars, a compass and a map. Dad had some in his desk. Halfway down the stairs he remembered his camera and went back for it. It took great photos and his dad had shown him how to transfer them to his computer. He hit the kitchen like a whirlwind.

"Mrs. Jackson, I'm going out on my bike, it's clearing up a bit. Can I have some sandwiches, please. Cheese and sausage and pickle too if you have some, Oh, and a tomato." She laughed and set about gathering it all together. Thomas grabbed a bottle of water from the fridge, keeping one eye on the weather. Yes, it was getting clearer every minute.

Mrs. Jackson tucked a rosy apple in with the sandwiches amused at his eagerness to be up and gone. She had been cleaning for the Greystones for almost a year now and always looked after him when his parents were away, which was often. Shame he was an only child she thought, he could do with some company he was too much on his own.

"Now Tom," she chided, "Remember to take a warm jacket. It gets powerful cold up on the hills. Not too late mind, be home before six, I don't want to be fretting over you."

Thomas struggled into his anorak. "Yes Mrs. Jackson, I'll

try to be back by four thirty." He zipped up his jacket then paused and looked up at her. " Mrs. Jackson, you've always lived around here haven't you?"

"Aye, all my life thereabouts," she said, wiping her hands on her apron. " I know it like the back of my hand, none better,"

" Then can you tell me where I might find some interesting places to go, I mean really interesting. You know like old ruins, caves, stone circles, Standing Stones and things like that?"

Mrs. Jackson leaned against the sink folded her arms over an ample bosom and regarded the thirteen year old with a curious look in her eyes. " What would a young lad like you be wanting with the old ways?" she asked quietly. "That's for those Arkywhatsits, it's dangerous to go wandering around places like that unless you know what you're doing," She paused as if reluctant to say more then went on.

"Of course there's The Singing Stones, but that's a fair ride. Best you try Old Friar's Folly, that's nearer. And then there's Misselthwaite Manor, nothings been done to that place for twenty years or more, and its got more than its share of nooks and crannies. As for caves, there's plenty o' them up on Toothill moor, but if its stories you're after, you need to find Bald Bessie. She knows all there is to know about these places. But she won't talk to just anyone. Half daft she is, though they do say she's worth a mint o' money. A real balmpot is Bessie. These places are all on the map. You can't get lost." She turned away to open the dishwasher.

"The Singing Stones," whispered Thomas, "what a marvellous name. How can I find them Mrs. Jackson. Can you show me on the map?"

Mrs. Jackson Drew in a sharp breath and stopped stacking the dishes. She turned round sharply and shook a finger at him. "No lad, I can't and you'd best not to try and find them. They might just sing you under the ground, like the legend says. They do say them Stones move from place to place, and never have been able to put them on a map accurate like. Only those who are called by the Stones can find them. I've heard tell they only appear at certain times of the year, the old festival times. But decent people don't hold with such things now." She paused, as if aware that she was making things sound more exciting than she should. "You'd best be going lad; Friar's Folly is better than an hour away. Don't stand there like a stale bun in a shop window, get going, I'll not have you under my feet all day, so off with you."

She sounded almost cross, but Thomas was determined. "Well where can I find out about the Singing Stones? Is there a book about them or someone who would know?"

The woman turned to face him. "Look lad, forget I ever told you about them cursed Stones. Promise me you'll not go looking for them," her voice changed again, almost pleading. "Promise me Thomas or I'll have it on my conscience all day."

Thomas stared at her and shivered at the intensity of her words. "Alright Mrs. Jackson, I promise I won't go looking for them, and I'll be back by four thirty or thereabouts." He grabbed his backpack and slung it over his shoulder making for the back door and the bicycle shed. "Thanks for the sandwiches." And he was gone.

Alone Mrs. Jackson sat down at the kitchen table and

berated her runaway tongue. Why had she mentioned the Stones? The lad was bound to come across some idiot who would tell him more. Well, what was done was done. He was a sensible lad, almost too grown up for his age at times. An only child was often like that. He looked a lot like his grandmother, with fine flyaway hair and eyes the colour of cornflowers, and like her he was stronger than he looked. God willing he'd not take after her in darker ways. She got up and began cleaning the kitchen energetically as if to banish her thoughts. But they remained at the back of her mind all through the day.

The rain had washed everything clean and the March winds had swept the clouds out of the valley and up onto the high moors. For the first time since he had come to live in Deepdale Thomas felt happy. With the wind behind him he raced through the village and out on to the winding road that led to places with strange names, like Shipton-under-Tor, Gigglestown and Barmby-by-Willows.

He took his time and savoured the feeling of freedom. He didn't really dislike school, but it got in the way of things he wanted to do. He enjoyed listening to tales of druids and witches and the strange things that happen to ordinary people in out of the way places like the Derbyshire Dales. On the other hand, Old Friar's Folly was a disappointment when he got to it, just two mouldering ivy covered walls, some fallen masonry, and nothing more. He spent just half an hour there before setting off for the next stop, Misselthwaite Manor. He remembered reading that 'missel' was an old name for a thrush and made a mental note to look up the meaning of Thwaite when he got back.

He'd thought the Manor might be private land. But there was no 'Keep Out' notice when he arrived so he figured it was safe to explore. He slipped through a pair of rusted iron gates and leaned his bike against a tree, then turned to look at the house

It was not as large as some Manor houses and only about two hundred and fifty years old, though obviously built on a much older site. It had three stories with elegantly carved shutters on the windows, some of which had fallen askew. The grounds however were much bigger than he expected and he wandered around the overgrown gardens to his heart's content.

He found the remains of a herb plot and gathered several bunches to take home, as well as some late snowdrops for Mrs. Jackson. The house itself was locked but he peered through the dirty windows at the back but saw only a few pieces of old fashioned furniture and some broken crockery. Then he came round to the front to look through the main windows but again there was little to see. The heavy oak door caught his attention, it was huge and carved with what looked like acorns, holly leaves and berries. Set fairly high up was a strangely shaped door knocker badly in need of cleaning. Thomas knew what it was, he had seen it in some of his dad's books. It was a Green Man with leaves and berries coming out of the mouth and ears. It must have been made specially as he'd never seen one like it before. He bent and lifted the flap of the letterbox and looked through.

A face peered back at him. It was an old, wrinkled face with piercing blue eyes and a thatch of white hair. Thomas yelped and sprang back his heart thumping, but when nothing happened he cautiously lifted the flap again. Then laughed, embarrassed at his show of fear. Facing the front door was a large portrait of an elderly man. It was so lifelike that in the dim light it seemed real and frightening. Now he looked again seeing it for what it was. Behind the figure, a landscape showed a ring of tall stones with a full moon rising above them.

Thomas drew back from the door. Perhaps the stones in the painting were the Singing Stones Mrs. Jackson had spoken about. After all, if what she said was true they should be somewhere around here. Then he remembered that he'd given his word not to look for them. He looked at his watch: it was nearly half past one. He'd left the house just after nine and had done about twenty miles. He should think about turning for home, but not until he had found a place to eat lunch.

He walked down the weed covered drive to where he left the bike and stopped to look back. The house seemed sad and rather lonely, as if it had hoped he would stay a little longer. He found himself making a silent promise that he would come back. Then he slipped through the gates and rode off.

A few miles further on he came to a steep hill and got off, partly to stretch his legs and partly because it looked too steep to peddle up with any degree of comfort. At the top he stopped and looked round him feeling a deep sense of belonging to this wild country. Mile upon mile of moorland lay before him, one side rising up to a steep limestone cliff, the other gradually dropping down in a series of gullies towards the distant ribbon of the Pennine Way. He guessed he was on what was known as The Spine of England, a place of legend and a haunt of the old ways since long before the Romans had walked the land. His ancestors had lived in this area for almost a thousand years, maybe more. It made him feel as if he had come home.

He found a spot out of the wind with a great view down the valley and opened his backpack. It was a good place to have lunch and Mrs. Jackson had done him proud. He sat looking out over the hills his grandma had loved so much, remembering her brought back memories and he told himself it was the wind that made his eyes water.

He sank his teeth into a satisfyingly thick sandwich. It was a favourite he and his father shared. A real man's sandwich his dad called it made from farmhouse bread, spread with butter right to the edge then covered with home cured ham, or cold sausages sliced long ways and decorated with pickle. The final touch being slices of Red Leicester cheese. Add a firm ripe tomato and both of them were as happy pigs in clover, his grandma used to say.

Thomas thought about his grandma as he chewed. Her death almost two years ago had been a bad time for him. She had lived the last three years of her life in an old people's home because there was no room for her in their small flat. She used to sit and look out of the window of her tiny room to a distant view of the hills with longing in her eyes. She had never been happy away from her beloved dales.

Thomas had visited her twice a week without fail, sitting and listening to her stories of when she was young. It was from her he learned to love the old places, ways and customs of the Dales. When his father's book had begun to sell they had tried to get her to move to a much nicer place, but she said she was used to this one and it would be a waste of money. But Thomas thought it was because she was too tired to make the effort. He missed her very much.

When he'd finished his second sandwich he reached inside his shirt to draw out a silver chain on which hung a small sphere of some strange substance that swirled with different colours. His grandma had given it to him a few days before she died.

"Keep it safe Thomas, it's important that you never take it off. One day you'll understand why I gave it to you and not to your father. I told him I meant to give it to you, and he knows why. I love you very much Thomas lad, I'll be looking out for you, so don't forget me."

When he saw her next she was lying in her coffin. She looked very peaceful and had a slight smile on her face. His mother had not wanted him to see her, but Thomas had in-sisted. "I'm not afraid, its only grandma and she loved me, I want to say goodbye to her. And he had, leaning close to whisper as if she could still hear him. "I love you grandma, lots and lots. I've got the little sphere you gave me, I wear it, and I always will. I hope it's nice in Heaven, like the Dales."

He sat silent, looking out over the hills she had loved so much, and remembering blamed the wind again for his tears. Then he tucked the sphere back under his clothes and went to get his bike. The wind had picked up and it was much colder than before and there were rain clouds gathering on the hills. It got dark more quickly here than in the city where there were streetlights. He bent to the pedals and pushed hard.

The road ahead twisted and turned and he began to feel

worried when, after half an hour of riding he saw no sign of a village, or even a farmhouse. He stopped to look at his map. There was little in the way of landmarks, it all looked the same, but he was certain he had taken a wrong turning somewhere. He might be only thirteen but he knew the dangers of being alone on the moors at night. It was now half past three and he had promised to be back by four thirty Mrs. Jackson would be worried.

He had ridden a couple of miles when he saw someone coming towards him. It was an old woman with a thick shawl wrapped around her head and dressed in layer upon layer of assorted clothing, thick knitted stockings and what looked like several sweaters. She was pushing a rusty supermarket trolley filled with assorted plastic bags full of odds and ends. At her side padded a skinny Jack Russell terrier.

Thomas thought it might scare her being suddenly faced with a stranger in a lonely place, so he waited for her to come closer. As she came up to him she stopped and peered at him with watery eyes. Her shawl slipped back and he saw she had almost no hair. Bald Bessie, the recluse who lived in a cave up on the moors in the spring and summer and only came down when the cold weather came on.

She eyed Thomas with more curiosity than fear then spoke in a harsh raspy voice.

"Thee'll be Jennet Carrick's grandson. I heerd as 'ow her son'd coom back. Thee looks like 'er. What's tha' doin' up 'ere lad. T'is getting dusk tha' knows. The Moors be dangerous at night. Best be off 'ome." She wiped her eyes on a scrap of cotton as grey as the few hairs she had left. Thomas touched the brim of his baseball cap and the woman's eyes gleamed with approval at the old fashioned gesture of respect.

"I'm afraid I've taken a wrong turning and missed the way ma'am. Could you direct me towards Deepdale please?"

Bessie leaned on her cart and the Jack Russell sat down on the grass to scratch.. "Happen I could seein' as 'ow yer dad taught you yer manners. I don't usually get a polite word or called ma'am. Now then, ride on fer about two mile and yer'll see t'crossroads. Tak' the one on yer left past the owd gibbet and the road'll tak' thee ter Barmsby. Yer can find yer way from there. Next time, watch fer the starlings, they allus roost in the yew trees in Barmsby church come dusk, follow 'em home and yer'll be alreet."

Thomas grinned happily. "Thank you ma'am," he rummaged in his pocket and brought out the uneaten apple and offered it to her. "Something in return for your help." He leaned forward to offer it and as he did the sphere dropped into view.

Bessie's eyes widened and she grasped it in a hand with dirty, broken fingernails. " 'Ow came thee by this lad?"

"It was my grandma's, she gave it to me before she died." Thomas pulled back, the old woman smelt bad.

"See tha' keeps it close, 'tis a powerful thing fer a young'un to wear." She let go the chain and snatched the apple from his hand. "Thank 'ee kindly Thomas Greystone, an apple in 'change fer knowledge, things hav'na changed much since Adam." She put it away in a hidden pocket, picked up the dog and dumped it in the trolley and without another word, trudged on.

Bemused by her words Thomas watched her for a while, then climbed on his bike and set off towards the crossroads.

It wasn't until he had past the old gibbet (pedaling a little faster and looking over his shoulder) that he remembered he'd not given her his name, yet she had called him Thomas.

It was gone four as he raced through Barmsby stopping only to call Mrs. Jackson " I'm running late, but I'm okay, be home about five-thirty." As he turned homeward he mulled over the events of the day. He was determined to find out about The Singing Stones, maybe he should have asked Bessie. He also wanted to know about the old man in the picture at the Manor. He'd bet a week's pocket money Bessie knew the answer to that as well. Mrs. Jackson might not want to talk about it, but Bessie was different. He liked her she'd be good company and he could learn a lot from her.

Shipley and Gigglestown disappeared behind him and he was on the road to home, and a hot dinner. There' d be a lot to write about in his diary tonight. He planned to look up local history on the Internet and see what he could find out about the Manor. If he was lucky he might find something about the Singing Stones at the same time.

It began to rain as he rode into the High Street and the streetlights were coming on in the houses. It looked warm and welcoming, but somehow Thomas felt here was something older, darker, and stronger under it all. He wondered if the Stones were a part of it and what Bessie knew about them and the Manor. He cycled up the lane still thinking about it.

Up on the moors Bessie sat by the fire brooding over the flames, and spoke to the dog beside her. "He is the one Grim, he has the Mage Sphere and he is a Carrick. The Stones will sing for him I'm certain of it. She had lost her rough accent and spoke with authority as if she had once been obeyed without question The dog whined and crept closer to the fire. Bessie began to chant as she rocked back and forth.

> *The Tall Stones they are sleeping as they have this thousand years,*
>
> *But their dreams are strong and wakeful and full of ancient fears,*
>
> *The men who raised them now are gone, but what they guarded then,*
>
> *Lies waiting for the destined one to make them strong again.*
>
> *Not yet a man, but not a bairn, his power will raise them up,*
>
> *And by the Shield and Sword and Rod be guided to the Cup.*
>
> *Twelve Tall Stones and one to lead, the thirteen voices they,*
>
> *Lie waiting for the lad whose name will match their colour grey.*
>
> *Then the powers now buried deep will to the surface rise,*
>
> *Awakening the twelve who rule and the one who holds the prize.*

TWO

It was dark when he got home and Mrs. Jackson was waiting at the door. Thomas put away his bike and opened the kitchen door to light, warmth and the warm smell of dinner filling the house. He was glad to sit down and be warm after the long cold ride, but curiously his appetite had deserted him and he pushed his food around his plate until the exasperated Mrs. Jackson took it away. He listened half-heartedly to her and Frank talking and thought about the weeks of loneliness ahead of him. He wondered if Bessie had chicken for dinner and baked apple with honey in the middle. Did her little dog get enough to eat? " It looked rather skinny. Maybe he could take her some little luxuries and they could talk. The idea cheered him up a little.

"May I leave the table Mrs. Jackson," he asked. "I'd like to go to my room and watch TV."

"Alright dear, I'll come up later to say goodnight." She watched him a little anxiously. " Frank and I will down here if you want anything." Thomas nodded and went up to his room to make plans for tomorrow.

Lying in bed, he went over things in his head. He'd get up early, it would be a long day so he needed to be prepared. He had already partly filled his backpack, only food and water needed to go in. The tins of dog food and biscuits for Grim and a bar of chocolate for Bessie he could buy in the village, or better still in another village altogether. On the map he had traced the route through Shipton-under-Tor and Gigglestown to the crossroads where the gibbet stood and from there to where he had met Bessie. He doubted she could walk more than a mile or two in either direction, so her cave had to be fairly near.

With the aid of the dog food and chocolate he hoped to get some information from her, at least enough to make some sense out of the bits and pieces he had so far. If he couldn't go to Hollywood with his parents, he would make his own excitement. He couldn't do much on Sunday, he had to get ready for school the next day but he could plan for the next weekend. Satisfied he'd done as much as he could Thomas turned out the light and snuggled down under the duvet.

In the driveway below his window a solitary figure stood looking up. It was wrapped in a long dark cloak with a hood drawn over its face and it watched silently for a while. Then, it lifted a hand and made a circle in the air that shone with blue-white fire, A finger pointed directly into the circle and a voice sang a low vibrant note. The centre of the circle shimmered and glowed briefly with a deep blue light and rose into the air. It floated up to Thomas's window where it paused for a moment then, silently passed through the glass and hovered over the head of the sleeping boy.

Thomas stirred restlessly and half opened his eyes. Before him glowed a brilliant circle of fire pulsing in a mesmerizing rhythm then it widened and opened and he could see into the centre of it. A hill with a flat top dipped into a hollow, as if long ago it had been the crater of a volcano. In the centre of the hollow stood a ring of tall stones that seemed to hum in deep earthy voices. Before each stone floated a sphere of light just like the one he wore. He struggled to wake up fully but his eyelids were too heavy and he slipped in to a deep sleep to dream he was talking to his grandma in the centre of the circle while around them the tall Stones sang a wordless song.

Below his window the cloaked figure waited until it was sure all was well, then lifted its hand to summon back its messenger. The circle of fire emerged from the house and floated back to the hand that had created it. The figure gave a satisfied sigh and turned away to drift down the driveway and melt into the darkness. A second later an owl soared into the night sky and flew south. But Thomas slept and dreamed with a smile on his face.

The next morning Thomas wandered down in his dressing gown to eat the fluffy scrambled eggs Mrs. Jackson had prepared for him as a treat. With his head still full of his dream Thomas could hardly wait to be off on his adventure, he had so much to do today. The rain had cleared overnight and a brisk wind had swept the low-lying clouds into the next county, it was cold but bright and Thomas planned to cover a lot of ground.

Mrs. Jackson turned to him with a cheery smile. "Well Thomas, Frank and me're going go into Stokewell today, we thought you'd like to come along and see a film. Would you like that?"

"Thank's very much Mrs. Jackson but I'm meeting with one of the boys from my school." (He crossed his fingers firmly behind his back) "We're going to Daniel Marshall's house in High Cross to go over the holiday projects for Monday. I've done mine but I'm going to help Dan with his. But thank you for asking."

"Oh." Mrs. Jackson was a little taken aback. "Well since you'll be with someone I suppose it's alright. But I'll want you back for supper mind. It'll be on the table at six. Sausages and mash and baked beans it'll be. I know that's a favourite of yours. Now do you want sandwiches? I've a nice piece of ham, or there's bacon, and I can do egg and watercress. Which is it to be … or do you want one of each?" She was well aware of a growing boy's appetite having raised three of her own.

"One of each please Mrs. Jackson, and could I have a couple of apples as well," Thomas remembered Bessie's delight at his gift of the apple.

"Aye, that you can, nothing like fruit for a growing lad. Make sure you dress warm Thomas, its gets bitter cold up in High Cross."

Thomas gave her a grin and raced upstairs to dress. Mrs. Jackson shook her head over the waywardness of boys. Yesterday he'd been devastated at the thought of not being able to go with his parents. Today you'd think he was pleased they'd gone. She got on with making the sandwiches.

Upstairs, while he showered and dressed, Thomas went over his strange dream. He thought he'd woken up and seen a sphere of something very bright in his room, at the same time he was aware that there was someone outside his window. The sphere talked to him about light, and colour, and sounds, but it was all mixed up. The one part of the dream he remembered clearly was talking to his grandma. They were standing in a stone circle that sang to them as they talked and she told him that this was where he was meant to be. He shrugged, and bent to lace up his trainers. His dreams were always a bit weird but maybe it was because he'd been thinking about the Singing Stones so much. Well, today he might get some answers.

Downstairs Wally Meakin the postman delivered a pile of letters and stopped for a cup of tea. He greeted Thomas with the news that he had a letter addressed to him. Thomas was surprised, the only time he got letters was on his birthday and Christmas. It looked very official with a name on the top left hand corner. Hawkins, Hawkins and Johnstone. Solicitors. 23/28 Oldham St West. Manchester. Thomas turned it over in his hand and looked at it. A strange feeling came over him and he knew without a doubt that it concerned his grandma. Watched eagerly by Mrs. Jackson and Wally he opened it. Its message was short and terse and informed him that he was to get in touch with the above persons at his earliest convenience, when he would receive some news greatly to his advantage. It was signed;

Bernard. H. Johnstone Esq.

Thomas looked up at his interested audience, and handed the letter over to Mrs. Jackson. "What do I do about this?" he asked her. "Dad's away and I think it's important, something to do with grandmas will, but I don't know why it was addressed to me."

Mrs. Jackson looked thoughtful. This was unplanned and she didn't like the feel of the letter. In her opinion it boded no good for the way she had been instructed to proceed. She thought for a minute and then reached for the phone. I'll call your dad and ask him." But there was no answer. "Well," she said pouring another cup of tea. "Solicitors don't work on Saturday, so we'll wait until Monday then I'll ring Mr. Johnstone and tell him your Dad's in America and they'll have to wait."

"But what if its very important?" asked Thomas.

"It says that it's 'news to your advantage' that means it's good news and good news can keep without going sour," said Mrs. Jackson confidently. " We'll wait until your Dad phones. He said he would as soon as they got settled. We'll tell him then and see what he says. If need be Frank and I'll take you to Manchester and see what it's all about. Now lad, there's your sandwiches and apples. See you're back before 6 o'clock, now off you go." She sounded glad to be rid of him.

Thomas cheered up at the thought of a whole day doing what he'd planned and went off to get his bike. Mrs. Jackson turned to the postman and asked curiously. " What do you think Wally is the letter important ?" The postman looked after Thomas with a thoughtful look in his eyes. He had a feeling that it was indeed very important, and not just to Thomas.

Mrs. Jackson went on. "I think things are beginning to wake up Wally Meakin, Old things, and when that happens people get hurt. That young lad is from an old bloodline and it's beginning to show itself. I'll lay six fresh eggs to my best hat he's not going to a friends house at all. He's off hunting for something." Wally shook his head, finished his tea and filed the information away for his own use, and left.

Thomas felt bad about lying to Mrs. Jackson but he knew she would not approve of him seeing Bald Bessie. But he had remembered something from his dream conversation with his grandma. "Place no faith in Bettina Jackson," she'd said.

He whistled cheerfully as he spun through the village and past the little church with its old Yew trees and ancient Bell tower. As he passed the post office a group of women on the corner watched him with curious eyes.

"That'll be Jennet Carricks' grandson I dare say," said Annie Heywood thoughtfully.

"Betty Jackson was saying t'other day as 'ow 'e has his gran's leanings. He asked about them Singing Stones up on t'moor, wanting ter know where to find 'em. No good'll come of it, that's fer sure." Mumbled Granny Salter.

" 'Ere's Betty now," said the third woman and they made room for the newcomer.

"Well now," said Bettina Jackson, full of her news. "Wally Meakin just brought the post and there was a solicitors letter for the lad, from Manchester. It said he would hear something to his advantage. Now what do you think of that. It comes to my mind it'll be about the Manor and old man Carrick." The women nodded to each other in agreement and began walking towards the local tearoom to continue their conversation.

Thomas reached Shipton-under-Tor in good time and stopped at the little grocery store to buy dog food and chocolate. On impulse he added a packet of biscuits and a small jar of honey and stuffed it into his backpack along with a Mars bar to chew on as he rode on towards the moors. The weather was holding well and with luck he should be at the spot where he met Bessie by half past twelve or thereabouts. Of course, then he had to find her cave. He stopped a few times to check out the road on his map and as he came up to the old gibbet decided to stop for a breather.

He put the bike down by the side of the road and walked over to the gibbet and stood wondering when it had last been used and who had been the unfortunate victim. He shivered and was about to turn away when a cold wet nose pushed against his hand. He jerked his hand away and looked down. Bessie's terrier stood by his side looking up at him, then it sat back on its haunches and offered a paw.

Charmed by the welcome, Thomas bent down and shook it, then walked over to his bike and took a dog biscuit from his pack and offered it. The dog took it very gently and put it down on the grass, then it barked twice, ran a few paces along the road barked again and returned to Thomas, and the biscuit.

"Do you want me to follow you?" asked Thomas. The dog barked again.

"Okay, I suppose your mistress sent you, so lets go." He shouldered his pack and got on his bike. The dog picked up the biscuit and ran ahead with Thomas following. They took the next turning and began to climb the hill. After a while Thomas got off and pushed the bike. Finally he stopped.

"Its alright for you," he told the terrier who sat down beside him with the biscuit firmly in its mouth. He took a swig of water. "You've got four legs and a lot less to carry. I hope its not much further."

" Well if an owd woman like me can do it, I'm sure a young 'un like you can make it," said a raspy voice above him.

Thomas sprang up and turned. Bessie leaned on a stout walking stick and regarded him with bright blue eyes. I watched thee from the top of the Tor and sent Grim down to show thee the way. Come on, I've a brew of tea waitin' fer thee." She turned and led the way along an almost invisible track.

"What about my bike?" Thomas asked. "I don't want to leave it by the road"

"Thee can leave it 'unner the gorse bush, 'tis thick enough to hide it." Said Bessie over her shoulder.

Thomas heaved the bike up a few yards and put it under a bank of gorse where it was hidden from the road, then followed the old woman. The track wound from side to side and in some places was totally overgrown. But in fifteen minutes they had come to an overhang of limestone covered with thick branches of gorse and scrub. Pushing them aside with her stick Bessie led the way into the cave behind. Grimm made for a nest of dried grass and leaves and settled down to enjoy his biscuit. Thomas stood and looked around entranced.

One wall and the roof of the cave were covered with

prehistoric paintings like the ones he had seen in books. He knew they must be thousands of years old. The unpainted walls were covered with old pieces of threadbare carpet salvaged from skips and empty houses. The floor had a thick coating of grass and rushes and in the centre was a fire pit filled with a cheerful blaze of logs on which was balanced an old cast iron kettle, singing gently to itself.

"This is wonderful its like a little palace in here. These paintings are very old, if people knew they were here they would be queuing up to see them."

"Which is why I don't tell anyone about 'em," chuckled Bessie, taking the kettle off the fire. She set a piece of bread on the end of a pointed stick and put it to toast before the flames, then poured the hot water into a cracked brown teapot along with several pinches of black tea and set it on a stone near the fire to brew. Thomas remembered his groceries and took them out of the backpack and offered them to his strange hostess.

"I thought you might like these," he said diffidently. "I didn't know what you would need so there's chocolate and I've got two apples and some biscuits and sandwiches to share and a pot of honey. There's something for Grim as well." He laid them down on a flat stone near where Bessie was sitting. She looked at the food and then at him. Thomas felt a little uncomfortable, it seemed so little, but Bessie reached out and touched the chocolate and then the biscuits and smiled. It transformed her face lit up as it was by the fire.

"Summat given freely demands a return," she said, "What can I give thee Thomas Greystone?" Thomas sat down on a rickety wooden stool near the fire and leaned forward eagerly.

"There's so much I want to know about the places around here. My grandma used to talk a lot about it, but it was never all of it if you know what I mean. I feel there's much more to know, but I don't know how to find out. Mrs. Jackson, our cleaning lady told me about you. She said you know a lot of things about the area."

"Ah," said Bessie, pouring tea into two thick mugs, "Said that did she? Nowt goes on down there that Bettina Jackson don't hear of and passes on." She added a spoonful of condensed milk and two big spoons of sugar and handed a mug over to Thomas. "Now lad, lets see what you 'ave in them sandwiches, I'm fair starved."

Eagerly Thomas unwrapped his lunch pack and displayed its contents to his new friend. Grim appeared at her side ready to share in the bounty. Thomas settled for the egg and watercress, Bessie took the ham and Grim the bacon. For afters they had biscuits and a bit of chocolate and Grim had two more of his biscuits then he curled up in his nest of grass and went to sleep.

Thomas sat and watched as Bessie filled a clay pipe with some form of herbal tobacco and settled back to smoke. The sweet smell filled the cave and for a while there was silence. Then he said quietly "Please ma'am, will you tell me about The Singing Stones and Misselthwaite Manor and why my grandma left Deepdale when she loved it so much. There's such a lot I want to know."

"You can call me Bessie, Tom Greystone, an' there's precious few as I'll allow ter do that. There's things you want ter know an' things you have ter know, it's not allus the same thing. But you have ter go slow. Tis like a puzzle. Yer 'ave ter know which piece goes where, then you 'ave to unnerstand why it goes there. Thee'll 'ave to 'ave patience Tom, and come ter the truth bit by bit." Thomas stared at her.

"You make it sound as if everything was planned as if, as if there was some reason why we all came to Deepdale, especially me." He added thoughtfully.

"Aye," agreed Bessie puffing on her pipe, "especially you Tom Greystone, and that's the truth. So. What does tha' want ter know fust?"

Thomas tried to sort the questions out in his mind. Then he spoke slowly as if the ideas were drifting up from deep inside him. "Why did we come here to Deepdale, my mum and dad and me?"

"Because this is wheer tha' belongs and wheer tha' must stay."

"What do you mean 'where we belong and must stay.' Do you mean we can't ever leave here?"

"Yer mam and dad can go where they please. You must stay Tom. Tis you must make things right agin. It'll soon be the Time of Opening and the Thirteen must be ready. It only 'appens once every hunnerd years, tha knows." The boy blinked.

"What is it that happens ever hundred years?" He leaned forward his eyes alight with excitement.

"Why the comin' o' the once and future King o' course."

"That's what they called King Arthur, but he's been dead over a thousand years." Thomas sat back again disappointed. Bessie chuckled.

"Yer niver heerd of Avalon then." Her listener was indignant.

"Of course I have but it's a legend … isn't it?"

"Well now, there's legends and then there's secrets that the legends hide."

Thomas thought about this for a while then decided to change the subject. " Why did my grandma left Deepdale?"

"She followed her heart and broke her word t'the Stones and for that she were cast out. But now tha's here and that'll heal it all."

"What exactly does 'cast out' mean Bessie." Asked Thomas holding his breath.

"Her Da wouldn't let her coom bak, He were that broke up ter see his own lass forgo 'er duty ter the Stones. She held the bloodline o' the Carricks yer see, and wi'out the Mage o' Stones the King's Chamber canna be op'd. An' now be the time, after a thousand yeer or more when another Arthur will return. Yer Gran gave the Sphere ter thee lad, coz she could niver coom back but she knew if thee held the Sphere, thee'd be able ter do what she should 'ave done."

"She was so sad." said Thomas, staring into the fire. "She talked about the Dales all the time, but she never tried to come back."

"She knew she were not allowed Tom, once the word is given 'tis not ter be broken, and if 'tis broken then exile be the only way. But the wound didna heal and the Stones can't sing true, when one note be missing. She allus planned that thee would be the one ter complete the task." Bessie watched him keenly, waiting for each question and answering with as little as might be given. He must go slowly, she could see he was trying to piece it all together.

"Grandma's name before she married Grandad was Carrick, and she was part of something that concerns the Singing Stones, but then she ran away and married Grandad so her Dad wouldn't speak to her anymore. Is that it."

"Tis near enough for now lad. Jennet were born for a purpose, but she was a wild 'un. Wanted her own way no matter that it broke the old laws, and she gave her heart to an outsider. The Stones don't forgive lad, so be warned." Bessie puffed on her pipe and stared into the fire. "But she'll mak amends through thee an' it'll all come areet."

"Bessie, I don't understand this. I'm beginning to be afraid. I can feel something coming towards me and I can't stop it, it's too big." Thomas's voice shook.

There was silence for a moment, then Bessie spoke gently, "I know Lad, I know, tis allus scary when thee' comes to it. But thee'll have the Stones and their Guardians wi' un and they be strong as the land when they do sing true. You have a ways to go Tom, but thee'll be helped niver fear."

"Does my dad know any of this?" asked Thomas wearily.

"He knows summat that's why he writes, but he wern't born ter sing wi' the Stones, He be too much o' a Greystone fer that. But he knows a little. Then there's The Others." The boy raised his head and stared at her.

"The Others?"

"Them as wants what the Stones guard. There be some in the village as are different from Deepdale folk. They'll try to keep thee from the Stones and what is rightfully yourn. Tha's special Tom, tha's a very special person."

"Why am I special Bessie, What is it the Stones guard?

Why do they sing and how, what exactly is the Mage sphere and what does it do. Tell me Bessie, please."

Bessie knocked out her pipe and put it aside. "Easy Tom, easy, there be some things as yer must find out fer tha'sen. Tis a kind of test tha' knows. Thee must ask the right questions at the right time."

"Like a school test?"

Bessie laughed, a deep belly laugh that rolled around the cave and woke Grim from his sleep. "Nay, these tests 'll mak' a man of ye Tom. Now, tis late and you'd best be off, Grim'll show thee a shorter road. Thank 'ee kindly fer the things you brought especially fer Grim. Tha'll be back at school on Monday so we'll not see each other fer a while, but I'll be watching thee and there be others as'll do the same."

Reluctant to leave with so much still to ask and learn about Tom settled his back pack on his shoulders, his watch said four o'clock so he'd better hurry. As they went down the little path he remembered something.

"Bessie, I meant to ask you about Misselthwaite Manor. I went to look at it the other day. Its practically empty but I looked through the letterbox and saw a picture of an old man with white hair. He seemed to be standing by a ring of stones. Were they the Singing Stones?" As an afterthought he added, "and who was the old man?

Bessie waited until he was astride his bike and ready to ride off, Grim waiting in front of him. Then she spoke firmly and with an authority that had Thomas wide-eyed.

"You are learning to ask the right questions lad. Misselthwaite Manor you say. Aye they are the Singing Stones, the ancient Guardians of the land and the royal symbols of that land, and the old man in the picture is Sir Piers Carrick, Baronet. He was your great grandfather Thomas, and the Manor, its title and everything he owned rightly belongs to you on your fourteenth birthday."

THREE

"I think Thomas is coming down with something Rosie. He was real quiet all yesterday, and this morning. Frank said there was not a word out of him the whole ride to school. It's not natural for a lad." Betty Jackson sipped her tea and shook her head over the vagaries of children and boys in particular, then continued. "I feel responsible being left in charge like this, and now it looks like his parents will be away longer than was thought. Heaven alone knows where he went on Saturday. Almost the whole day out on the moors, he could catch his death of cold. I'm worried stiff."

Rosie Boothroyd finished her tea and rose to her feet. "I'd not fret just yet Betty. Lads are like that, down one minute and up the next. I must be off, the men'll be back by now and wantin' their supper. Thanks fer the tea, petal. Cheerio." She disappeared into a fog that had drifted in during the night. Mrs. Jackson cleared the dishes and set about the pile of washing in the laundry room. Lordy, what did boys do to collect so much dirt on their clothes?

As she shook out Thomas's shirts something tinkled and fell to the ground. She looked down frowning and bent and picked it up. It was a silver chain some sixteen inches long and from it hung a small sphere that looked like glass. But it wasn't glass, that she knew. She had seen things like this before. Then it began to glow.

Something flashed into Betty Jackson's eyes. Her face contorted with fear, then she yelped as a sudden heat seared her hand and she flung it away from her. It landed on the shirt and lay there, its glow slowly fading. But the palm of the woman's hand was red and blistered.

Sobbing with shock she ran back to the kitchen and plunged her hand into cold water, then applied cooling witch-hazel to reduce the pain further. She covered the burn with a dressing and went back to the laundry room to look at the sphere.

She could hardly believe it. The lost Mage Sphere was here in the house. The key to the power of the Stones. She had to think fast. Thomas would know he'd lost it by now and no doubt would be looking for it. She had to let him think it has just been mislaid, for the moment at least. She needed to get advice on this and quickly.

She must let the others know that the object they thought was lost was here in Deepdale. Hurriedly she filled the washing machine with clothes and turned it on. Then, with a pair of wooden tongs she picked up the chain and took it upstairs to Thomas's bedroom and put it on his desk. She looked around the room searching for any clues it might hold to answer the questions filling her mind.

It had been no accident that she'd offered her services to Nora Greystone a few days after the family arrived in Deepdale. News that the Greystones were returning to the village had sent shock waves through the small community. The fact that Thomas was the spitting image of his grandmother, and, more especially, his great grandfather, had been the subject of gossip right from the beginning.

Betty Jackson had made great efforts to get herself well in with the family right from the start. Now, almost a year later she was trusted enough to be left in charge of the boy while his parents were away. So far she had seen no sign the lad knew anything of his ancestry. They, the Others, had hoped Jennet had passed the Mage Sphere to her son. But Steven Greystone seemed too occupied with fame and fortune to wonder what his mother might have been doing in her youth. Now they knew who it had been given to. But did the lad know what it was and did he know who he was, and what kind of task had been laid on him?

She put on her hat and coat and grabbed her purse. As she prepared to leave the phone rang and hesitated. With a muttered curse she waited for the answering machine to take the message then pressed the button. Thomas's voice was breathless and worried.

"Mrs. Jackson, I've lost something important to me. It's a silver chain with a small glass ball on it, it was given me by my grandma and I wondered if you might have seen it in the house while you were cleaning. If not will you have a look round please, thank you. I really hope it's not lost."

"Yes Thomas Greystone, you've lost something important alright. More important than you know."

She hurried out of the house and walked quickly down the lane into the High St. Looking both ways to see if anyone was around she crossed the road and followed a flight of steep stone steps down to the lower part of the village. The house making a corner with the passage was very old as the carved date above the lintel proclaimed;

1690 AD Prudance and Makepeace Allsop

She knocked on the door twice and waited. After a few minutes a bolt was drawn back and a key turned in a lock. The door opened and a man's face came into view. Not overly tall but with a trim athletic build he held himself with the assurance of someone used to commanding others. His dark hair was lightly streaked with grey that contrasted sharply with the youthfulness of his face. Dark eyes narrowed when he recognised his caller. He did not appear to welcome the intrusion.

"Bettina, what brings you here at such an early time?"

"I had to come Marcus, there's things afoot and we need to talk. It's the Greystone lad. Jennet Carrick gave him the Mage sphere before she died, I've seen it. The cursed thing burned me badly. If the Mage sphere is back in Deepdale they'll be able to open the Kings Chamber come Lammas."

"Come in, come in and stop yammering woman. You'll have the whole neighbourhood listening in!" He stood back and let her into the hall then carefully locked and bolted the door behind them. Turning he led the way along a dark passageway into a small kitchen at the back of the house.

"Sit down," he ordered shortly. "I'll make some tea, then we'll sort things out. It's no good getting in a flurry about things until we know the whole story."

Mrs. Jackson sat quietly feeling ill at ease, as she always was when visiting Marcus Allsop. She had never felt comfortable in the man's presence. He was too overpowering, too sure of his ability to command, and to instil fear.

He poured two cups of tea and sat down, settling back in his chair and regarding her over the rim of his cup. "Now," he said calmly. "Tell me what has brought you here in such a state." Mrs. Jackson took a deep breath and began.

"The Greystones have gone to America, they'll be away for about a month or even more. They left the lad with me to look after. I thought the boy knew nothing about the Stones or the King's Chamber but now I'm not so sure. The parents are so took up with all this new money and fame that they can't see more than the end of their noses. The father may know a little of the old stories, but I'd lay odds he doesn't know his son is the new Keeper of the Mage Sphere." She took a sip of tea to calm her nerves, and leaned forward.

"The lad's been taking off on 'is bike all over the place lately, and like as not 'he's met up with some of the Guardians of the Stones. With the Waking due this Lammas and Arthur's Crown to be offered to the Rightful King, they're bound to be making plans, same as us. It's the chance we've waited for. Well, you've waited for," she added hastily as the man raised his eyebrows. "Now we know where it is and who has it. We…"

"Can bide our time and let them do the work for us," interrupted Marcus Allsop. He finished his tea and stood up.

"Thank you Bettina, you've done well. Now go back and let the boy know his trinket is safe. Act normally. Our next task is to make sure he doesn't get to know how important it is, until nearer the time. Try to keep him away from the subject. I still have a lot of research to do. The Royal Regalia has to be found and the Guardians themselves identified. Time is short, but with a lot of work and a little luck I will be the one who will wear Arthur's Crown at Lammas." As he spoke he seemed to grow taller and more threatening.

He saw her out, drawing the bolts and unlocking the door with the same care as before. Then, satisfied that she had gone he climbed the narrow stairs to a room under the eaves where shelves floor, and tables were covered with books and ancient pieces of armour. Sitting at a well-worn desk he opened a small leather bound diary written in ancient Latin and began to read.

Mrs. Jackson hurried back to Deepdale House to take the washing out of the machine and set it to dry. Then she phoned the school and left a message for Thomas with the secretary saying she'd found his "good luck charm" and it was safe on the desk in his room.

At twelve, just as she was finishing a ham and cheese omelette, she happened to look through the kitchen window. In the middle of the lawn was a skinny and rather dirty terrier. It stared at her, its head slightly to one side. Then it walked deliberately to the apple tree in the middle and lifted its hind leg against it.

Outraged Betty grabbed the broom and shot out of the back door. The dog raced across the lawn, jumped the fence and disappeared into the woods at the back. Breathing heavily Betty Jackson returned to find Bald Bessie sitting at ease across the table from her. She blinked, then opened her mouth. "And just what do you think you're doing, coming in here without so much as a bye your leave. If you're looking for a handout, you can think on!"

"Now is that the way ter talk to summ'un who's come wi' a present. I found some wild fennel down in Lower Field and thought you might find a use fer it. Goes well in a bit o'broth does fennel. The door were open an' I saw thee chasing t'dog so I thought I'd come in an' wait like. Any chance of a cuppa?" She smiled displaying toothless gums. "I saw a lone magpie in yer garden just now. Seems like some bad news might be coming yer way Betty Jackson."

"One cup, and you're gone Bessie!" was the reply, as Mrs. Jackson poured out a mug of tea with a shaking hand, added milk and pushed it across the table.

Bessie beamed and plunked a plastic bag full of wild fennel in front of her unwilling hostess. " 'Appen I can do summat about that magpie afore I go." She drank the tea in swift gulps and got to her feet. " I'll see meself out." She hobbled down the path and as she closed the gate a second magpie flew down to join its foraging mate.

"Told you I'd do summat. Now ye can sleep easy Betty me gel!" And she went off down the lane laughing.

Mrs. Jackson slammed the door shut. "Wretched woman," she muttered and began to clear away the remains of her lunch.

Upstairs Grim, who had sneaked back into the house, now padded quietly onto the landing to look over the banisters. The crabby woman was vacuuming the front room so he ran down the stairs and leapt up on to the kitchen table where a pound of beef sausages had been left to defrost. Seizing them in his mouth he jumped down again and disappeared through the old cat flap. Bessie was waiting by the back gate.

"Good boy Grim." She patted his head. That'll do us nicely fer supper tonight" She put both dog and the sausages in her trolley and set off down the lane.

A small, battered van swung round the corner and came to a halt. A heavily bearded face thrust itself through the window.

"Ow do Bessie" said the Beard, " Happen I was thinking on thee last night. Saw an owl sitting in my old oak round midnight, just as I was 'aving my last smoke. You bin flitting around 'ave yer?" He laughed.

Bessie came close to the van. "More than flitting Stan Simonite, I was guarding. The Singer of the Mage Stone is here in Deepdale. We are all gathered as of now."

Bessie's departure from her North Country accent did not startle her listener. Her news however did.

"The Mage be here, now, in Deepdale. Is it Steven Greystone as you thought? "

"No Stan, it is his son, young Thomas who wears the Sphere and he's asking the right questions. We have four months near enough to prepare him and tune the Stones. It will be tight, and there's no margin for error. I have sent word to the High Places and it has been received and answered. He will come at the appointed time. But we must be cautious, Bettina went to see Marcus Allsop this morning and that bodes no good. We must call a meeting as soon as possible, agreed?"

"Agreed Bessie me dear. I'll pop in to the surgery and let the Atkinsons know, and Posy at the shop. I might even see Maggie on her rounds. " Tis half moon tonight, so there'll be light enough at the Stones. Best be after eleven for Drew won't be able to get there till after closin' time. I'd best be off, see thee later Bessie."

Bessie looked after the departing van for a moment then set off on her errands. Few people took any notice of her and that was how she liked it. Every once in a while she disappeared for days on end, but again, no one noticed. Had they known where she went and how the village would have ground to a halt in shock. She pushed her trolley along the High Street with Grim riding shotgun and collected bruised fruit and vegetables from the grocer and some bones from the butcher. Along the way she rummaged in a skip outside the local Pub and came up with a couple of old pieces of carpet and some wood for the fire. Drew Docker must be tarting up The Carrick Arms so she went round the back to see if he was there.

Drew Docker was a big man, and he needed to be to lift the beer barrels as he was doing now. He caught sight of Bessie as she came round the corner and grinned.

"Hello m'dear, come fer a drop o' the hard stuff?" He leaned on the dray and winked at her and she laughed.

"Rascal, you know well I cannot abide the stuff." He dropped what he was holding and came closer, "What be up then Bessie m'dear?"

"Be at The Stones tonight Drew Docker and you'll know. Come after closing without fail, and tell Wally Meakin the same when he comes in for his lunch pint. Young Thomas Greystone is holding The Mage Sphere. Stan's gone to tell the others and I'm going to find Edna Pugh."

Drew's ruddy face beamed with delight. "That be great news Bessie, I'll pass it on to the others to make sure. Les and Ben are over at Barmsby, they've had a coach go off the road there. They'll be back before six o'clock I reckon, time enough to get them word."

Bessie nodded, "I'm passing the school, I'll get one of the children to tell Edna." She paused as some drinkers came out to sit in the weak sunshine, then spoke loud enough for them to hear. "Thank 'e kindly Drew Docker, I'll sing thee a charm fer tha' kindness". She pushed the cart back to the High street and hobbled off to the village school. There was only the *Annointer* to summon now.

When they saw her the children crowded to the railings. Without exception she was a favourite with them, always ready to tell a story and give out few sweets. They were not disappointed today. She paused by the rails and produced a bag of lollipops.

"There, one fer each o' yez and no cheatin' mind. Now, 'oo's going ter tak a message ter Miss Pugh fer me?" A forest of hands shot up in the air. "Jessica Dawson, you'll do," she said to a small freckle-faced girl with untidy plaits. "Tell 'er as how I think she could do with some extra singing lessons ternight. Here's summat fer yer trouble." Bessie pushed a closed fist through the railings and dropped a stone into the childs hand. "That there's a fossil, an' its millions of years old. Found it up on the moors. You ask Miss Pugh ter tell 'ee about it. T'will bring 'ee good luck Jess."

The child ran off to take the message and Bessie sat down on the school wall and began to tell the others a story while she waited.

* * *

His mind was at rest now he knew the sphere had been found so Thomas didn't bother to rush home. Instead he went to find Father John, the Head of the History department. John Foxton had been a noted archaeologist in his day and still acted as a consultant for the BBC. Given Thomas's love of everything old it was inevitable they would have a lot in common. Though now a Jesuit priest, John Foxton had an open and inquiring mind that often placed him in a difficult position with his superiors and, occasionally, with his own conscience. He had made a study of the Dales and its legends over the last thirty years and was considered an expert on the subject. Today Thomas had a lot of questions for him.

"Come in Thomas, "he called on hearing his knock. "Make yourself comfortable. Have you rung Mr. Jackson to tell him you'll be staying late? We don't want to worry him or have a search party scouring the moors for you, do we?"

Thomas laughed. "No sir, I did ring, and he'll pick me up at five thirty. If that's alright with you."

"Of course, of course. Now lets see, you mentioned The Singing Stones, Thomas, and on looking through books and notes I found very little." "However," he went on, noting Thomas's look of disappointment. "What I did find made very interesting reading. I found out a great many things that lead back to you Thomas. What brought this to your attention lad?"

Thomas squirmed in his seat. He was a little in awe of Father John, and wondered if his questions would sound stupid. "My grandma came from Deepdale, and there's some mystery about why she left, but she never talked about it, neither did my Dad. Before she died she gave me something to remember her by, a silver chain with a funny little sphere on it. It seems to change colour all the time, and it gets hot when I'm with people I don't really like. Not everyone, just certain people. When we came to live here the village people were very curious about us, about dad mainly, because he's a famous author. But now, they seem to be curious about me as well.

"In what way Thomas? Are they hostile or rude or just curious?"

"Mrs. Jackson, our housekeeper is quite nice, but she watches me all the time. I sometimes meet her in the village on my way home and if she's with her friends they stop talking when I pass. Then of course there's Bald Bessie. She's really interesting to talk to. She's like you, I mean." He paused, embarrassed. "She knows a lot about old things."

"Yes, she does. I've already made the acquaintance of Bessie. I met her years ago when I was walking on the high moors and got lost in a sudden fog and hurt my ankle falling into a gulley. Her dog found me and brought her to where I was lying. Bessie got me back to her cave, a marvellous place with all those prehistoric paintings, and looked after me until the following morning. We spent a fascinating time discussing local customs. I re-paid her kindness by forgetting what I'd seen on those walls so she wouldn't be bothered by hoards of archaeologists and tourists. She went off early the next day and got a friend of hers, the carpenter Stan Simonite, to pick me up in his van. How did you meet her?"

"I was on my bike and I got lost like you sir. It was her dog who found me as well he's called Grim."

"Yes, well he would be wouldn't he," said Father John with a slight smile. "There are more than two hundred legends of dogs called Grim all over the British Isles, most of them however, are very large and black. Would you like some hot chocolate Thomas? I'm partial to a cup this time of day, especially when it's cold."

"Yes please sir," said Thomas eagerly. Father John busied himself preparing the drink and setting out some biscuits to go with it. He used the time to think over what had been said about Bessie and what he needed to say to Thomas. The boy had asked him about The Singing Stones a couple of days ago and (hiding his shock at the directness of the question) he had contacted the other Guardians. They had placed the task of explaining on his shoulders. He set a mug of hot chocolate and a plate of biscuits in front of Thomas and sat down with his own cup.

"Tuck in, it's a while to dinner time." He watched as the boy sipped at his drink, then settled back in his armchair. "Now, what exactly did Bessie tell you Thomas?"

"Well," he licked chocolate off his fingers, "That first time she just gave me directions to get home. Then the chain with the sphere on it fell out from under my shirt and she saw it. All of a sudden she changed, and got sort of, excited. She told me to keep it safe, that it was something very powerful. But I think it's only a sort of charm. I promised my Grandma

I'd always wear it for her sake. That was all the first time. I got on my bike and went home."

"Have you met her since then?"

"Yes sir. I saw her the following Saturday. I told Mrs. Jackson I'd be out all day and she made me sandwiches and stuff. I thought if I went back the same way, Bessie's cave would be close by. She doesn't walk very well you see. I took her some chocolate and honey and some biscuits and something for Grim. Grandma always said you should give something if you're going to ask for something?"

The Priest hid a quiet smile, recognising the ancient custom of exchanging food in return for information or teaching. "Go on Thomas," he said.

"Well I got as far as the Old Gibbet and found Grim waiting there for me. He took me straight to Bessie and from there we went to her cave. We sat and talked the whole afternoon and it was great, really interesting. But I didn't ask her about the Stones until much later. Mrs. Jackson had told me about them some days before but when I asked her where they were, she looked frightened and made me promise I wouldn't go looking for them. She was quite upset when I asked for directions. So I decided to try and find some information about them by myself."

The priest nodded thoughtfully and Thomas went on.

"Bessie told me lots of other stories about the moors. She said some of the caves were supposed to be doorways to the Fairy Kingdoms, and that sometimes the Fairies misled people who got too close to them, with lights, and voices and weird things like that." He grinned cheekily at the priest over the rim of his cup. "Was that how you got lost on the moors sir?"

Father John smiled back and shook his head. "But what about the Stones ,Thomas, what did she say about them?"

Well, I'd kept my promise to Mrs. Jackson and I didn't go looking for them that first day, I went to Misselthwaite Manor and Friars Folly instead. But when I went to see Bessie that second time, she said that The Stones didn't stay in the same place all the time. They move around, I've read about Stone Circles in Cornwall that are supposed to do that. Anyway, then Bessie said that each stone had a guardian and they had special tasks and important things that they were responsible for. But it was all mixed up with talk about the guardians handing over their places to their children, and how every hundred years it all had to be re-done, or re-conned or something like that. I didn't really understand that part very well."

"Re-consecrated, was that the word she used?"

"Yes, sir, I think it was, I'd forgotten it. What does it mean sir?"

"To consecrate something means to make it special, holy, and to be used only for a special purpose. You can consecrate an object or place or a person as in the consecrating of the King or Queen in a Coronation."

"But if its been done once, doesn't it stay like that?"

"Usually yes. But sometimes with special objects one has to redo what has been done before, to keep the level of power at the same strength. Go on Thomas."

"Then she said that I had to find some things out for myself and that it was a sort of test. It would prove to the guardians that I was the right person to hold the Mage

Sphere. She seemed to think they had been waiting for me to come." He leaned forward his voice dropping. "But the really weird thing came just as we said goodbye. I told her I'd been to Misselthwaite Manor and that I'd seen a picture of an old man hanging in the hall. Behind him in the picture was a stone circle. I asked Bessie if they were the Singing Stones and who the old man was."

"And did she tell you?"

"Well sir, she told me something, but I don't know if it's true. She said that they were the Singing Stones and the man was Sir Piers Carrick. Then she said that he was my great grandfather and the Manor and the title belonged to me, but I don't think that can be true."

Father John steepled his fingers together and looked at the boy before him with serious eyes and a little sadness. "Why do you think that Thomas?"

"Because I've read a lot about this kind of thing and I know that if there's Baronet after the name, it's a title that is handed on. So IF there's a title it would go to my father not to me and I don't think he knows anything about it, because he would have said something before now wouldn't he?"

Father John rose from his armchair, walked to the window, and looked out. "There are certain circumstances Thomas, when a title is withheld and passed to the next in line. Your paternal grandmother was Jennet Carrick the only child of Sir Piers Carrick Baronet. Many years ago she ran away from Deepdale to marry Thomas Greystone against her father's wishes. Sir Piers however lived long enough to know of your birth and he went to a lot of trouble to make certain that his title, land, and property passed to you on your fourteenth birthday."

"On August 1st this year you will become Sir Thomas Carrick of Deepdale, Lord of Misselthwaite Manor, and other properties in England, Scotland and elsewhere, as well as a great deal of money. You will also inherit a task that is over a thousand years old. You will become The Mage of Spheres, Master of The Singing Stones, and Guardian of the High Crown of England, also, if you prove worthy of the title, the Archmage of Britain. I must also tell you that there are people here in Deepdale who will stop at nothing to prevent you from reaching your fourteenth birthday."

There was silence behind him, and he turned. A crumpled heap lay on the carpet. Thomas had fainted.

FOUR

"Yes of course Mrs. Jackson, I do understand your sense of responsibility, but the Matron assures me it is not serious, merely a bump on the head. He was out for just a few minutes. She thinks it would be best if he stayed over night in the school infirmary, just as a precaution. No, its no trouble at all, he will be quite safe here. Your husband can collect him at the usual time tomorrow and please do not worry we'll take good care of him. Good night."

Father John replaced the phone and turned to a pale-faced Thomas who was now lying on the sofa before the fire. "That's settled, you'll stay here tonight and sleep in the infirmary. You came over a little dizzy that's all, it's all been a bit too much for you I think. Now I'll go and get us some dinner and we'll eat it here in front of the fire. I believe its shepherds pie tonight with braised celery hearts and sticky toffee pudding with custard to follow. I'll make the tea here.

Won't be a moment."

He closed the door gently after him and stood thinking about what had happened. It was just as well the boy was kept here in the Priory. Tonight's meeting might stir something up from the dark side that might well have caught him unprotected. Here, on holy ground, he would be out of their reach. He set off towards the kitchens. Poor lad, it was a lot for him to take in at such short notice. But with just four months to go time was of the essence.

Upstairs in the cosy fire warmed room Thomas lay back against the cushions. He had fainted! Yuk! Of all the idiotic things to do, how embarrassing. He felt inside his shirt for the little sphere and then remembered it was back home in Deepdale. But for a moment, when Father John had called him the Master of the Singing Stones he had felt as if it was around his neck, the sphere warm and tingling against his skin. He settled back and tried to sort things into some kind of order.

1. The Singing Stones really existed and they held some kind of power that had to do with the sphere.

2. There were two kinds of people in Deepdale, some were helpful and some were out to get him.

3. His great grand father had had a title, a Manor House and, so it seemed, a lot of money. All of which would come to him on his fourteenth birthday

4. He, Thomas Greystone was to become The Mage of Spheres and the Master of the Singing Stones, whatever that meant.

5. The Stones were guarding something very important and other people wanted to get it.

6. How was he going to explain all this to his mum and dad when they came back?

7. How on earth did two people as different as Bald Bessie and Father John come to be mixed up in this together?

He sighed, it was one big puzzle inside his head, a head that ached terribly at the moment. The door opened and Matron came in to set down a tray on a small table beside him.

"Now then Thomas," she said taking a thermometer out of her top pocket. "Let's make sure you're not running a fever." She stuck the end in his mouth. Father John, followed her with another dinner tray and set it before his armchair and watched while Matron fussed. Eventually she said brightly. "I've made up a bed in the infirmary, but you'll be the only one there. You don't mind being alone?"

"No, I'll be fine," said Thomas politely, "Thank you for all your trouble Matron."

She beamed at him and turned to Father John. "Such a well mannered boy Father. Enjoy your dinner both of you, I'll send someone to collect the plates later. Now don't stay up too late, Thomas. I've put out pyjamas for you, a toothbrush and a new tube of paste, and a towel. I'll wake you in the morning and see if I think you're fit for lessons. Good night to the two of you." She went off, her starched apron rustling as she closed the door behind her.

"Well now, let's tuck in while it's hot" Father John brought the little table close to the sofa then sat down to his own dinner. At first Thomas felt hungry, but after a few minutes he slowed down. Suddenly he was very tired. It was only seven p.m., but he felt as if he had been up all night. He drank half of his tea and let his head fall back on the cushion.

He'd shut his eyes for a few minutes and then eat some more. Within seconds he had fallen sleep.

The priest put aside his dinner and got up to observe him as he slept. Satisfied he would sleep until morning he lifted him into his arms with surprising strength for a man of his age, and took him to the infirmary where he and the matron undressed him and put him to bed. Then he returned to his own chambers and locked the door.

He crossed the room and pulled an old fashioned armchair away from the wall ,behind it was a small safe. Father John opened the neck of his cassock and took out a silver chain on which hung two items. One was a glass sphere that glowed with a deep blue flame the other was a small brass key. He opened the safe and took out a book bound in flaking leather and secured by a brass lock.

Seated at his desk he opened the lock of the book and turned to the first page. It was written in a flowing script and decorated with fantastic creatures that writhed and twined and entangled themselves around the borders of each page. Father John touched the page with careful fingers and read aloud, softly and with great emotion.

HEREIN IS WRIT THE HIGH HISTORY OF THE CROWN OF BRITAIN ACCORDING TO THE WORDS OF MERYDDN AP HELIPHON.

THIS SHALL BE PLACED IN THE CARE OF SIR CARRICK OF THE NORTHERN MARCH AS REQUIRED BY ARTHUR PENDRAGON. SIR AMICUS CARRICK TO BE THE MASTER OF THE SINGING

STONES AND THE GUARDIAN OF ARTHUR'S
REGALIA UNTIL SUCH TIME AS AN ARTHUR
SHALL SIT UPON THE THRONE OF BRITAIN
ONCE MORE

Signed in the royal presence:

Sir Launcelot dulac
Sir Pellinore of Wirral
Sir Bedivere of Caerleon
Sir Perceval of Corbinec
Amicus Carrick of Deepdale

Arturus PENDRAGON
REX BRITTANICUS

He turned the fragile yellowed page with care.

Set upon the moorland above the hamlet of Deep-Dale lies the
stone dance called by The Wise The Singing Stones. 'Tis held
by them that they were raised for a purpose of great high magic by
the ancestor of Merddyn named by him as Heliphon. He was a
priest of renown in his own land which had been lost beneath the
sea. By his art Merddyn knew of the outcome of the last battle
with Mordred and made plans accordingly. A sennight before the
battle the King met with certain of his knights for whom he had
great trust and love. Among them was the youngest, Carrick of
Deepdale barely fourteen years and not yet knighted.

They rode long and hard to the place of the Stones where
seven moons before Merddyn had brought together a group of

wise men and women. From each of them he had taken a single drop of blood by which he bound them one by one to certain stones and taught them the note of that stone. Then he gifted all with a chain of silver set with a round jewel containing the magical power to shift their shape. To young Carrick he gave the same but with an extra power, one that would bind all the others together. For it was he who would be the Mage of the Sphere and the Master of the thirteen stones.

But one stone was without a Guardian and Merddyn called into the darkness and there came forth the Lady Guenevere, wife to the king. She knelt at his feet and wept, asking for forgiveness and the chance to prove herself worthy of his trust. Then did Merddyn raise her up and bless her and she did take her place by the empty stone.

On the night of Lammas eve all came together with the King and his knights in the middle and each stood by their stone, the twelve notes were sounded and hung upon the air like stars, From young Carrick came the thirteenth and at its sounding the Mage stone slid aside to display steps leading down into a stone walled chamber. Herein the King did lay his crown. His sword and shield and various other precious things pertaining to the crown he gave to the Guardians and bid them, hide them well. Then all partook of bread and wine in the old way and swore to uphold the name and power of the once and future King. Then Arthur knighted young Carrick and gave to him the lands thereabouts and the deeds also. He bade him stay and to forgo the battle that he might begin his guardianship. Arthur and his knights then departed to return no more.

Here follows the Company of the Singing Stones, their powers and the object of their guardianship. Each was enjoined to hand on their task to a son or daughter, and once in every hundred years, at Lammas Eve they would gather to open the chamber of the Crown and bring it forth. At this time the future king would come to the stone to be crowned and adorned with all things royal as a symbol of the future of Britain's Royal Line.

Sir Amicus Carrick. Master of the Stones, Mage of the spheres, Guardian of the Crown.

Ralf's son of Atkins, Farmer.   The King's Chain of Office.
Marjory, wife of Ralf.   The King's ring.
Master Lovell, Scrivener and Freeman.   The King's Sword Belt & Scabbard.
Mistress Pugh, Midwife and Freewoman.   The Royal Seal.
Jarvis, Keeper of the Manors Warrens.   The Orb of Rulership.
Widow Kate Fairchild, Landowner and Freewoman.   The King's spurs.
Lady Gueneverre, Wife to the King.   The King's Cup.
Simon of Ely, Carpenter.   The King's Sceptre.
Loveday Pym, Sir Amicus' Nurse.   The King's Shield.
Edmund Doker, Tavern Keeper.   The King's Sword.
Makin the Pig Keeper, Serf.   The King's Horn.
Dickon Reynard, Forrester.   The Holy Oil & Ampulla.

His voice faltered to a stop and he bowed his head. No matter how many times he read them the words never failed to move him. His love of the ancient ways and its people had been the lynchpin of his life and his work. Since he was a child he had known that in his lifetime the King's Chamber would be opened and that he would be the Guardian of the Sacred Oil and Ampulla. He loved this land with a deep and abiding passion as did all the Guardians and would fulfil his duty no matter at what cost.

When young he had married and raised a son and a daughter to adulthood to ensure the Guardianship, in case another generation would be called to take on the burden. Only when his wife died did he turn in his loneliness to the life of the cloister. Now the high point of his life was approaching and all his energies and knowledge must be tested to the limit. For the one who was heir to the Kingdom of Britain bore the name of Arthur, among others. This time Arthur would return, this time would bring the fulfilment of their Guardianship and this time would bring danger close to them all. For he knew without doubt that there would be a battle between good and evil at the Singing Stones on the next Eve of Lammas.

He looked up at the clock; ten forty-five. It was time to be going. This was the part he always dreaded, and yet at the same time found exhilarating. He took a black cloak from the closet and made his way to the infirmary where he checked on the sleeping Thomas. Then, leaving the door slightly ajar he went quietly down the stairs like a shadow to the front entrance where he disabled the security alarm with deft fingers. Grim was waiting in the doorway, at Father John's nod of approval the dog scampered up the stairs and slipped through the open door of the infirmary. After making sure Thomas was safe, it curled up on the beside mat and waited, alert and ready.

Once in the driveway Father John looked around and along the rows of windows. All were dark with no sign of activity . The air was crisp and cold and the half-moon shimmered against a clear frosty sky. He raised a hand and drew a circle of white fire before him, then seizing it he threw it into the air where it spread out to enclose the school and its grounds within its protection. He waited until it had settled and all that could be seen, and then only to a very observant eye, was a certain glimmer of white light at the boundaries.

Satisfied that all was now guarded he spread his cloak wide and turned his face to the night wind. It billowed beneath his cloak and caught him up. As it did so he changed, shrinking, turning, twisting from man into bird. Seconds later a black-tailed hawk sailed into the air and circled the buildings below. Then it turned into the wind and flew northwest towards the Singing Stones and the Meeting.

* * *

High up on the moors the Stones waited patiently as they had for thousands of years. From the track they were all but invisible, standing in the hollow like gaunt grey shadows. Time and weather and the changing of the land had distorted their original shape and angle and indeed that of the circle itself, but not enough to erode its power. That lay upon it like an ancient benediction conferred long before the last wolf had roamed the land. As they waited the ground beneath them began to vibrate. Slowly the sound built up until a distinct humming sound could be heard. Each stone contributed a single note the whole blending together in a cadence of majestic power and beauty. As they waited, the Stones Sang.

The Mage Stone lay lengthways outside the others and apart from them. While the others exuded a latent power, it alone seemed to be unaware of itself. It was still to be awakened by the presence of the Mage, its note still to be added to the others. There was an air of expectancy hanging over the high moors and a soft grey mist began to gather as the waxing moon rose higher into the clear sky.

Inside the circle there was a flurry of movement, a flash of grey and white feathers and a large Barn owl settled on the top of a stone and fluffed itself up against the cold. It was not the first arrival, huddled against another stone a grey muzzled badger snuffled in the grass and rooted a juicy worm out of its damp resting place.

Nearby a dog barked short and sharp, and was answered by another further away. A few minutes later the lean shapes of two greyhounds entered the circle. They stopped and sniffed the air. The owl turned its head and elongated its body, voicing a soft Hoo-oo-oo in a soft welcome. The dogs circled the Stones and settled down against one using its bulk to ease the bite of the wind. The night became quiet again and still the Stones waited and sang, softer now.

The Moon climbed higher.

Suddenly the dogs leapt up, noses catching a scent, ears alert . They stood close together as if on guard, then relaxed again as a large black faced ram stepped into the circle and stood for a moment looking round as if to check out its friends. Riding on its back, with its claws latched firmly into the thick wool was a sleek black and white cat. It leapt down gracefully and began to wash. The ram ambled over to a stone and settled down, to graze on the grass inside the circle.

Next to arrive was a ferret slipping in almost unnoticed and curling up against one of the smaller stones A delicate roe deer stepped daintily forward, looking at each one and touching noses with the dogs before taking her place. A hare and a huge tusked boar arrived a few minutes later and were greeted by the others with muted growls, squeaks, purrs and a soft *Hoo* from the owl. Finally the drumming of hooves brought every head up, and the scream of a hawk overhead announced the coming of the last two arrivals. A grey stallion entered the circle and trotted round as if counting the others before taking its place. The hawk flew in low and fast, its wings scooping the air to break its speed, talons outstretched to grasp its stone perch. The Stones fell silent.

The Moon reached her zenith.

The mist rose and swirled, filling the circle, then cleared again leaving twelve human figures where the animals had been. The Guardians had arrived. They waited silently for a moment then from the Ring of Stones came a sound. Soft as first and then growing into a deep rumbling roar that rolled across the ancient moorland like distant thunder. Three times the sound rose and fell then died away. The Stones had welcomed their Guardians.

* * *

Back in Deepdale the man named Marcus Allsop was raging. He strode up and down in the small room under the eaves and hit out at a vase of flowers with his hand. It crashed to the floor the glass splintering and allowing the water to seep into the carpet. On the desk stood a large crystal ball set into a carved wooden rack and glowing with a pearly iridescence. The picture in it was fading fast but the outline of a small white bed in which Thomas Greystone lay sleeping could still be seen. Above his head a circle of white fire pulsed in time with his gentle breathing. At the foot of the bed stood a small Jack Russell Terrier its hackles raised and a ridge of stiff fur along its back. A low growl came from between its exposed teeth. The Mage had not been left unguarded as Marcus had hoped.

Well there were other ways in which to bait a trap and he would find one. So, the Guardians were meeting were they? Well, let them meet if they wished, he would best them yet. The Crown would be his, he had waited long enough, schemed and dreamed and twisted the very fabric of time itself to obtain his desire. He had paid dearly for it. The hate and greed that had increased his lifetime had also steeled and blackened his heart. But he would win. His father's crown would rest on his head this time. After a thousand years of bitterness the desire for revenge instilled by his mother still boiled within him.

He flung himself into his chair and reached for the crystal. With a swipe of his hand he cleared the last image and began to summon a new one. He reached back through time moving from link to link with the ease of long practice. He looked into the crystal.

The scene was silent but he supplied the noise and shouts of battle from his own memory. He watched as Arthur's charge began and saw the wedge driven through his own lines. It went deep on that first charge and then spread out into the three line fighting format that had always been so successful for the King. But Mordred knew this tactic and was ready, letting his men thin out and fall back before the charge, then swinging round to enclose their enemy within a tight circle.

God, how good it had felt to slaughter those mealy mouthed knights. He had felled young Geraint with his own sword and watched him fall beneath his horse, Gareth, his own half brother had fallen in the first charge. He saw the ageing Pellinore take a lance through his throat and laughed. He laughed now, watching the battle as it was played out in the crystal. He saw Arthur before him, raising his sword, it was not Excalibur but another, saw his shield with its Royal Device and knew it for another forgery. He could hear his father's voice in his head, ringing across the centuries.

"Mordred you have lost what you most desire. The Crown, my sword, my shield and all that belongs to the High King you will never have. They are well hidden from your greed and your desire for power, safe and well guarded until I come again. Farewell ... my son."

The crystal went dark, leaving its owner in darkness, a soul searing darkness that he had suffered for centuries. Marcus Allsop, once Prince Mordred, flung back his head and howled like a mad dog. "Oh but I will have it, I will wear your crown Father, Arthur the Great, Arthur the Glorious, Arthur the Beloved King of Legend. Well I, Mordred, will have the last laugh and the best." But he bent over the crystal again with Arthur's last two words beating in his brain and put his head in his hands and wept.

* * *

"When will he come John, when can we see him here, at

the Stones. We need to talk to him." Edna Pugh wrung her hands nervously. "There is so little time."

"We have time enough Edna, don't worry so. We have had so much help over the years and I am sure that when Thomas knows the whole story he will be able to help us." Maggie Pym spoke with more conviction than she felt and sent an imploring look to Father John. But it was Bessie who answered. A Bessie who was no longer bent and worn. Her eyes were as bright as ever, but she now stood tall and straight.

"Listen to me well. It is true we have only a few months before the Opening of the Chamber, and it is true that we have yet to find some of the Regalia. But I believe that Thomas has the 'far memory' and will know how to find those things that are lost. Our main task is to keep him alive until Lammas. We have enemies in Deepdale, powerful enemies, and there is one who guides them but whose name as yet is unknown to us. We must find the head of the snake and deal with it."

Drew Docker, wrapped in his night dark cloak and leaning on his stone, spoke now with deep foreboding. "I think Bessie is right we must find the leader of the Others but it comes to me that before this is over there will be spaces to fill here at the Stones." The Guardians fell quiet at this dark warning. For all his bulk and his blunt ways, Drew was a gifted Seer, respected by them all for his clear sight.

John Foxton looked up at the moon, now falling from her high position. "It is late and we must leave here. Too much time spent in this place can leave traces of power by which we could be found. I will talk to Thomas again and I think all of you should begin to introduce yourselves to him. Speak to him of what you guard and why it is lost, let him know we have need of his help. Good night and may all here be blessed."

He spread out his arms and as if obeying his summons the mist returned filling the circle with its soft dampness. As gently as it had appeared it drifted away. The circle was now empty, but a black tailed hawk circled the sky, watching and guarding its companions as they made their various ways home in their travelling forms. Only then did the hawk turn, flying swift and sure towards the school where the Hope of Britain lay sleeping.

Standing at the foot of the bed he watched the boy intently. The guards were thanked blessed and dismissed, the Circle of white fire blinked out with a quiet sigh. Grim came forward to lick the hand that had blessed him then followed him downstairs to be let out. The dog trotted off into the night, pausing once to lift a casual leg against a tree, then broke into a run heading for the moors and his mistress.

FIVE

Thomas woke up feeling hungry and for some reason very happy. He'd slept better in fact than at home. Matron beamed at him and, having made sure his temperature was normal sent him off to breakfast. Then she went to see Father John.

"He's fine, Father, you know how boys go up and down with things. There's nothing wrong with him that I can see. So he's back in class and can go home as usual."

He thanked her and rang Mrs. Jackson with the news. She seemed eager to get the boy back under her care, and though that was natural in the circumstances, he detected an undercurrent of anxiety that struck him as being out of place. Being apart from the villages as the school was, he had little to do with the folk who lived in them. He thought for a while, then decided to phone Drew Docker at The Carrick Arms.

"The Carrick Arms here, and whoever you are, a good morning to you." The priest smiled at the verbal welcome.

"And to you my friend. Father John here. Can you spare me a few minutes Drew?"

"Of course Father, just let me switch to the house phone." The line crackled and then the Landlord was back again. "That's better, now we can talk with no one to overhear us. What can I do for you?"

"What you said last night Drew, its has been on my mind. I was awake during the night thinking about it."

"Aye. t'was a sudden 'knowing' that comes on me at such times. Normally I can sit and let the pictures rise up, as you know Father, but this was like a window that opened up in my mind. I could see the circle clear as day, but there were two empty stones and a sadness surrounding them. I felt such a pain at that moment. A sense of loss yet at the same time a feeling of freedom and well-being."

Father John drew in a sharp breath. "Drew, can you tell me which stones were empty, it could be important?

"That was the strangest thing of all. The spaces kept changing, I think what the vision was trying to tell me was that who will leave the circle, depends on how things will happen. I've never had such a clear 'knowing' nor one that seemed to offer a choice in what is to come. Have you any thoughts on this Father?"

"Yes, I think I have. I prayed for help last night as I have seldom prayed before. What we face is darker than we think and if it cannot get what it wants, it will lash out at those it sees as standing in its way. I fear for the Twelve Drew, I fear for the boy, and I fear for the one who is to be crowned. I have traced what I can of the past Opening Times, and a lot of information has been lost, but of the five of which I have the most knowledge, all of them have claimed a sacrifice."

"There are three of which I have only partial and very limited information. All missed their time. The sons of Edward IV were murdered in the Tower and the blame misleadingly laid upon their uncle Richard, and the throne went to the Tudors. Mary Tudor sent her Inquisitors to Deepdale in her stead, and many of the Guardians paid with their lives. We all but perished then. Charles the First refused to come and was murdered by Cromwell bringing about the Commonwealth. When you said what you did, my heart failed me. If more is revealed to you my friend, I beg you, let me know at once."

"That I will Father you have my word on that. Is there anything else?"

"Yes. Who, in say the last five years has come to live in the village, yet does not mix with the locals? Apart from Thomas's family of course."

"Well now, the only one as comes to mind is Marcus Allsop. When old Ben Allsop died it caused quite a stir, as no one knew if he had any family left. He were all of ninety three when he were taken. Took a year or more afore the solicitors found Marcus. Seems he was a distant cousin. Leastways he had the papers to prove he could inherit the house. There was a fair bit of interest there, it being a Landmark property and all. I know him by sight but to my knowledge he's never been here in the pub, nor the church. Though there's a few folk as goes to his house. Bettina Jackson for one."

A cold feeling ran through Father John's veins. "Are you sure? She works for the Greystones and Thomas is in her care. If Allsop is part of this Thomas could be in danger. See what you can find out but be discreet."

"Right Father, I'll get on to it right away."

Later that day Thomas went to say thank you to Matron and got a smile and a hug for his thoughtfulness. Now he stood outside Father John's door and knocked gently. It swung open almost at once.

"Thomas, its good to see you recovered, my boy. Is Mr. Jackson coming to pick you up?"

"Yes sir, he'll be here any minute, but I wanted to thank you for your help with … with everything," he ended in a rush, "And I wanted to ask you, well, what do I do now. I still have so many questions."

"Come in Thomas and sit down, we do not have much time and I need to tell you some things before you go home. Some may seem strange and some you may not understand as yet. Firstly, you must not tell Mrs. Jackson, or indeed anyone what we talked about last night. This is important Thomas. Secondly all that I have told you is true and can be verified. Thirdly there are people who will be prepared to harm you and your family if they know who and what you are. Do you understand?"

"Yes sir. Sir, is Mrs. Jackson one of The Others?"

The priest swung round and fixed him with an eagle eye. "Why do you use that term Thomas. Have you heard it before?"

"Yes sir, I've heard Mrs. Jackson use it on the phone. She calls her friends like that. She'll say things like … I must tell the Others, and she makes it sound like she's talking in capital letters, if you know what I mean."

"I do indeed Thomas. Listen, certain people will begin to introduce themselves to you in the next few days. Some will be people you can trust, others will not. If, and only if, they mention an animal or bird in their conversation can you be sure they are friends."

"An animal or a bird and they'll be a friend. I understand sir. Sir, my parents will be coming home in a few weeks. What am I going to tell them? I mean about what's to happen on my next birthday, and the Stones and all of this … stuff. And what about the letter the solicitor sent"?

"What letter Thomas?"

"Well, the day mum and dad left, a letter came addressed to me. It was from a firm of solicitors in Manchester. It said I was to go and see them and I would hear something to my advantage, something like that. Mrs. Jackson said she and Mr. Jackson would take me to Manchester if need be."

Before he'd entered the priesthood John Foxton had used bad language when the occasion demanded a release of tension. Years of self -discipline in Holy Orders had taught him to control his tongue, that control left him now as white hot anger ripped through him. "Bloody hell, why can't that damned woman cease her meddling."

Thomas's eyes and mouth opened at the same time. "Sir?"

"We are too late Thomas, if she knows, then all of them know. We must move swiftly. When you get home is Mrs. Jackson usually there, in the house?"

Yes sir, always. We have a cup of tea and some cake or biscuits, then I go upstairs to do my homework while she makes dinner. Mr. Jackson comes in about six o'clock and we all have our dinner together."

"Well today things will be a little different. When you get home I will make certain she is not there, go in and find your silver chain and put it on AT ONCE do you understand Thomas, at once. While you wear that, they can do you very little harm. If they suggest taking you to Manchester to see this solicitor tell them you have decided to wait until your father can take you, alright?"

"Yes sir." Thomas sounded a bit frightened. Father John bent down and took hold of his shoulders in a strong grip.

"Don't be afraid, but be on your guard. Think of yourself as a knight, like your ancestor. You're green in power as yet, but you will grow stronger I promise you."

He paused as a car horn sounded below the window. "You'd better go now, and remember what I've said lad. I'll see you are protected."

Thomas closed the door behind him and stood for a moment in the hall feeling as if he had wandered into a horror movie. As he made his way downstairs he suddenly felt like running away and hiding up on the moors in Bessie's cave. But then he'd be a coward, and not like Sir Carrick at all. No, he would have to see this through.

He squared his shoulders and went out to the car, watched by Father John from his window. Yes … the lad would do alright. John turned away and went to the phone and punched in a number

" 'Flowers For All'. Posy Williams speaking," said Deepdales' one and only Florist. "How may I help you?"

"Posy, its Father John, and yes, I do need your help and quickly."

"Certainly sir, I quite understand… a rush order. Let me go and see if I have enough of that particular flower." He waited trying to be patient, understanding she had people in the shop and had to be cautious. A few minutes later Posy spoke again. "Father John, it is safe to speak now, I had someone in the shop but Ruby is taking care of them. How can I help?"

"Posy I have need of your powers of mimicry and right away. I need to get Bettina Jackson out of Deepdale House by the time Thomas gets home, and he is on his way now. Can you mimic one of her friends on the phone?"

"Well now let me see, there's old Sadie Jackson her great aunt she's nearly ninety hard of hearing and a little touched in the head bless her. Betty is hoping for a mention in her will and if the old lady were to call and sound a little… shall we say distraught. Betty would be off like a shot. Old Sadie would never remember phoning anyway, she seldom does. Would that do Father?"

"Admirably Posy, I don't like stooping to deception, but things are moving fast. I have reason to believe Bettina now knows who and what Thomas is and, even more worrying, that on his fourteenth birthday he will come into his full inheritance as Sir Carrick's heir, which means his powers as well.

"Enough said Father, I'll phone her now and get back to you late." She rang off.

John Foxton rubbed the back of his neck distractedly and wondered how he was going to deal with his next confession. At this rate he would be on his knees for several hours.

Posy sat down by her private phone and drew a deep breath. She closed her eyes and summoned up a mental picture of old Sadie Jackson. Then she began to imagine what it would be like to BE Sadie, her arthritis, her sense of age, her loss of mental ability, and, lastly, her voice. When she felt ready she picked up the phone and with a suddenly shaky hand dialled the number of Deepdale House.

Betty Jackson was singing to herself as she took a fruit cake out of the oven and set it to cool on the rack. "Tonight, Tonight," she carolled, slinging the tea towel over her shoulder, "won't be just any night, tonight there will be no …" She stopped in full flight as the phone rang and lifted the receiver. "Deepdale House, Mrs. Jackson speaking."

"Betty, is that you dear," the quavering voice at the other end held a distinct note of panic. "Betty I need some help dear … feel so dizzy and weak … I can't remember the doctor's name. Oh dear." There was thump and a clatter and then silence.

"Aunty, Aunty!" Mrs. Jackson yelled down the phone. "Aunty are you there, did you fall … Oh dear, Oh dear." She slammed down the receiver and re-dialled the local taxi service. "Bernard, thank God you're in, I need a taxi over to Shipton, Aunt Sadie's bin taken queer. Yes. I'll meet you at the top of the lane." She grabbed her coat and purse and ran out of the house leaving the phone off the hook in her hurry and the kitchen door wide open.

In the little office at the back of her florists shop Posy Williams listened to the panic and smiled. That should keep Betty Jackson busy for at least a couple of hours. She picked up her glasses and went back into the shop.

A few minutes later Frank Jackson turned into the drive and parked the car round the back. He noticed the open door and called out as they entered but there was no reply. Thomas pretended surprise when it became obvious that no one was in the house.

"Maybe she was called away, that happens with my mum sometimes, look the phone's off the hook."

Frank dialled a number and spoke into the phone, "Dora, 'ave ye seen Betty? No, she's not in the 'ouse, left the door wide open she did. Not like 'er ter do summat daft like that. Could've bin burgled, silly cow. No tea on the go, and no dinner neither. I'll give 'er what for when I sees 'er." He rang off and looked at Thomas and shrugged.

"Put the kettle on lad and lets have some o' that cake, I'm fair famished." Like most Dalesmen, Frank was of little use in the kitchen, so he sat and filled his pipe while Thomas set out two mugs and the teapot, milk, sugar and two plates for the cake. Then he excused himself and went upstairs to his room.

The chain and sphere lay on his desk. As he entered the room it lit up and pulsed through its rainbow of colours as if in greeting. He picked it up and went to place about his neck, then paused. Pictures flickered through his mind, as if he was seeing a memory of something that had just happened. He saw Mrs. Jackson holding the chain, and the burn on her hand. He saw, and heard her dialling a phone number and talking to someone called ... Mack ... Max ... Mark ... no ... Marcus. Then she left the phone and ran out of the house. He shook his head as the pictures faded and looked at the sphere with astonishment. It was talking to him, talking with pictures, telling him what had happened. He sat down on his bed and tried to make sense of what was going on.

"Tea's up Thomas, come an''ave summat t'eat lad".

"Coming Mr. Jackson."

He jumped up and ran down the stairs, the chain safe about his neck once more. It was well over an hour later when Mrs. Jackson returned. She was red faced with hurrying and very cross and took out her anger and frustration on the two of them.

"Well now, I do think as 'ow you could've laid the table Thomas and as fer you Frank Jackson, you surely know 'ow ter peel a potato after all these years, seems I 'ave ter do everything around here."

Thomas and Mr. Jackson looked at each other. He raised his eyebrows and Thomas shrugged his shoulders and began to lay the table for dinner. Frank inexpertly peeled the potatoes while his fuming wife slammed a large meat pie into the microwave, and went on with her tale of woe.

"Old Sadie rang up, said she needed help, and felt dizzy. Then there was an almighty thump and I thought as how she'd fallen over. Fair gave me a turn it did. So I phoned Bernard to take me over there and what do I find? Her ladyship and Maggie Pym supping tea and eating chocolate éclairs. Said she'd not phoned at all. Well, I told 'er. Well, if you think I'm so daft I don't know yer voice Sadie Jackson, then think on."

She went on complaining all through dinner until Frank got up and said he was heading off to the Carrick Arms. Thomas claimed he had homework and escaped upstairs to his room leaving Mrs. Jackson to knit in front of the television. In actual fact he had very little to do, and that could be done tomorrow during break.

He sat on his bed holding the sphere in his hand. He suddenly felt a lot older and wiser than thirteen. As if he had so much 'knowingness' in his head it might burst. He wished his parents were home, and in the same breath was glad they were away. All this stuff about Arthur's Crown and Singing Stones might freak them out. He didn't want to think about how he would tell them about all this when they did come home.

He got up and went to sit on the window seat, his favourite place for thinking, and looked out on to the night-shrouded garden. In the apple tree that stood in the centre of the lawn he caught the flutter of wings and held his breath as a barn owl edged into view. He and the bird looked at each other, its amber eyes glinting in the faint light from the kitchen windows below, and he felt the sphere grow warm in his hand. Not hot as it did if any of the Others were around, just comfortingly warm, as if someone was holding his hand. Downstairs the grandfather clock began to strike nine. He yawned and rested his head against the window frame, his eyes closed and he was drawn into sleep. The owl watched as he dreamed.

He was riding hard across the moonlit moors, on either side of him rode men in bright armour that caught the moonlight. Ahead rode three other men, two of them slightly behind the king, his king, Arthur Pendragon. The destination that lay before them was an ancient stone circle, the Singing Stones that he had known since childhood, a childhood now behind him, for tonight he would feel the touch of Arthur's sword on his shoulders and he would become Sir Amicus Carrick of Deepdale.

Ahead they saw the outline of the sacred hill and within its hollow lay the stones and the work that was to be done by the king and his most trusted men. Waiting for them was Merddyn ap Heliborn, the Archmage of Britain. After tonight Deepdale would become the hiding place of the royal regalia. All that made Arthur the anointed king he was, and would always be, and Mordred would be denied his greatest desire. Somewhere, deep inside the head of the young rider, Thomas was living this wonderful night with him. He knew this was Amicus Carrick, and at the same time HE was Amicus Carrick. They were one and the same in a way he didn't really understand. He also knew that one day he would understand and was content to wait.

They left their horses at the foot of the Tor and climbed the rest of the way. The Stones stood silvered by the full moon. Before each one was a cloaked figure wearing a silver chain with a shining sphere, a gift of protection and power from the Arch-mage. Merddyn himself was standing in the centre of the circle. He came forward and bent the knee to his king and kissed the hand that wore the royal ring, a ruby red as blood, and set in thick Welsh gold. Around them the Ancient Stones raised their voices in a muted roar.

Vivat, Vivat, Rex Arturus, Rex Brittanicus!

The other knights came forward carrying carefully wrapped bundles and laid them at Merddyn's feet. He undid each one and laid out their contents until the whole of the Regalia of Britain was before them. The Mage blessed it all in his sonorous voice.

"May the Gods of the Ancient Land long hidden beneath the sea bless and keep these sacred objects. May they guard them against the dark desires and hatreds of those who would desecrate them. They will lie hidden from the eyes of the world until Arthur shall come again in name to rule the Blessed Isles."

The High King Arthur now came forward to speak to those gathered in his name.

"Ladies, Freemen, knights of the realm. In three days time I will fight my last battle. I already know the outcome, and that for a while, the High Kingdom of Albion will be no more. Therefore, on the advice of Merddyn I have come to this ancient place of power to hide the sacred regalia of the High King. I know that Mordred my son and sadly, my enemy, desires them and that he wishes to feel the weight of my crown upon his head, to hold my sceptre and wield my power. But that he will never do.

In ancient times on this night, the night of Lammas Eve, the Corn King was sent to his death that the harvest might be prosperous. Soon I too will go to my death, as it has been foretold. But I go willingly, and the willing sacrifice dies with great power. This power I now share among you, and at the same time I lay a task upon you that will pass from generation to generation until I lay claim to the crown again."

Arthur took the gold chain from his neck and went to the first man who knelt and kissed his hand saying, "I am Ralf son of Atkins, freeman and farmer of Deepdale, I swear fealty to you as the Once and Future King."

"To you Ralf, son of Atkins of Deepdale I pass the Kings Chain of Office for safe keeping and the power of the swift running greyhound. He placed the chain about his neck and passed to the next stone and the woman who stood beside it. She knelt and kissed his hand bathing it with her tears.

"I am Margery, wife to Ralf, I swear fealty to you my Lord King, now and forever." Arthur raised her gently and kissed her hand, as he would have done to a great lady, and placed on her finger the royal Ring.

"Marjory, wife to Ralf, to you I pass the King's Ring for safe keeping and, because you are a loving wife I give to you also the power of the greyhound that you might share the work together."

Now he took from his waist the sword belt and scabbard and came to the next man. He too knelt and swore fealty and kissed his hand.

"I am Richard Lovell, Scrivener and Freeman of Deepdale your devoted servant Sire."

"Richard Lovell, Freeman, take this Belt and Scabbard and guard it well. I pass to you the power of the Badger, strong and resourceful."

Next he came to Docker, a big man more than six feet who cried like a babe as he held the king's hand and swore his oath. To him was given the King's Sword and the power of the Stallion.

The king passed to the next stone and paused not knowing what to say to his errant Queen who now knelt at his feet. "My Lord and King I have begged this place from Merddyn, that through its power I may undo the wrong I have done and earn the right to your forgiveness and mayhap one day join you in Avalon. I offer these herbs to ease the path you must tread, the *people here call them Tansy, but their real name is Asphodel."*

Arthur took her gift and smelt them then raised Guenevere to her feet. "Let there be no blame between us Gwen. I shall wear your gift next to my heart when I go into battle and I place in your hands the cup from which I drank at my crowning and pass to you the power of the Owl." He kissed her hand, her cheek and her lips and passed on.

So he came to Jarvis the Warrener and from him also he took allegiance. To Jarvis was given the Orb of Rulership and the power of the sleek, swift Ferret.

Widow Kate, a free woman and landowner, swore allegiance and offered, as was the right of any freeman, to die in his place. He blessed her and spoke gently, but declined and gave to her his Spurs and the power of the Hare.

Then he came to Mistress Fairchild the Weaver, She knelt dry-eyed and pricked her finger with her spindle and with her blood anointed him, an ancient offering to take on his sins, that he might die in purity at his death. Arthur wept at her gift and knelt for her blessing, then gave into her hands the Royal Seal and the power of the Cat.

Simon of Ely, a carpenter, was next to kneel before the king and swear his oath. To him was given the Kings Sceptre of English oak, topped with a sapphire of great worth, and with it the power of the Ram.

Loveday Pym, the nurse of Amicus knelt before her king and bathed his feet with her tears. He comforted her as best he could and passed to her his Shield, for, he said, Love was the greatest shield of all. To her he gave the power of the Deer.

Meakin the pig keeper and a serf, now stood before him and apologised for not having had time to wash. He did not know why he had been chosen as he was not a Freeman. The King gave him there and then his freedom and the right to the cottage in which he lived. He also gave into his keeping his Hunting Horn. "Do not blow it until an Arthur stands before you again," he told him. "Your power is that of the Boar."

Finally he stood before the last of the guardians, Freeman Dickon Reynard the Forrester. "Merddyn tells me you are to be the leader of these people. To you therefore I give the Ampulla of Holy oil. It will be your descendants who will anoint the once and future king every one hundred years and to you I give the power of the Hawk."

Now at the last, he stood before the child-man Amicus Carrick. He accepted his oath of allegiance, then called for the sword of Launcelot and with it dubbed him knight. Raising him to his feet he bade him take his place as the Guardian of the Mage stone.

"Merddyn, now it is your turn, open the chamber beneath the stones, that the Crown may be interred by its true Guardian."

Merddyn had trained them well during the weeks before and at his signal the first guardian took breath and sang out a pure note, then each one joined in until the night was filled with a long graceful musical cadence ending with the clear high note of young Sir Amicus. The Stones replied with a descant of their notes and with a harsh grating sound the King's Stone slid sideways to reveal a flight of stone steps. The king took the crown of Britain from his head and held it for a few minutes. "I remember when this was placed on my head and the Kingdom of Albion was placed under my protection. Now I surrender it to another Arthur who will come on a night such as this in the far future. May God be with us all."

He wrapped it in his mantle of purple velvet and placed it in the hands of his newest and youngest knight. Amicus descended into the chamber beneath the stone and laid it on the altar already prepared there and bowed before it. Then he returned to his place and the same notes were sung but in reverse. Obediently the stone covered its secret.

The king turned to the gathering "To all of you I say this, Live long, live in grace, and pass on the knowledge and the powers you have been given." He came to Amicus and placed his hands on the slim shoulders of the young knight. "Stay Amicus and guard these treasures. To you I pass the power of the King's Stag, which power was once my own, and the Guardianship of the Treasures of Britain, to you and the heirs of your body until your task is done." He bent his head whispered to the young man some private words. Then Merddyn served wine and bread to all to seal the promises made and the King and his knights descended the hill and took to horse. They rode away from Deepdale, leaving the legend behind them.

* * *

The grandfather clock downstairs was striking the last of nine strokes as Thomas woke, unsure if he was Thomas or Amicus, but knowing that what he had seen would, from now, on be the meaning of his life.

The full knowledge of who and what he was, and what he was destined to become had been passed to him in those few moments of linkage with the past. The last words of Arthur lingered in his mind.

"Amicus, for these few moments I see into the future and I foretell that from your line will come one who will restore my

crown to the rightful Pendragon, and, mayhap if the heart is true and brave, restore to me what I most desire."

But for now he was still only a boy, and he wept silently for he knew that this was the last real day of his childhood.

SIX

The Thomas that had cried himself to sleep was not the Thomas that woke the next morning. It was as if another, stronger and more aware Thomas had crept in overnight. Deep within, the child was still there, and would continue to be a part of him forever, something he had heard his dad call 'The Forever Child.'

He washed and dressed as usual and went down to the kitchen where Mrs. Jackson was bustling about getting breakfast. "Morning Thomas m'dear," she said brightly, then stopped and looked at him. "Goodness, we'll have to see about getting you a new uniform, you're fast growing out of that one." Thomas smiled and sat down to eat, opposite Frank who was deep in the morning paper.

Later, driving to the school Frank made the same comment. "They do say as 'ow thirteen is the grow-fast time. Looks like ye'll be needing a whole new wardrobe Tom lad. If'n I didn't know better I'd say as 'ow ye've growed overnight. Yer mam and dad'll not know thee."

Thomas looked down at his blazer sleeves and was quietly amazed to see that his wrists stuck out. He had a nasty feeling his pants were much shorter as well. Maybe Mrs. Jackson could let them down tonight, otherwise he was in for a lot of ribbing from the other boys.

Wednesday meant Geography with Father Timothy, Science with Father Laurence and a break period through to the afternoon session. He planned to spend that time in the library looking through local land records of ownership.

But his mind wandered badly during lessons and an exasperated Father Laurence made him stay behind to complete his experiment a second time so making him late for lunch. "Drat," he thought, less time to spend in the library. When he arrived there however he found Father John waiting for him in one of the small reading alcoves going over a pile of books and papers set in front of him.

Thomas looked at them and then at his mentor and grinned. "Looks like I'll be here till going home time."

Father John smiled back, "Funny you should say that, I'm the one who arranged for you have a lesson break this afternoon. You'll be working on a special project for me. Now here," he sorted through a pile of papers and extracted one from the pile. "Now here you will find the history of Misselthwaite Manor and a list of its owners. You'll see that around 1490 the name changes from Carrick to Misselthwaite. This happened because there was no male heir and the ownership passed to the eldest daughter who married a William Misselthwaite."

He paused and went to a marked place in a large book. "However, when we come to 1587 almost a hundred years later, we find a Royal Charter granting a Baronetcy to Charles Misselthwaite in return for help and favours offered to the Crown. There is an interesting corollary to this. Charles Misselthwaite had to change his name back to Carrick on command of the King as the charter stipulates that this name must be taken in order to claim the title."

Thomas read it through several times then looked across the table at his companion. "Does this mean I'll have to change my name as well on my birthday."

"Yes Thomas, but you can add the name of Greystone to that of Carrick and become Sir Thomas Greystone-Carrick of Misselthwaite Manor. "It has quite a ring to it, and it will please your father to know that his name will not be set aside completely."

Thomas looked down at the papers and frowned. "I will also change the name of the Manor. It will become Carrick House as it once was. It is only right and fitting considering the circumstances, that the ancient name is restored."

Father John's head came up, his eyes startled. The statement had been made with an authority far beyond the boy's age. He looked at him carefully and began to notice the differences in him from yesterday. He seemed taller, more assured, as if he had already taken on his inheritance and the responsibility it entailed.

Thomas looked up and smiled, "It's alright Father John, it's still me, but last night I stood with the King, and with Amicus back at the beginning when it all started, I saw them all and I will recognise them again. There are still some things I need to learn but it will come back to me bit by bit. But I need to see inside the Manor House. Do you know who holds the keys sir?"

John Foxton took a deep breath and said carefully, " I do Thomas. I am the executor of your grandfather's will. Your grandmother insisted you came to the Priory School of St Edwards when you moved and left money for your education. When you leave here you will go on to Cambridge, it has all been arranged."

"I don't really have any say in the matter do I?" Said Thomas wistfully. But then that's what happens to some people." He stared out of the window.

Father John cleared his throat and said gently, " Er, Thomas, what did you mean when you said you had been with the King last night, when it all started?" Thomas turned back to him, his eyes bright with the memory of his experience.

"I dreamed, only it wasn't a dream, it was something much more than a dream. I seemed to be Amicus Carrick, the boy who was the first Mage of the Stones. I was inside his head, or he was inside mine, it's difficult to say. The King and his knights came to the Stones and Merlin was there, only they said it differently, something like Merthin. There were people standing by the stones and the King went to each one in turn. They knelt down and put their hands between his, it was like ... a promise to him."

"Fealty, Thomas, they were swearing fealty to their King."

"Then he gave each one something to keep and guard.

A golden chain, a ring, a sword ... things like that. Then he took a sword from one of his knights and knighted Amicus, only I was Amicus and he was me. When the sword touched me it seemed to leave a sort of 'mark' I suppose you'd call it only the mark was on the inside of me where it can't be seen, only felt.

Then the people sang a kind of song and the Stones answered, it was tremendous I could feel the ground shaking with the power of it. Then a special stone, the one that was outside the circle slid aside. There was a little room down there and a stone table. Arthur took his crown off and gave it to me, I mean Amicus, and said I was to guard it. I, well we, took it down into the little room and left it there. Then they sang the song again and the stone closed up. The King said something privately to Amicus, I can't remember exactly what it was, but I think I'll remember when the time is right. After that Arthur and the knights rode away. There was some other stuff, but I can't remember it."

"I think that you remembered it very well." Said Father John. "Almost too well."

There was a silence in the deserted library as Father John watched a boy take hold of his future and become a man." Thomas looked through the tall window at the moors for a long moment, then turned back. "Since I have the afternoon free sir, could we go and see the house."

"Yes of course. I have seen to it that everything has been kept in fair order. We can go now if you like." They left the library and walked down the wide stairway to the front door. " Sir Piers let things go when his daughter left, he seemed to lose heart in the day to day running of the estate. Most of the furniture was antique and very valuable so I had it put into store. It will need re-decorating of course, but then it will be sometime before you go to live there."

"Maybe," said Thomas absently as they got into Father John's old Ford. "A lot depends on what happens when I am fourteen." He turned to his companion as he eased the car into the main drive. "I believe some of the regalia has been lost?"

The car swerved a little and recovered. "How do you know that," demanded Father John. "I didn't tell you!"

"Well, it's a little complicated to explain, but I can feel Amicus in my head and every now and then he tells me something I should know." He turned and laughed. "It's alright sir, I'm not going bonkers, he won't be there for long, he's just come back to help me until Lammas Eve." He rummaged in his pocket and brought out a bag. Would you like a toffee sir, there's plenty to spare." They drove on in companionable silence.

* * *

In the sitting room of Marcus Allsop's house a small group of people crowded together while Mrs. Jackson took round mugs of tea and wedges of her famous fruit cake. From his armchair beside the fire he looked round at the gathering.

Len Thorpe from London was a small time mugger and thief, lounging beside him was his friend Fred Harris who was fresh out of Brixton prison for receiving stolen goods. Then there was Jack Farrell a local layabout with a reputation for brawling. The last and most reliable was Pete Willis, clever and devious and willing to do anything for money.

They were a long way from the knights he had once commanded as a Prince of the Realm, and who now lay sleeping until he summoned them to the battle. But they were good enough for the menial tasks that needed doing. It would all change when he had the wealth and power Arthur's crown would bring him. He knew and accepted that he could not overthrow the present monarchy. But he could and would become the power behind it, and the line he would found would marry into it, he would see to that. In a few months he could take on his real form as a Prince in all but name. Then he could settle old scores. He would enjoy that, he would enjoy that very much.

"Mr Allsop, Marcus, are you alright, can I get you something?" Mrs. Jackson stood at his side looking anxious. " You look quite pale."

Marcus Allsop collected his thoughts and gave her a thin, cold smile. "Its quite alright Mrs Jackson, I have a great deal on my mind at the moment. Let's get on with the meeting shall we? Now, if you will kindly give me your full attention everyone we can begin." Marcus uncovered a large crystal ball in the centre of the table and stared at his audience.

Fools, every last one of them. They thought they would soon be rich and powerful, but he doubted more than one, maybe two would survive the coming battle. Those who did would be eliminated quietly, one by one in the weeks that followed. It was all falling into place very nicely. By the end of August he would have the power and the wealth. Within a year he would be a member of Parliament. Within five years, he would be Prime Minister and the virtual ruler of England ready to plunder the land and its people.

"I want you all to fix your eyes on the crystal," he said, "and watch the pinpoint of light in its centre."

Obediently six pairs of eyes focussed and within seconds were linked mentally to their dark leader. His voice flowed over them like syrup.

"You are comfortable and relaxed and you will not be frightened by anything you experience. You are no longer aware of your bodies. You feel very light as if you are floating. Your attention is fixed on the light in the crystal. You are drawn to it and into it, passing into the crystal itself. As you enter the crystal your body is changed into that of a bird, a black crow. Now you are flying over the moors towards a circle of stones, there are people inside the circle, one standing in front of each stone. They are our enemies and will harm us if we allow them to do so. Just outside the circle is a tree.

"Fly over and around it imprint its location, shape, and size in your mind. This is important.

"Whenever I tell you to 'enter the crystal' you will change your shape and fly in the form of a crow to this place and perch in this tree. You will look and listen to anything that occurs in that circle and you will report back to me. When I say, 'return through the crystal,' you will return to your own form. After you have reported to me, you will forget what you have heard. Do you all understand?"

A muted 'yes' whispered through the room.

"You will withdraw from the crystal and resume your normal form, you will give an unshakable loyalty to me at all times. When our objective is realized you will receive wealth and position as a reward. You will wake in five seconds from now."

There was a rustle of movement as they stretched and looked around. Bettina Jackson bustled off to make a final cup of tea. Marcus handed sealed envelopes containing money into eager hands. He believed in paying for service, but not for very long. They were expendable, every one of them.

* * *

A little before sunset, dressed entirely in black, Marcus left his house and walked to his car. The streets were empty. Most of Deepdale was watching Coronation Street. The rest were in The Carrick Arms.

He drove the dark green Morgan through the deepening twilight, taking small side roads that gradually became little more than tracks. Finally he stopped and got out. He took a pair of Wellington boots from the car and put them on, slung a back pack over his shoulders then, with a strong walking stick in hand and a large torch he set off across the moors towards a distant outcrop of limestone. His objective formed a high ridge three miles long, running from Whitley-by-Foss to Charnley Cross. As he walked a large black crow flew overhead cawing loudly. He looked up and smiled.

Thirty minutes of hard walking brought him to the base of the ridge, and he began to climb. From the ease with which he moved he had done this many times before. A third of the way up a thick shrub hid an opening to a cave. With a quick look round Marcus disappeared into it. It smelt of damp earth and decaying leaves and the floor underfoot sloped downwards.

Taking the torch from his pocket he pushed on. The way became narrow and twisted from side to side until without warning, he came to a smooth wall of stone. Setting his shoulder to it he pushed with all his strength. With a deep groan the stone swung inwards.

The cave was large and reached up into dark shadows overhead. In the centre, on a stone table stood a sphere of faceted crystal that glowed with a pale blue light. On one side lay a horn with a silver mouthpiece and on the other a wooden rod tipped with a Lodestone. Marcus took a torch from a wall sconce and lit it with a match, then used it to light several others until the cave sprang into full view.

The walls were hung with rich tapestries, lightening the starkness of the stone beneath. It was cold, so cold that Marcus' breath hung on the air like mist. He shivered glad of the warmth of his black leather jacket. But the other occupants of the cave seemed not to mind.

They lay, all twelve of them, on couches arranged in a circle around the central pillar, each covered with the banner of their house and lineage. At the head of each couch stood a wooden cross piece bearing a full suit of armour complete with helm, the shield lay against it. A sword lay along the body of each knight, the hilt clasped in his hands. Marcus felt a surge of pride run through him. These were his knights, not Arthur's, sworn to him alone. They had come here willingly, enduring a sleep of near death for over a thousand years to be with him when he called. And now at last it was time.

He moved purposefully around the cave, arranging

things he took from the backpack. Soon an aromatic scent began to fill the air as he burned incense in a bowl. He took a silver cup from the pack and filled it with red wine and the contents of a small packet of specially mixed herbs. As he worked the crow fluttered into the cave and walked into the centre. It spread its wings and dissolved into a mist that swirled around the crystal then finally melted away to reveal a woman with handsome but cruel features. Her black hair curled to her waist and her eyes, the colour of rich amber, took in the preparations with a smile.

"I bid you good even Mother," said Marcus quietly.

Morgana moved to his side giving him a cold smile. "Is all ready for the Awakening?"

"Yes, all is ready".

Morgana took the incense and moved to the Northern quarter of the cave. There she blew the smoke into the air where it formed a spiral that began to turn anti -clockwise. She repeated the gesture at each quarter and returned to the centre leaving the four spirals spinning in the air . Then she picked up the crystal and circled the cave three times each time pausing at the quarters to thrust the crystal into the spinning circles with a muttered Word of Power. Finally she lifted the cup up high and began to chant, turning in a circle as she did so, her dark red gown swirling around her. The cold began to disperse and the air to warm as her voice woke the hidden powers of the dark that had slept for so long.

"By my will and by my power, on this day and in this hour
I summon up and summon in, all that's owed by kith and kin.
Life to life as it must be I call you all to come to me.

Warm the blood and deep the breath, all ye who have defeated death.
Life to limb and strength to arm, roll back sleep and mind be calm.
Time to keep the oath once sworn, time to face the new made dawn.
Live and breathe and stand and fight, time to serve with sword and might.
Knights of Valour wake to war, stiffen sinew, set the jaw.
I claim your sword, your shield, your skill, For Mordred fight, for Mordred kill.
Warriors wake from aeons sleep, the time is now your oaths to keep."

She swung round to Mordred. "NOW" she screamed, "BLOW THE HORN NOW!" Mordred seized the horn, and blew.

In the enclosed space the sound became an agony that ripped through their minds. It ricocheted off the walls and echoed down the narrow passage before erupting into the outside world. Startled birds rose in flocks and fled screeching into the evening air seeking to flee the thunderous sound.

Back in the cave Morgana and Mordred stirred from where they had fallen, blood running from ears and noses. The air in the cave was filled with a deep humming sound that slowly died away. Morgana rose to her feet and wiped the blood from her face with the hem of her gown. Mordred was already standing by the side of the first couch, his eyes bright with hope, his face eager.

"Agravaine," he whispered. Then louder "Agravaine it's time, wake up!

The lashes on the pale cheeks fluttered and slowly lifted revealing eyes so dark as to appear black. The thin mouth lifted at the corners and a voice, rough and hoarse from lack of use answered him. "Mordred, by all that's unholy, it worked. The spell worked."

Morgana came with the cup and held it to his lips. "Drink, it will strengthen you. Mordred start awakening the others."

It took hours to get them on their feet, stretching limbs and learning to stand and walk and talk again. There was laughter and jokes as they compared doublet and hose with the black jeans, roll necks sweaters and black leather jackets Mordred had provided. But all were eager to begin their mission. They gathered round the glowing pile of crystals that Morgana had empowered to heat the cave and listened as Mordred told them of the changed world they were about to re-enter.

Morgana left them early, unable to sustain her human form for very long. But Mordred stayed through the night bringing them up to date, setting soup to heat on the camping stove and slowly introducing their bodies to long denied nourishment. He wondered if Arthur had felt the same pride in his Knights as he felt as he watched them laugh and talk and speak of the battle to come.

Hugh De Courcy stocky and belligerent, always arguing. Gervaise of Brittany elegant and deadly with a blade. Vigo a minor Prince of the Orkneys and one he never trusted entirely. The twins Garth and Gregory, Ranulf and Mawg, and

Ossa skilled swordsmen all three and Wulf the dark browed Pict with his heavy battle axe, Agravaine his half brother and second in command. Niall the silent and menacing Fenlander and Sorne the viper tongued Cornishman, nephew of the murdered Gorlois. All of them were sworn to his command and his alone.

Mordred left just after dawn bidding them rest and promising to come with more food and transport at night. He smiled to himself as he walked with a jaunty stride. His long awaited ambitions were falling into place. Within weeks he would wear Arthur's crown, wield Arthur's power and at last he would take his rightful place not just in this little kingdom, but on the world stage. He whistled as he walked.

From a gnarled and stunted tree an owl watched him go. And a small black and white dog scrambled up to the cave where it listened for more than half an hour before returning to its mistress.

SEVEN

"This is quite an occasion Thomas, and one I have long awaited." They stood before the front door of the Manor looking at the ancient knocker. In his hand Thomas held the keys to the house. He thought back to the first time he had been here, just a few weeks ago, so much had changed in such a short time that he felt torn apart. He stepped up to the door and turned the key in the lock. The house held its breath.

Thomas stepped into the hall and faced the portrait of his great-grand-father. He could see faintly, the resemblance to his grandmother and his father. What he could not see, but which struck his silent companion like a physical blow, was his own amazing resemblance to the picture. The same determined stance with feet planted apart. The slim wiry build, the hair swept back from the broad forehead. But most of all the eyes. Fierce, proud, and intense. He could almost see the outline of a stag's rack of antlers, Then the moment faded.

Thomas turned and smiled. "He looks very fierce but I think behind the fierceness he could have been quite jolly."

"Yes. He had a great sense of humour. He was also a fine horseman and worn prizes at Bisley for shooting. In fact in his day, as you will find when you read the entry in Debretts he represented England at the Olympics. He was also good at languages and spoke very good French and Italian. You would have got on well with him Thomas."

"Lets explore." Thomas ran off abruptly all boy once more. Father John followed more slowly, smiling at his charge's enthusiasm.

For the next two hours Thomas went over the house from top to bottom. There were attics with all sorts of fascinating things in them, an old rocking horse, chests of clothes going back a hundred years, portraits of his family far older than that. Boxes of books, and toys generations of Carricks had played with. He found a high backed chair carved with fantastic beasts, a bow and a quiver full of arrows, swords, uniforms, helmets and the bric-a-brac of countless years of family treasures.

The other rooms, all thirty-two of them were mostly empty, but imposing, with high exquisitely moulded ceilings and tall arched windows. Those in the hall and lighting the stairwells were inset with stained glass depicting the knights and ladies of Arthurian times, but it was the first landing that held Thomas's attention the most. It showed Arthur handing the Crown of Britain to Amicus. He turned to Father John who stood watching him with alert interest, then came slowly down the stairs.

"Father John, as each one takes up the Mageship, do they also feel Amicus inside them, like a voice telling them things?"

"I am not a Carrick Thomas, so I can't say for sure, but I think it is very likely. One of the things I have learned during my lifetime of study, is that there are things we cannot, maybe are not meant to, understand. I have my own thoughts on the matter, but as yet I think this is not the time to speak of them. Come it is time to get you home. I called Mrs. Jackson and told her I would be bringing you."

As they went towards the car Thomas stopped suddenly. "Wait sir, I have to go back, there's something to take with us." He turned and raced back fumbling with the keys.

"Wait Thomas, its getting late." But Thomas was already inside. The main staircase rose to a square landing overlooked by the stained glass window that had so taken his fancy. Thomas stood looking intently at the picture. It was framed by long sections of red glass, each section holding a different pattern. On the right hand side the lowest section showed what looked like a rod topped by a brilliant blue stone. Thomas turned excitedly.

"Look Father John, it's the King's Sceptre."

"Yes I know. Each section shows one piece of the Royal Regalia. It was designed like that."

"Yes, but what you didn't see was this." Thomas pointed to the banisters. The palings had been carved in three sections, each section joined to another by a wooden ring. The pattern was exactly the same all the way from top to bottom of the main staircase. At the beginning of each landing was a carved newel, a wooden sphere inset with pieces of different coloured glass. Thomas grabbed Father John's hand and pulled him to the landing, then pointed to the newel heading the stair to the West Wing. The inset was blue.

"Don't you see?" he asked impatiently. "Look." He put both hands on the newel post and pulled upwards. There was a click and it came away in his hands leaving behind it a brilliantly blue stone. Then Thomas took hold of the paling itself and tugged. Another click. He turned and held out the sapphire crowned sceptre of King Arthur. "The window is a sort of map of where the rest of the regalia can be found. I think it was hidden in the Abbey that used to stand where our school is now. When Henry the Eighth pulled it down the monks hid the treasures they had been guarding all over the place. Look, this window has the date when it was made, *1541,* just about the time when he was closing down all the shrines and monasteries. It all fits. We just have to find the answers in the picture."

Father John stood open mouthed. The hands holding the relic were trembling as the power of the consecrated sceptre flooded through him. Then he looked at Thomas and shook his head. "And a little child shall lead them." He quoted. "It took the clear eyes and uncluttered mind of a young boy to see what we have missed all these years. But Thomas, the Guardianship and the power that will be yours on your fourteenth birthday, these are things best kept to ourselves for the time being." Eyes alight with excitement Thomas nodded.

"Of course sir, I understand."

They drove back to Deepdale in silence until they reached the house. Father John drew up in front of the driveway. "Be careful Thomas, there is danger all about you. I know you are guarded but nevertheless do not relax your vigilance. Good night, dear boy. God bless you."

"Good night sir, and thanks for all your help. See you tomorrow." He ran inside and dumped his books on the hall table. "I'm home Mrs. Jackson," he called out. "Just going to wash and I'll be down for dinner."

In the kitchen Betty Jackson took a steak and kidney pie out of the oven and began to fill three plates. "If you asked me I think he's spending too much time with that priest fellow. I don't like it Frank. That's twice this week he's brought him home. What's he up to I'd like to know?"

Frank grunted and went on reading the racing results. "'Appen he's just interested in the boy, he's bright, is Thomas, 'as the makings of a University type I reckon. Talks my 'ead off every morning. Them mathymatiks fair makes yer 'ead hurt to listen to. Let the lad be Betty lass, and stop fussin'." He put down the paper and attacked his pie with gusto. Thomas, hands and face shining came in and sat down beside him.

"Evening Mr. Jackson. Have you had a good day?"

"Aye lad, won a fiver fer a one pound bet. That makes it a good day as far as I, know. 'Ow about thee Tom?"

Thomas dug into a piece of steak. "Great, I got a gold star for my Geography essay. Then I did some research in the library in the afternoon." A bubble of mischief broke inside him and he just had to tease Mrs. Jackson. "Did you know that Misselthwaite Manor was once called Carrick House?"

Mrs. Jackson lost control of the milk jug and spilt milk over the tablecloth. "Drat," she said. "Now look what you've made me do. Eat your dinner, Thomas." She mopped up the milk and went to get the treacle tart she'd made for desert muttering to herself.

Thomas had two slices of the tart, then excused himself to do his homework. There was not a great deal of it and when he'd finished he switched on his computer and surfed the Net for information about King Arthur. There were several different versions of the basic story, but what interested him most was the account of the last Battle between the King and his son Mordred. It seemed so very sad that Arthur's son hated him so much. Thomas couldn't imagine hating his dad so much he'd want to kill him.

He turned the computer off, cleaned his teeth and changed into his pyjamas. Before he got into bed he drew a big red X over the date on his calendar. His mum and dad had been away almost four weeks. Their last letter said the script writing was going well and they hoped to be home in early June. There was a P.S. asking him to think about what he would like for his birthday. But Thomas had other things on his mind. What would they say when they came home and he told them he would become Sir Thomas Greystone-Carrick of Carrick House on his fourteenth birthday!

He climbed into bed, put out the light and lay quietly listening to the sounds in the house. Frank was locking doors and windows, while Mrs. Jackson set the table for breakfast. The grandfather clock chimed ten-thirty as their bedroom door closed. Most Deepdale folk were up early, so they went to bed early as well. Thomas turned over and snuggled down. But sleep wouldn't come. Twenty minutes later he gave up trying, nothing had helped. Half an hour later he was just about to go down to the kitchen for a glass of milk when he heard a clunk at the window, then another. With the third one came a soft bark.

He got up and went to the window and looked out. Bessie stood in the driveway with Grim. She waved an arm, gesturing to him to open the window. He leaned out and said as loudly as he dared. "Bessie what on earth are you doing out there? Is there something you need?"

Bessie grinned at him. "Ye're a sweet kind laddie but I've not come for help. Tis you I need Thomas. You'd best be coming quickly we don't have all night."

But I've got my pyjamas on." Thomas said foolishly.

"Then get dressed ye balmpot! And hurry!" She sat down on the front step.

Thomas grabbed for underwear, then jeans and a thick cabled sweater, socks and trainers followed. Then he crept downstairs and opened the front door.

" 'Bout time too. Come on we've a ways to go," grumbled Bessie.

"Where are we going Bessie? Shall I get my bike?" Thomas hopped on one foot tying the laces on his trainers.

Bessie cackled. "You'll not get to where we're goin' on yer bike laddie. 'Tis the Second Road we'll be taking."

Thomas stopped tying his laces and stared at her. "What's the Second Road? It sounds spooky." But Bessie was already ahead and lifting the latch of the gate.

"It's like this," said Bessie, moving more quickly than an elderly woman should. "We've bin called to a meeting. It seems the Kings Sceptre 'as bin found and they want ter know about it. Besides, 'tis time you met the Guardians of the Stones laddie."

Thomas stopped in his tracks. "The Guardians, I'm going to meet the Guardians," he stammered. "But, but, they're all dead long ago." I saw them with the King."

"Aye Thomas that ye did. But the Guardians ye'll see tonight are the descendants of those who were honoured by the King. They've kept the promises their ancestors made for over a thousand years. Now it's your turn, for you're the Mage of the Stones, or will be come Lammas Day. Now, look lively, here be the entry to the Second Road."

She stopped and looked around to make sure they were alone. Before them was a narrow footpath leading between high hedges that Thomas did not remember ever seeing there before. Grim darted through and disappeared. Bessie turned to Thomas her blue eyes serious now.

"Do you remember what power the king gave to young Amicus?"

"Yes," said Thomas, wondering how she knew about his dream. "He gave him the power of the King Stag."

"Well that be your power now Thomas. As you pass through the entrance, just think about the Kings Stag, and you'll be alreet. I'll go ahead and wait fer 'ee."

She passed between the hedges and vanished into the darkness beyond. Thomas hesitated. He had no idea what this was all about but he knew, deep down that he had to follow her even though he was scared. He took a deep breath and pushed his way through the hedge and on to the little track, thinking about the King Stag.

Suddenly there was pain. Once Thomas had broken his leg and two of his ribs in a fall but this was far worse. He felt as if he was being torn in two, turned inside out, and shaken to pieces, it went on and on. Then he was on the other side of the hedge and on a wide path that seemed to give off its own light. He stooped trying to catch his breath.

"You did well Thomas, the first trip is always painful, but it gets easier. Come now, there's no time to waste." The voice came from an owl sitting on a branch above him. Thomas moved forward and stumbled. His feet felt wrong. He looked down and saw hooves where his trainers had been. He reared up in fright and found his head tangled in branches. No, not his head, a different head, a head with tall branching antlers. He stepped forward slowly and the owl fluttered her wings.

There's a pool a few steps down the track, go and look at yourself."

The pool was deep and clear. He looked into its depths and saw..! A King Stag. Twelve tined, muscular, strong and proud looked back at him. With a surge of realisation Thomas knew without any doubt at all that this power was now his by right and the might and power of his ancestry welled up in him. He swung around and bowed his regal head to the owl above him. His thoughts touched hers.

"Lady, it is time, Let us go to the meeting."

The Second Road opened before them broad and green and mysterious. There were many others of his kind on the road tonight, but none were taking his path. Swift and free he broke into a gallop and set off across the moors, the owl flying above, Grim following. As he ran Thomas flung up his head and bellowed full -throated, letting the others know he was on his way.

* * *

The dream, always the same dream, no matter how he tried. No matter what barriers he put up it kept returning. Mordred turned and twisted on his crumpled bed then sat up sweating and trembling and shaking his head to rid himself of the insistent images. He got out of bed and went down to the tiny kitchen. Perhaps a hot drink would help. He set out a mug, milk and sugar then, with a curse he put them back, and went into the front room and poured himself a glass of brandy.

Leaning back against the chair he let his thoughts run on. He was so tired. There were even times when he wondered why he was hanging on to this idea of revenge.

Such thoughts had become more frequent of late. For over a thousand years he had defied time and age by holding to the hate inside and letting it fill his every waking moment. But, was it all worth it?

He allowed his mind drift back to childhood and memories of his mother. She had been so beautiful with her milk white skin and dark hair tumbling in curls to her waist. Her voice could be so soft when she had her own way, then strident and cold when she didn't. He remembered the insistent hammering of her words.

"He is an upstart, he fears me because he knows that I am the true daughter of Gorlois and Igraine and he is just the bastard son of Uther Pendragon. No matter that Merddyn has put him on the throne, it is ours by right as descendants of the premier Prince of Britain. My father would have been High King if it were not for him."

Only once had Mordred has ventured to contradict her. "But he didn't ask to be born. How can you blame him?

Blame Uther yes, but why Arthur? You say he is a Bastard, but then so am I."

The pain of the beating that followed was a haunting memory. After that it was easier to believe what she said, do what she asked, be what she wanted him to be. So many centuries, so many different names and places but always the same goal. Always the same loneliness, the same drive to find the Royal Regalia, to be crowned King as was his right as Arthur's son.

That last battle had brought him face to face with his father. Arthur had taken off his helm and looked him in the eyes. " Mordred, let this stop, now, before more gallant men are killed. It is not too late. Let go this hatred your mother has instilled in you and end the feud. Why did you not come to me when you were young? I would have acknowledged you, loved you, cared for you."

He had wanted to believe. Dear God, for just one moment he had longed to feel his father's arms around him, and to know he was loved by just one person. His mother had never loved him, he knew that, had known it all his life. He was just a weapon of hate and revenge conceived, borne and honed for her use. He remembered how royal Arthur had looked in his armour, and how small he had felt on that battlefield, knowing with envy in his heart that he could never be like him. Then rage had taken over, he lifted his sword and brought it down on the unprotected head of the king.

That was always where the dream ended. With Arthur at his feet and he, Mordred, sobbing with fear and guilt, looking up at Lancelot looming over him, sword raised. Then spinning down into the darkness screaming. " Father, Father,

I didn't mean to do it, I didn't mean to do it!"

He remembered dawn and waking on the battlefield surrounded by the dead. Despite Lancelot's blow he seemed to be unhurt and had staggered from the field. Hidden behind an overturned cart he saw the arrival of the three Queens in the Death Barge and watched Bedivere lay the wounded king in their arms then wave them out of sight, on their way to Avalon.

That was when Merddyn had come to him. He had talked to him for a long time, but, as always in the dream, he couldn't quite hear what he was saying. After that it was all dim and hazy. He walked for a long time. He must have done other things but couldn't remember what. He kept hearing Arthur's voice in his head saying he would return to claim his kingdom. He remembered him saying he had hidden the crown and the regalia with the youngest knight of the Round Table, and recalled his feeling of total despair. Since then he had but one desire, to find his father's crown and claim the kingdom.

The long empty years had been bad. He'd had to forage for food and had stolen to live. As the years lengthened he had come to realise with horror that he did not grow old as others did. At first he had fled into the forest, terrified by the thought of an unending guilt ridden existence. But slowly he'd learned to deal with it. Gradually, all those who might have recognised him had died and he began to feel safe again.

More years went by and he made a new life for himself, changing names, places, livelihoods and slowly amassing new wealth. He watched as the Normans overtook the land and had sided with them, and won favour at William's Court. But he took care not become too prominent lest people asked questions that could not be answered.

As a mercenary he fought for Richard in the Holy Land and again with Henry at Agincourt. Time and again he sought shelter in monasteries when life in the outside world grew too much to bear. But he always returned to the outside world with the same aim, searching for the hiding place of Arthur's crown.

Sometimes his mother came to him in her crow form, her punishment of an ageless existence the same as his. He would let her take enough energy from him to take human form for a few hours. But her fury and hatred would engulf him dragging him down into her personal maelstrom of pain. Then she had told him of her plan. Of the small band of knights loyal to her and to him that she had placed in a magical sleep deep in a cave on the Derbyshire moors. There they would wait until woken to fight the last and greatest battle, when Arthur's crown would finally be his. It had given him hope and the strength to search and keep searching for the lost regalia. Now at last he was within grasping distance of his dream. He drifted at last into an uneasy sleep

For the second time that night he woke, sweating. He sat for a minute, swallowed the last of the brandy and went back to bed, but not to sleep. He lay staring into the dark and wondering what would have happened if he had not struck that fatal blow, if he had taken Arthur's hand and asked for forgiveness, if he had called a halt to the battle, if, if, if ...!

He thought of young Thomas Greystone and the obvious affection, and yes, love, he had for his father. What would it have been like to have felt Arthur's arms around him as a child? Would he have let him ride before him on his charger? Let him sit in his chair at the Round Table?

They would have gone hunting together, flown their hawks together, laughed and joked together. It would have been, could have been so different. It might even have been possible for him to become king when his father died. He wondered if Arthur would still have been taken to Avalon, or if he would simply have been buried in the chapel at Camelot.

A long forgotten memory stirred within him, of a time when Guenevere had given him a blue velvet doublet sewn by her own hands and embroidered with golden leopards. It had been a birthday gift. His mother had never given him anything on his birthday, ever. He had wanted to throw his arms around his stepmother, but with his own mother watching he'd mockingly told Guenevere that blue was not his colour. She had turned away to hide her disappointment and Morgana had laughed.

He felt a strange sensation come over him and put a hand to his face. It came away wet. After a thousand years he was crying. What did it mean? Was it a sign that the end was in sight? Would he reach his goal this time? His mother had wanted revenge so much, and he would do it for her, and if not for himself. He sighed and turned over and finally he slept.

EIGHT

The King Stag ran like the wind. Under the starlit sky of the Second Road he raced over the high moors and down into the valleys. The earth thundered beneath his hooves and the night wind sang through his antlers. The World here was quite different to the one he knew, but he felt at home just the same. It was as if he had been waiting for this moment since he was born. He could feel his link with the past, his link with his family and all who were a part of ancient Albion as surely as he knew his name.

Standing high on the skyline he could see the Stones. Here on the Second Road they were no longer hidden in a fold of the hills, but stood proud and regal under the full moon of the ancient track. Up the last slope he came and stopped by the Mage Stone, his flanks heaving from the long gallop. Then he stepped delicately into the circle where they all waited The hare, the badger, the ferret and the ram, the cat curled against her stone, the stallion alert and watchful, the two dogs lying close together. The deer pressed shyly against the cold granite started as the owl came to rest on her stone. The boar snuffled and rooted in the grass for a few minutes then sprawled at ease on the night cool grass.

Slowly the Stag moved around the circle, touching noses in greeting, then moved out to stand before the Mage stone and waited with the others. Grim stayed outside the circle and lay quiet but watchful.

The hawk came in low and landed on its stone, silent as a whisper. The dogs started to their feet and lifted their muzzles to send a long low howl into the night. Then all of them rose to their feet, elongating as the outer forms dropped away and twelve cloaked figures stood in the soft twilight. As one, they turned towards Thomas and bowed, acknowledging his authority as the Mage of Stones.

Around and beneath them the earth vibrated as the Stones gathered up their power and let it out in one mighty note that rang through the night of the Second Road, alerting all within hearing that a destined moment had become one with its Time.

As the form of the King Stag fell away from him Thomas found himself on his hands and knees. Embarrassed, he scrambled awkwardly to his feet and made a hasty bow back to the Guardians. They remained silent, as if waiting for him to speak, then from the shadows close by him came a voice he knew well.

"Welcome to The Singing Stones Thomas. We have waited a long time for this night."

Thomas turned. "Father John," he whispered in amazement.

"Yes Thomas and many others you will recognise. Come let me introduce you to the descendants of the first Guardians." With a hand on his shoulder John Foxton led Thomas around the circle.

"Dr. and Mrs. Atkinson, Drew Docker, Ben Warrener, Wally Meakin, Nurse Pym, Miss Petronella Anderton we call her Posy by the way, Constable Les Finch, Miss Edna Pugh, Stan Simonite, and of course you know this lady well, if not in this form."

The golden haired, blue-eyed lady with a brilliant smile who now took his hand bore no resemblance to anyone he had ever met, but as soon as she spoke Thomas knew the voice.

"Welcome Thomas, this is a most joyous occasion for us all. I am the only original Guardian and I hold the King's Cup and the power of the Owl." She swept him an elegant curtsey.

"Bessie, is it really you? But ... but you're not, I mean ... well." He blushed and shuffled his feet.

Bessie's laugh rang out, and the circle joined in. "No Thomas I'm not bald. Bald Bessie is the form I wear in Deepdale. Here in the lands of the Second Road I can be as I once was. If all goes well come Lammastide, I may be allowed to fulfil my task and be forgiven at last. But see, there is someone else for you to meet. Though not a Guardian he is a part of the story that concerns all of us." She turned and held out her hand, "Barney, come and show Thomas your true form."

Out of the shadowed places beyond the Stones a strange

shambling figure shuffled forward. The shortened body and awkwardly bowed legs were topped by the head of a young good looking man. His thick chestnut hair fell in a calf's lick over a broad forehead but the lustrous brown eyes shone with intelligence, mixed with deep seated pain. Bessie drew him to her side.

"Thomas this is Barnaby. When I was… well before I was what I am now in your world, Barney was my jester. Now he is my companion and my friend. When my former friends deserted me, he alone remained true. Without him, my time in your world would have been lonely and intolerable. Because he stayed for love of me and not to do penance, he was given a form in which he could be my protector. You know him as Grim."

Thomas turned and looked at the little man. He recognised the eyes of the Jack Russell terrier, shining with devotion for his mistress. Thomas grinned and held out his hand.

"I'm delighted to meet you Barney. I'm sorry about the dog biscuits. I hope I didn't offend you."

The dark eyes crinkled with laughter. "They were very tasty Thomas though next time something a bit sweeter would not come amiss." Laughter echoed round the circle, then their leader called them to order.

"Ladies and Gentlemen, there is much to do before Lammas, and Thomas has a lot to learn about the great event that comes full circle at that time. The Cadence must be perfect in tone and pitch and the boy must learn his Magus note. I will undertake that task myself, since it will cause less notice if done at the school. But I have some good news for you all. The King's Sceptre has been found." The gasp of delight went round the group.

John Foxton threw back his cloak and produced it for them to see. The Sapphire gleamed and glistened in the moonlight as it was passed from hand to hand. When it came to Bessie she held it close to her heart and shed quiet tears before passing it back to Father John.

"Stanley Simonite, it was to your ancestor that the King's Sceptre was given, now it is in your hands until Lammas-tide. Guard it well, for all depends on every piece coming together at that time."

Stan Simonite came forward and took the beautiful thing in his gnarled carpenter's hands, and held it to his forehead in reverence. " With all the life and strength that is in me I will guard it until it is placed in the royal hand once more."

The priest turned to the others. "We now have some idea of how to find the missing pieces of the Regalia, for their hiding places are shown in the stained glass window of the Manor. Each one must help to train Thomas for his part in the coming event. I have given the keys of the Manor to him and that is where such meetings will be held, out of sight of curious eyes." He paused, his voice taking on a serious note.

"But there is other and less welcome news. We know the King's son, once Mordred, now known as Marcus Allsop has gathered together a group to oppose us. Some of them are hired thugs and thieves working for money. But in the last few days with the help of his mother Morgana he has awakened the twelve Sleepers under Ragnock Tor. They are his original band of knights, sworn to his cause and it is with their help he plans to steal the Regalia. I know his mind, he will wait until we have found all the pieces and the Once and Future King is on his way. Then he will strike and attempt to take the crown for himself."

"More dangerous is the fact he now knows that Thomas is the Mage and the key to all our hopes and efforts. He must be guarded at all costs. Without his note the Cadence will not open the Hidden Chamber. Without him, the king cannot be crowned. Without the knowledge that has been born with him we will fail in our task. Do not under-estimate the power of Mordred or the strength of those who follow him. For even as you have kept faith with the promises your ancestors gave to Arthur, so have they remained loyal to his son down the centuries.

That there will be a repeat of the last great battle I do not doubt. My fear is that it will burst the boundaries of the Second Road and spill over into our own world." He paused looking round at their serious faces then went on.

"We must be prepared for this, and for the possibility that a price may be demanded for our victory. The fate of the Blessed Isles of Britain hangs upon our ability to keep faith with the coming King. Thomas has yet to come into his full power and until he does, he will be vulnerable. One of the Others is actually in his home, supposedly taking care of him, but actually reporting his movements to the enemy. You must protect him as far as possible and with your lives if need be." He paused as a sudden cold wind blew across the circle, and a cloud passed over the moon.

Instantly Barney turned towards the North and moved into the darkness beyond the stones with his unsteady, shambling walk. A moment later they heard Grim's low voiced growl. The moonlit sky overhead was suddenly darkened by a flock of crows that swooped and soared and fluttered in the area beyond the stones filling the night with raucous, menacing sounds. With the crows came a growing feeling of menace. Danger and Dark Magic began to stalk the night beyond the circle.

The Guardians came together in a tight group standing back to back with Thomas in their midst. Father John spoke over his shoulder. "Thomas are you wearing the Mage Sphere? If you are I want you to hold it over your head. Everyone lift their spheres, NOW!"

Trembling, Thomas pulled his from beneath his sweater and with the chain wrapped round his hand he lifted it as high as he could. Thirteen spheres flashed in the moonlight. Twelve of them each lit with a different colour fed its light into the Mage sphere. Filled with their combined energies it emitted a blinding flash that lit up the entire circle. A rumble began deep in the earth as the Singing Stones added their ancient power to those of the Guardians. The sound became a single chord that grew and grew until it culminated in an ear-splitting clap of thunder that deafened them for a moment. It was followed by a flash of lightning that scattered the dark intruders. Before they could re-group a fierce wind swept up from the valley and the birds fled before it cawing shrilly as they flew.

"Quickly, into your forms," ordered Father John. Before his bewildered eyes Thomas saw the Guardians melted into their animal shapes and within minutes the circle was empty but for Thomas, Grim and the black cloaked figure of Father John.

"Thomas, you must hurry back. In the real world it is almost dawn, and I must also leave or I will be missed. Grim will guide you back to where you entered the Second Road. Use your power, reach with your mind for the shape of the King Stag and let it flow over you."

Thomas thought hard for a few minutes trying to imagine the shape he had used, but nothing happened. Miserably he looked at his companions and shivered. "It won't come" he whispered, "I can't seem to get hold of it. What can I do?"

Grim suddenly charged across the grass and snapped at his legs, nipping and snarling. Thomas yelled and sprang back, but the little dog continued to bait him until, with a sudden burst of irritation he turned on his tormentor and flowed into the form of the Stag. He lowered his antlers as if to charge, then realised the change had happened. Father John laughed softly and patted the little dog's head.

"Nice work Grim. There's nothing like a shock to get things moving. Now Thomas, be off as quickly as you can. In the morning tell Mrs. Jackson you don't feel well and want to stay home and she is to ring me at the school. I want you to rest and think about all that you have seen this night. One's first time on the Second Road can be an unnerving experience. Off you go, and God Speed."

He watched them as they left the circle. On reaching the top of the rise the Stag stopped, looked back and reared up on its hind legs pawing the air and bellowing. Then it turned and disappeared into the predawn light. Wearily Father John shifted into his Hawk form and took wing towards his own bed and rest.

High on a tree some way from the circle a single black crow sat watching. When the circle was empty it continued to sit and watch for a long while, then rose into the air and flew towards the north and the village of Deepdale. Silent and sinister it passed over the fleeting figures of the King Stag and its smaller companion, but made no move to follow them.

Thomas stepped from the opening in the hedge in his own shape once more and bent down to stroke Grim's head. "Do you want to come home with me? I can find you something to eat and you can go back to Bessie in the morning." Grim leapt up to lick his hand. "Ok then, you can sleep on my bed and I'll sneak you out after breakfast while Mrs. Jackson is cleaning the house."

They ran down the lane together and crept in through the back door. The fridge yielded some sausages left over from yesterday's dinner so Thomas cut them up for Grim, then made himself a cheese sandwich and a glass of milk before they stole up the stairs to his room. There they both climbed wearily into bed. Grim circled a few times then settled down at his feet, one paw covering his nose. Within minutes both dog and boy were fast asleep.

* * *

Mrs. Jackson knocked on the bedroom door for the third time. "Thomas, Thomas, wake up lad, it's time you were downstairs, you're going to be late for school. Thomas, wake up there's a good boy."

Thomas dragged himself up from the depths of sleep.

He ached all over and his head felt as if it had a Black and Decker drill inside it. Grim had disappeared under the bed and was keeping quiet. The door opened and Mrs. Jackson bustled in. She stopped when she saw Thomas's face. "Well now, what's wrong with you my lad. You look fair washed out. Let's see if you have a temperature. Hmm, a bit warm, do you have a pain anywhere?"

Thomas shook his head, and immediately wished he hadn't because it felt like it was going to fall off. "No, but I ache all over. We did a cross country run yesterday and I think I overdid it. It was chilly out on the moors." He crossed his fingers firmly under the duvet and told himself it was almost true. "Perhaps if you rang Father John at the school he might let me stay home today. Its mostly revision anyway." He sat up and tried to get out of bed but felt so sick and dizzy he sat down again.

Mrs. Jackson muttered under her breath and got him back under the covers. "I'll go and ring him, meantime you stay here and keep warm and I'll bring you up some breakfast. What would you like?"

At the moment he felt as if he never wanted to eat again, but he asked for tea and a bacon sandwich. He might not be hungry but Grim needed to eat. The housekeeper bustled away and as soon as he heard her going down the stairs Thomas leaned down and looked under the bed. Two bright eyes glinted at him from the shadows, then the little terrier emerged and leapt on to the bed. Thomas hugged him.

"Thanks for staying with me Grim. Should I call you Grim or Barney? Well anyway, there's a bacon sandwich for you in a minute and I'll get some water for you from the bathroom when Mrs. Jackson goes down again. She'll start doing the cleaning soon and while she's doing the upstairs I'll let you out the front door. OK? Give me your paw if you understand." Grim put out a paw and waved it at him, Thomas grinned and hugged him again. A few minutes later Mrs. Jackson's heavy tread sounded on the stairs and Grim disappeared back under the bed.

"Well now, I've rung that priest fellow and he says you're to stay put for today and he'll come by after school to see you and bring your homework. He says a hot bath with a handful of salt in it will take away the aches and pains. So get this down you and then get yourself into the bathroom. I'll get on with the housework but you call me if there's anything you want or you feel bad." She watched while he sipped at his tea and took a half-hearted bite at the bacon roll. "You'll feel better with something inside you." She went out, closing the door behind her.

Grim appeared beside the bed, tail wagging furiously. Thomas broke the roll into small pieces and set the plate on the floor then filled his bathroom mug with water, Grim made short work of both offerings. Breakfast over he got his hair brush and groomed the dog's coat free from the burrs and mud.

"There now, Bessie'll be pleased to see you looking so smart. Are you sure you can find your way?" Grim lifted a paw and waved it. "Okay, let me see where Mrs. Jackson is." He went out on to the landing and listened. The sound of a busy vacuum cleaner overlaid with an off key rendering of "Oh what a beautiful morning," told him Mrs. Jackson was cleaning the back bedrooms.

"Okay Grim, she's busy, off you go and give my love to Bessie." They crept down the stairs and as soon as Thomas opened the front door, Grim was off. He paused at the top of the drive, and looked back to give a little bark, then disappeared.

Half an hour later, lying in a warm bath Thomas went over all that had happened since they had come to live in Deepdale. From being an ordinary boy, living an ordinary life in an ordinary family, he now had a famous father, lived in a big house, and was up to his neck in a world of magic, danger, history, and legend. On top of all this, in a few months time he was due to become the thirty-seventh Baronet Greystone-Carrick of Carrick House. Surely it couldn't get any stranger than this ... or could it. He didn't feel like making a bet on it.

He suddenly felt much older than thirteen and three quarters and very tired. He climbed out of the bath and dried himself, put on clean pyjamas and crawled back into bed where he slept deeply and dreamlessly, clutching the Mage sphere in his hand.

NINE

When Thomas woke up it was well past lunchtime and he felt a lot better. He also felt very hungry. He put on his dressing gown and went downstairs to find the housekeeper and her friend Mrs. Maguire drinking tea and eating hot buttered scones. He greeted her guest politely but made a point of escaping to the front room to lie on the sofa and watch afternoon television's offering of black and white westerns.

A few minutes later Mrs. Jackson came in with a lunch tray, and he fell on it like a starving wolf cub. A bowl of homemade tomato soup went down first followed by apple pie with custard and finished off with a scone topped with butter and strawberry jam and a mug of tea. With a deep sigh he put the tray on the coffee table and settled back to watch yet another western.

Someone knocked on the front door and he woke with a start, amazed to find he had fallen asleep yet again. The television had been switched off and Mrs. Jackson had covered him with a blanket while he slept. He began to untangle himself as the sound of voices told him he was about to have a visitor. So when the door opened to admit Father John he was not surprised just grateful for some company.

"Just stay where you are Thomas, don't get up. I'll just sit on the end here. How are you feeling now? You look a little pale, but there's no harm done. Still I would rather you stayed home tomorrow as well. I've spoken to the Headmaster and he agrees. I have also asked Nurse Pym to come and see you in the morning. Just to be sure." He winked and tapped his nose.

Thomas understood at once. There was every chance there was an ear listening at the door. For a few minutes they chatted about, lessons, the latest letter from his parents and the end of term school concert scheduled for mid July. They were still talking when the door opened again and in came Mrs. Jackson carrying a tray with tea and a plate of ginger biscuits. She busied herself pouring two cups of tea and fussing with Thomas' blanket and cushions. When neither of them showed any sign of talking further she took the hint.

"While Father John is with you I'll just pop down to the shops before they close," she announced. Thomas nodded brightly and they occupied themselves with the tea until she walked past the window pushing a shopping trolley. They watched her disappear then the real conversation began.

The priest looked closely at his young companion and noting his pale face and listless attitude. " Now Thomas, how are you really feeling, I was worried about you. There is so much going on and it's a lot to take in I know but we cannot risk your health."

"I'm fine now sir, really I am," said Thomas reaching for another biscuit. "I felt awful this morning though, I ached all over and my head felt as if it was going to burst."

"Shape-shifting for the first time can have some side effects. You look a bit better now, but best take tomorrow off as well. I asked Nurse Pym to come along because it seemed a good opportunity for you to talk. She is the Guardian of the Shield, and she holds the power of the Deer. Her ancestor, Loveday Pym, was nurse to Sir Amicus. As you meet each of the Guardians they will be able to answer the questions that must be filling up your head."

Thomas thought for a moment then said, " Sir, there are some questions I would really like to ask right now if I may."

"Ask away lad."

"Well, first, who is Bessie really? She looked so different last night, sort of young and beautiful. And then there's Grim I mean Barney, what about him?"

"How well do you know the story of King Arthur Thomas," asked the priest. "I mean do you know why Mordred was so angry, and why Launcelot was sent away from Camelot?"

"Well, sort of. Dad told me the story many times, and he said it had different endings and sometimes different meanings that changed depending on who was telling it. He gave me several books to read by a man called John Matthews, Dad said he was the expert on Arthurian stuff."

"That's true. Let me take the story right down to its roots. When Rome recalled its army from Britain, some of the leaders decided to stay. They had grown to love the land and its people. But, as it disintegrated into small, petty, squabbling kingdoms one great leader arose from among the Celtic-Romanos. His name was Ambrosius. His dream was to unite all of them under one ruler, a High King. But he also knew it would have to be a younger and more able man than himself, so he chose Uther Pendragon."

"Some say he was his son, others say he was his nephew, we will never know. At first Uther did well and won many battles. But then he fell in love with a married woman, Igraine of Cornwall and though they knew it was wrong they created a child between them, Arthur. Igraine's husband Gorlois, was killed in battle and Uther was blamed for his death. Because of this Arthur was declared illegitimate, and Igraine was forced to give him up at birth. She placed him in the care of Merddyn Ap Heliborn, the Archmage of Briain and a descendant of an ancient and long forgotten Priesthood." He paused to gather his thoughts, then went on.

"There were two daughters from Igraine's first marriage, Morgana and Morgause. The elder girl Morgana, never forgave her mother and Uther for their illicit love and this hatred was transferred to their son Arthur. Merddyn or Merlin as you would know him best, had put Arthur in fosterage to Sir Ector, a good and honest knight. He trained him in all that he needed to know until he was 14. Then as you know from the legends, he was hailed as the High King after drawing the Sword from the Stone." He paused and then went on.

"Morgana nursed her hatred all through the years of Arthur's childhood and into his young manhood. He had never met or even seen her, but when she did come on the scene he fell head over heels in love with her, not knowing that she was his half-sister. Do you understand what the word incest means Thomas?"

Thomas frowned. "I think so sir. It means you can't marry someone like a sister or a brother, is that right?"

"Yes, though there are other extensions of that, but for now that understanding will do. Arthur had become High King at a very early age thanks to the help of Merlin, who had been trained in the lost arts of Atlantis. As you get older, you will be told that Atlantis never existed, but it did; though not in the place where it is said to have been, but it did exist. Its people, especially its rulers knew many extraordinary things and had the use of many powers that we have long forgotten, and nowadays are regarded as myths. Like us they had flaws and their powers were used in both good and bad ways."

Morgana had inherited these powers and used them to entrap Arthur. Like Igraine and Uther before them, they made a son. Then Morgana disappeared without telling Arthur anything of this. She brought Mordred up alone and taught him to hate and despise Arthur. She filled his head with lies and tales and her own desire for revenge and turned an innocent child into a weapon to be used when the time was right." Father John paused again, uncertain how much Thomas would understand then went on.

"Arthur married Guenevere, the daughter of King Leodegrance. It was the destiny of Britain to be the resting place of the Grail; the original Grail that is, not the one you read about in the stories. This one was far older. Had everything gone as they were intended to do, Arthur would have married Elaine, daughter of the Guardian of the Grail, and Guenevere would have married the man who became Arthur's dearest friend, Launcelot du Lac. But human beings have free will and Arthur was determined to have Guenevere for his wife."

"Didn't Arthur know about the Grail?" asked Thomas, completely wrapped up in the unfolding story.

"He didn't know then how much trouble his marriage would cause. As you get older you will understand that men and women do not always think with their minds. Most of the time they think with their hearts. However Arthur raised a company of knights specially trained in the laws of chivalry and they came together at a Round Table, where no one man was above or below the other and the King took his place among them. Thirteen seats and thirteen men."

"Just like the Guardians and me." Thomas broke in excitedly.

"Yes, lad, just like the Guardians and you. In fact the Company of the Singing Stones is based on the Round Table where all are equal. Arthur's marriage was not happy. They had no children and that worried his councillors who were thinking about the succession when Arthur died. Then along came Launcelot, and he and Guenevere fell in love. But they both loved Arthur as well, so they kept it a secret from him."

"It's like one mistake repeating itself with different people isn't it? That is so sad," said Thomas leaning forward. "What happened next?"

"Mordred arrived and announced himself as Arthur's

son and heir. As you can imagine this threw everything into confusion, which was what Morgana wanted. After the first shock Arthur tried to make things right and recognised Mordred as his son. But as Arthur and Morgana had not and could not marry, Mordred was declared illegitimate and so could not inherit the throne. This made him very bitter and because he'd been warped by his mother's desire for revenge he began to spread rumours and lies.

The country was at peace, but he told the knights Arthur was a coward and afraid to fight. Then he found out about Guenevere and Launcelot and spread tales about them as well. Then things began to get worse. Launcelot went away for a long time and during that time he met Elaine the Grail Guardian's daughter and the pattern repeated itself yet again, and they had a son."

"I know, that was Galahad," said Thomas bouncing excitedly on the sofa.

"Yes Galahad, who should have been Arthur's son and the Grail King of Britain after him. Through Mordred, Arthur found out about Guenevere and Launcelot and sent his best friend away. Some say Guenevere went with him for a time, but then returned to Camelot and Arthur."

Mordred undid all the good that Arthur had done and the land went back to fighting between small kingdoms. Then Mordred set himself up in opposition to Arthur and finally it came to war between them. But he could not claim the throne by conquest unless he also had the Royal Regalia. Three days before the battle Merlin sent for Arthur and those of his knights who were still loyal to him. He asked him to bring the Regalia with him to a small village in the North of the country.

Merlin had left Camelot many years before, he knew what would happen and wanted to prepare a plan that would prevent Mordred from ever becoming King. The rest you know, for you were privileged to see it for yourself in a waking dream. Mordred must have the crown and all the rest before he can take on the power that was his father's, and claim it by right of conquest."

"But how is it that Mordred is still alive after all this time?"

"His hatred, his desire for vengeance, and his mother's dark magic kept them both alive. Also, the same Powers of Light that guard this island decided to punish him for the slaying of his Father. In the heat of battle Arthur met him and offered him peace, told him he loved him still despite all he had done. Mordred listened, but then slew him. But Arthur did not die, he lives now in Avalon until there comes another Arthur who will be crowned as the Once and Future King."

Thomas was silent then asked. "Then why is the chamber opened every hundred years?" John smiled sadly.

"This is done to keep the link between the Arthur that was and the Arthur that will be. Although the regalia is brought to the circle and displayed before the one who will be King in his time, the crown is never set upon his head. Until now no King of England has borne the name Arthur. Many princes have had that name, but only one was in line for the Throne, but he died before he could be crowned. He was the last until now. That is why this time is so important.

Thomas was silent for a moment then he got up and

went to the bookshelf. He took down an encyclopaedia and began to turn the pages. John Foxton watched him silently. The boy has a brilliant mind he thought proudly, he is already following up the clues.

"Have you found it?" He asked as Thomas came back and sat beside him.

The boy looked up at him, eyes wide, then read from the book he was holding.

"Charles, Phillip, Arthur, George," his voice was shaky. "Duke of Cornwall, Baron Renfrew, Lord of the Isles and Prince of Wales. Father John is this what's going to happen this August?"

"Yes Thomas, this is what is going to happen. Now you see why it is so important to win this particular battle. We have a chance this time to bring it all to a close and lift the burden of Guardianship from those who have borne it for so long." There was silence in the room as they both contemplated what might be the outcome of it all.

"Well now, still here Father John, shall I make a fresh pot of tea for us all." Mrs. Jackson's voice shattered the calm of the moment and brought them back to earth. The man rose to his feet.

"No thank you Mrs. Jackson, I have taken up enough of Thomas's time and your patience. I'll be off now. Nurse Pym will pop round tomorrow morning to see him. Don't let him out of bed until she has seen him. Goodbye Thomas, sleep well. I'll see myself out Mrs. Jackson, and thank you for the tea." Betty Jackson's bright eyes watched him leave then she turned back to Thomas.

"Well, that was a nice long visit, what did you talk

about?"

"Oh mostly school work and the concert we're giving in July. It takes a long time to arrange it all. I think my class is going to do a one act play."

"Oh, well, that's nice. I'm sure Frank and I will be along to watch. Now, for dinner I thought a spaghetti bolognese would go down alright, and I have Strawberry ice cream to follow. You go up and have a wash to freshen you up and change your pyjamas and I'll make you a tray in front of the telly. Thomas climbed the stairs feeling tired again. He washed his hands and face, cleaned his teeth and put on some fresh pyjamas, but as he reached the top of the stairs he heard Mrs. Jackson on the phone in the hall.

"Yes, he was here for almost two hours. When I came back they were still at it, talking close together. I'm sure they were up to something. The boy was sick today and didn't go to school. He'll be home tomorrow as well, so I won't be able to make it in the morning, best leave it to the afternoon. Right, I'll do that."

She put down the phone and Thomas drew back in case she looked up, but she went on into the kitchen. When he was sure she was out of the way he went downstairs and sat in front of the television. But instead of watching, he went over the story of Arthur and Mordred. The more he thought about it the sadder he felt. He loved his own dad dearly, and even if they had disagreed he knew he would never love him any less, so why couldn't Arthur and Mordred make it up?

"Why do grown-ups make things so complicated?" he asked himself. Why couldn't Morgana see that Arthur didn't ask to be born. He was her half brother after all, and what about Mordred? All he really wanted was a dad, to love him and play with him when he was little. Someone who would teach him to ride and use a sword and fish and that kind of stuff. But he got a mother who used him to hurt her brother, and a father he couldn't talk to. Thomas began to see both sides of a very complicated situation.

He ate his supper half-heartedly and finally went to bed with his head still full of problems. After a somewhat restless night the morning brought a new excitement. An hour long phone call from his parents.

"It's amazing", said his dad, "the film rushes are just superb. They are saying now that it could well be nominated for another Oscar. I feel as if someone just gave me the Empire State Building." His mother came in on the other phone.

"Tell him about the new offer, go on."

"Well," said his dad. "They are talking about a sequel. I was talking with the producer the other day and just running things over in my mind about taking some of the characters into a new situation. They got so excited I freaked out. Suddenly they were talking sequels and getting new contracts out for the stars. I tell you Thomas it's amazing. We hope to be home about the first week of July I know that's putting it back again, but this is such a chance for us. But that's enough about Hollywood. What about you? Anything going on in Deepdale?"

Thomas didn't know whether to laugh or cry. "Er, well nothing really happens here. Nothing like your news anyway." Nothing remotely like yours, he thought to himself. "But I have lots to tell you when you get back. I've almost forgotten what you look like." For a moment he felt like Mordred, unloved and lost. Then he shook himself. " Oh, a letter came for me from a solicitor in Manchester. He wants me to go and see him. He says I'll hear something to my advantage. Do you know what it might be?"

There was silence on the other end of the phone, then his father's voice came down the line. "Yes Thomas, I know what it is about, I've been expecting it but I had hoped we'd be home before it came. It'll be about your great grandfather's Will and it will change a lot of things for us all."

"Mrs. Jackson rang them to say you were away and would be in touch when you got back. They said it would be alright." Thomas took a deep breath and went on. " Dad, I know about Sir Carrick and what happens on my fourteenth birthday. I've seen the Manor and looked it up in the land registry. I'm sorry great-grandfather didn't want you to have the title and the house."

His voice wobbled and tears came close, suddenly he knew very well how Mordred had felt when he came to Camelot for the first time. "Dad, you … you don't hate me do you, I mean because I'm going to be Sir Thomas and have a big house, if you want me to, I'll give it up, but there are some important things I have to do first. But Dad, please don't hate me." The tears came at last.

"Thomas, Thomas, are you there? Don't put the phone down …. Listen to me laddie, I don't hate you, I love you, always will. You know that Tom, my Tommy Tucker, you are my son, your Mum and I love you so much. I should have told you all about this before, but I didn't think you'd under-stand, until you were older. Then with the book being such a success, I didn't think straight. Oh God! This is such a mess.

There is more to all this than you know. Go to see Father John at the school. He'll tell you all about it. Damn, damn! Look, we're coming home as soon as possible. The film can get along without me. You are more important than anything else. Listen to me Thomas and believe what I'm telling you. I never wanted the title or the Manor. I always knew it would be yours one day I just didn't know it would be so soon. Nothing, nothing in this whole wide world would ever make me hate you Thomas. I might get angry, I might shout, but I will always love you."

"I love you too Dad, and you Mum, I'm sorry to be such a baby, but so much has happened and I don't know how it will end. I've already spoken to Father John and he's been great. But there are other things happening ... too much to tell you now."

"Thomas, if you're talking about the Singing Stones, your grandma told me most of it the night before she died. Oh, laddie, you've been trying to deal with this by yourself. Your Mum and I have been so caught up with this damned film and all the bright lights and stuff and you've been coping with something much more important. I am so proud of you lad, so proud. Your Mum and I will be home as soon as it can be arranged."

"Dad, you don't have to do that. I'm OK and I have a lot of friends in Deepdale who are helping me. I'll be alright honest, you don't have to drop everything and come back. This is what you've always dreamed of and it's right for you, just as what's happening here is right for me. Just as long as I know you don't mind me being a 'Sir'. Father John said I should add Greystone to Carrick when I'm fourteen, so your name will still be mine as well and it will go on. He said you'd like that."

Steven Greystone sounded close to tears himself. "Oh yes Thomas, I'd like that very, very much. Thank you son. God bless."

The phone went dead and Thomas put his head on the table and wept with relief. A gentle hand on his shoulder made him start and look up. Nurse Pym smiled down at him and offered a clean hanky.

"You are a very brave, very loving young man Thomas Greystone," she said. "I am proud to be your friend in this adventure. I met Mrs. Jackson down in the High Street and she said to come straight in. Let's make a cup of tea and get you calmed down. I think perhaps you have been carrying all this worry around for too long a time." Thomas nodded and sat down at the kitchen table.

"I know lots of people would like to have a title and a manor house and I thought maybe Dad would … would," his voice tailed off.

"Be jealous?" Suggested Nurse Pym. He nodded shame-facedly.

"Your father is a very clever writer, I have a lot of his books, and this new one is the best of them all. He deserves his success, but I think that if he had inherited the title, he wouldn't be able to write with the freedom he has now. The estate will take a lot of looking after, you know, but your father must be free to write because that is what he is meant to do. Now drink up. I'll stay until Mrs. Jackson gets back.

They sat quietly with their tea and Thomas told her what his father had said, and about the film and its sequel. " Well I never," she said. " To think I know someone who has spoken to all those famous people, well I never."

Thomas sat quiet for a few minutes then said hesitantly, "Miss Pym do you think Mordred might be sorry he behaved so badly to his father?" Startled she set down her cup and looked across the table at the serious faced boy sitting opposite her.

"I don't know Thomas. I've never thought about that possibility. After all this time I don't know if it would be possible. Perhaps Father John would be able to give you better advice about that." She poured a second cup. "What made you think of that?"

"Because when I was talking to my Dad, I suddenly knew he felt very lonely when he first went to Camelot. I think he was a bit afraid of his father and tried to hide it by being bad and telling lies. I was afraid my Dad wouldn't love me anymore and I was almost not going to tell him about the Singing Stones in case he hated me more. Then when I did tell him, it was like everything was lighter and I knew he really did love me. I thought if Arthur had taken more time to be with Mordred and talked to him and did things together, you know, like fishing and swords and bows and arrows and things, they might have liked each other more."

"Thomas Greystone, I have lived with this since I was a small girl. I thought I knew, all there was to know about Arthur and Camelot, but this is the first time I have ever been faced with this way of looking at it. You are a remarkable young man and a very wise one. Ah, here is Mrs. Jackson. We haven't managed to have the kind of talk I was hoping for, but this was just as important. I'll be on my way now. You can go back to school tomorrow, Thomas and I will see you next week, at the manor."

Mrs. Jackson came bustling in with her shopping, surprised to see Nurse Pym still there, but held her tongue. She saw her out then returned to the kitchen.

"Well now, you've had a lot of visitors haven't you . Hope they've not tired you out you look a little pale. I've got sausage rolls for lunch, we'll have them with baked beans on toast and you can have one of these little trifles for afters. I don't like store bought stuff, but they are quick and easy when you're pressed for time."

"I'm feeling much better Mrs. Jackson, I think I'll get dressed. Nurse Pym said I could go back to school tomorrow."

"Oh she did, did she? Well I suppose she knows best. Run along then, but it's an early night for you tonight."

That night Thomas slept deeply but towards dawn he began to dream. He stood in a boat draped with purple velvet, its prow carved into the form of a bear's head. Ahead of them he could see waves breaking on the shore of an island.

Arthur, still in his battle worn armour, lay with his bandaged head in the lap of an older woman who wore a circlet of gold. Two other women sat on either side of him, one as dark as night with hair coiled into an elaborate net of gold and silver.

The other was Bessie as Thomas had seen her in the Circle, golden hair spilling to her waist, her eyes as blue as a summer sky, but now red with weeping. At her feet, holding her hand sat a short misshapen figure dressed in the motley of a jester.

As the boat reached the shore, a procession emerged from the trees that edged the beach. They seemed to be priests of some sort, dressed in white and carrying a litter. A man in rich red robes and a woman in a long gown of sea blue walked ahead of them. With gentle hands the priests lifted Arthur and placed him on the litter. The older woman went with them as they carried him away. The other two stood waiting.

Merlin and the Lady of the Lake watched the litter out of sight then turned to the two women. Merlin looked first to Morgana who stood with her head up, defiant and proud. "Morgana, you have used your powers to destroy the Great Plan for the Blessed Isles. In your hatred for your half brother you warped the mind of a child, and caused Arthur to commit the sin of incest. You will return to Britain and seek to undo the harm you have caused. If you do not avail yourself of this chance Avalon will be forever closed to you and your powers will dwindle and fade. Loneliness and shame will be your fate. Find repentance within you, or you will never be allowed to return. Until then you are banished."

He raised his staff and the woman's form shrank in upon itself and where she had stood was a large black crow. It lifted into the air and circled Merlin's head cawing defiantly then flew away to the North. The Lady of the Lake turned to Guenevere who was still weeping.

"Guenevere, the blame is not all yours. You were intended to be the wife of Launcelot in the beginning. But, human nature intervened and over that, the Gods have no power. For you also there is banishment but there will be a chance for you to redeem yourself. When another Arthur claims the crown your chance will come. Until then you will return and your life will extend until that claim is made." She turned to the jester and smiled laying her hand on his head.

"Barnabus, you should not be here, this is Avalon where

heroes come to rest and wait until they may return to life. But, since you came for love of your Queen you may stay here and be with Arthur but to do this you must leave the service of Guenevere."

The jester limped forward and knelt at her feet, head bowed." Lady, grant me leave to go with my Queen until my life ends. She will be lonely and I want to do what I can to help her. It will only be for a short time, for my kind do not live long but I will do what I can."

Merlin and the Lady spoke quietly together then Merlin came to the jester where he knelt on the sand. "Barnabus, if you stay here I will give you the shape that was intended for you, strong and straight. If you go with your Queen you must stay as you are. Choose." There was no hesitation, the little man struggled to his feet and went to Guenevere's side and kissed her hand. He had made his choice.

"The Lady smiled and said, "Your loyalty will be rewarded, your life is also extended so you may stay with your Queen. But, so that you may better protect her I will change your shape." She bent and laid her hand on his head, power shone from her fingers and enveloped him. When the brightness cleared a small terrier stood where the jester had been. "Once in each month you may take your own shape for a while if you wish. When your Queen's task of repentance is completed you will also be welcomed here in Avalon. Return now, the boat will take you back to begin your exile."

In the dream Thomas watched as the boat sailed back over the silver sea into the light of a new day. He woke slowly, holding on to the memory of what he had seen, knowing it was important. That love, loyalty, and faith can overcome the darkness that sometimes lies hidden in the human soul.

He got up and went to the window and pulled back the curtains. A bright morning greeted him and in the lane beyond the drive stood Bald Bessie with Grim in her arms. She looked up and smiled. Thomas opened the window and made an awkward bow, then called down softly.

"Good morning your Majesty, Barney, may the day go well with you both."

Her smile became brilliant and she made a little curtsey. "And with you, my Lord Carrick." Grim gave a little bark and they both continued down the lane. Thomas watched them go and remembered the golden haired Queen she had once been. He lifted his head and squared his shoulders. He would see to it that this time, she could return to Avalon.

TEN

The whole of May continued fine and Thomas could almost believe the world was returning to normal. Father John had gone into retreat, schoolwork was going well and a large parcel arrived from America with books, DVD's, and some signed photos from the actors in the film of his Dad's book. But best of all was the arrival of a new Sports Master at the school.

Carl Mycroft had been an Olympic fencer in his younger days and when he put up a notice offering fencing lessons as part of the school sports curriculum Thomas was at the head of the queue. Football and cricket had never interested him very much, but he quickly proved to be a natural with a foil in his hand. He enjoyed the mental challenge as much as the physical and stayed behind to practice twice a week.

In the two months of his parents absence he had grown almost three inches and Mrs. Jackson, armed with a cheque from his dad had whisked him off to Manchester to buy a new school outfit. Along the way he had replenished his casual wardrobe, including, to the house-keepers' horror, a pair of low slung, wide legged rap pants.

He had seen little if anything of the Guardians. Even Bessie had disappeared. So he was relieved when one Saturday afternoon as he was lazing in the garden, Grim appeared and scampered over to tug urgently on his new jeans.

"Got a message for me have you?" He asked. Grim barked and tugged again.

"Okay, okay I'm coming, just let me get a jacket and my bike." Obediently the dog sat down by the back gate and waited. Thomas ran in, grabbed a jacket and a bottle of water and left a note for Mrs. Jackson to say he would be out for the rest of the afternoon.

With Grim running beside him he rode through the village and once they were out on to the Shipton road he stopped and poured some water into his hand for the little dog. "Where are we going Grim?" he asked. "I know, let's play twenty questions. I'll ask the questions and you must give one bark for yes, and two for no. Now, are we going to see Bessie?"

Grim barked twice. "Okay, then is it the circle? No, well then I guess it must be the Manor?" Grim barked once, turned a somersault and raced off with Thomas in hot pursuit. As they came in sight of the gates he saw a white van parked outside and recognised the man leaning against it at once. It was Drew Docker from the pub. He straightened when he saw Thomas and waved, then stooped to pet Grim who was leaping up at him.

"Afternoon young Tom," he said cheerily. "I thought as how we might get together seeing it's my day off. Not knowing were you were, I borrowed Grim here to find you. Hope that was alright?"

"Of course Mr. Docker, it was getting a bit boring being by myself. Mrs. Jackson's off with her friends, Frank is trimming the hedges and everyone else seems to be doing things except me. Let me unlock the gates and we can get the van inside. If you park it just beyond the house no one can see it from the road."

He re-locked the gates after them and followed the van on his bike. He stood for a moment looking at the house, feeling as always, a faint thrill that it was his and he had every right to be here. Then he looked across at the publican.

"Right, let's go in. I suppose you're here to look at the window." He unlocked the door and ushered his guest into the wide hall. "It's there on the landing." They climbed the stairs their footsteps echoing in the empty house and stood before the brilliantly coloured scene.

Against a star-filled sky the Stones looked taller and even more mysterious. The figure of Arthur had been done with great care, and the crown he held out to Amicus glittered with jewels. The Guardians, grey cloaked, were set back from the event taking place, the whole window depicting the importance of what was happening between the two main figures. But it was the border that held the attention of the man and the boy now standing before it. In twelve rectangular sections they edged the whole thing, each one displaying a set of symbols or a smaller scene.

"What are we looking for exactly," asked Thomas, squinting in the light coming through the glass. " Let me see, you have guardianship of the Shield, or the Sword, I can't remember ?"

"It's the Sword lad. Not *Excalibur*, that went back to Avalon with Merlin. This one was a gift from the Lady of the Lake. If you're right and the window is a sort of map of where they are hidden we must look for something that looks like a sword or might be connected to a sword." They looked in silence for a while then Thomas sighed.

"I don't see anything like a clue. Maybe I was wrong Mr. Docker, maybe it was just luck the first time, but I was so sure there would be something there."

"Tell you what, I've got sandwiches in the van, lemonade for you and some cider for me, let's have a break and then look again." They sat outside in the sun on the front steps and talked as they ate for Thomas had a question he wanted to ask.

"Mr. Docker, what did it feel like when you first used your power of the Horse?"

"Ah lad, it was grand. Such a feeling of freedom it was. I ran and ran and ran that first time. Of course I paid for it. Could hardly move for the next three or four days."

"Did it hurt the first time, the actual change I mean. It did for me, I thought I was going to die."

"Aye, it did, but it got easier each time."

"That's what Father John said, but I haven't done it again since that first time. I've been a bit, well, scared to do it alone and Father John is on retreat and goodness know where Bessie is." Grim who had been dozing in the sun pricked up his ears at the sound of the name, then went back to sleep. Thomas went on. "I was wondering, if you wouldn't mind, since we are both here and there's no one around, sort of ... watching while I try to change."

"Be glad to lad. Tell you what we'll do it together. Lets move round the back where there's more room."

The back lawn that had once been lovingly tended, was now a tangle of weeds but it was quiet and private. They stood facing each other and Thomas watched as Drew took a deep breath and let the change flow over him. His form blurred and became misty. Through the mist he saw the human outline shift and elongate into the horse form. The mist cleared as quickly as it had appeared and there stood a handsome stallion. Seventeen hands high, its coat gleaming in the sunlight it stepped forward and blew gently in Thomas's face.

"Now your turn, think about the King Stag, remember the feel of the wind on your face and let it come slowly." The thought-words were clear in Thomas's mind.

He took a deep breath, and tried to remember how it first time had been, the weight of the antlers, and the feeling of power. The pain was not so bad this time, a wrench of muscles and sinew, a sharp stab and then a feeling of being like a river and flowing into a new shape. He blinked and looked down. Four strong legs, gleaming hooves, he looked at the shadow he cast on the grass ... the shadow of a King Stag. "I did it, I did it, Drew... I mean Mr. Docker, I did it,"

"Yes, you did indeed Thomas, and Drew will do nicely from now on. How about a run through the woods and out on to the moors?"

Grim danced with excitement between them, then all three turned to the woods behind the house. The Stallion led the way leaping over the broken fence with ease, Thomas followed, with Grim scooting underneath. Through the little wood and out on to the moors they ran at full strength outstripping little Grim, who gave up at last and sat down under a bush to wait for them to return. On and on they galloped across the rough moorland scrub and on, up to the top of Tagg's Tor. There they stood and looked out over the rolling green hills embroidered with the white fleece of grazing sheep and their lambs.

The King Stag reached out with his thoughts. "It's a beautiful land Drew, I am so proud to be a part of it, and a part of what we are doing for it."

"All the Guardians feel that way Thomas. It's what makes England both great, and blessed. We have always fought for what we believed in. Did you know that Sir Phillip Carrick went on the second Crusade and took with him ten men of Deepdale? Sir Phillip's tomb is the oldest in our church, to the right as you go in. All crusader effigies lie with their feet crossed, some with a dog beneath their feet to symbolise fidelity, and they hold their sword hilt upwards the length of the body. We had some archeologists here a while back, they wanted to open the tomb and make some tests on the remains. But your great grandfather sent them packing. The Carrick Coat of Arms is on the side of the tomb."

"Yes I've seen it, it's a shield on a field azure bearing a crown d'or, pierced by a sword upright and surrounded by twelve stars argent. You can see it again in the Manor window at the bottom on the right hand side." His voice tailed off into silence. "Drew, do you think that might be it?"

" The clue we've been looking for. Yes Tom lad, I think it just might. Let's get back."

They wheeled in unison and raced back the way they had come, collecting the patient Grim along the way. Back in the Manor grounds they returned to their own forms. Thomas was so excited he completed the change without thinking and with little discomfort. They checked the window again and sure enough, there in the right hand corner was the Carrick coat of arms.

"Look" said Drew, " See how the shield is set askew. If you draw a straight line from the tip of the sword it points to my place in the circle."

"Wait Drew, think, is there any other place where you can see my coat of arms?"

"Well, it's over the front door here, and on the main gates but you couldn't hide a sword there. Then there's a smaller one over the big fireplace in the old hall here." They looked at each other and then, as one, they headed for the three hundred year old timbered hall that was one of the finest in the north of England.

The oldest and original part of the manor faced west with six tall windows each bearing in a stained glass roundel, the coat of arms of a family that had married into the Carricks. Overlooking the hall in the north was the carved minstrel gallery and in the east was a huge fireplace with seats set each side of its width. The grate and firedogs were not as old but Thomas could well imagine how it would once have looked on a winter's night with logs blazing and heavy curtains shutting out the wind and rain. Mentally he promised himself that it would look like that again, and soon, maybe this coming Christmas. Then he turned his attention back to the task in hand.

Above the fireplace an ornately carved mantle ran its full length. Set into its surface were small replicas of the shields set into the main windows. The larger centre shield bore the arms of the Carrick Family. They looked at it closely and Drew gently pushed it with a callused forefinger. Nothing happened.

"See if it turns or pulls out or something," urged Thomas, beside himself with curiosity.

"I don't want to damage anything," muttered the publican, "This is antique stuff, God alone knows how old."

"Yes, well, it belongs to me so I'm telling you to push it, pull it or twist it, just try. "

Drew grinned. " Right you are Sir Thomas. Here goes. "He took hold of the little shield and pulled. Nothing happened. He pushed it, hard, but again nothing. Then he tried turning it. There was a click, then silence. Drew gave it another quarter turn and with loud thud the whole front section of the mantle fell forward with a crash.

They both leapt back, but nothing else happened, so they inched forward to peer into the cavity. At first they could see nothing, then Drew put out a cautious hand and reached in.

Thomas took a step back. " Mind how you go Drew, there could be rats in there, or," he shuddered. "Spiders. You never know, it might be booby trapped."

"I don't think they had booby traps back then," said Drew, feeling about in the darkness.

"Oh they did, the Chinese invented them way, way back. I learned that in history," said Thomas eagerly. "Can you feel anything, anything at all?".

Drew's arm was now at full stretch inside the hole and he face lit up. "There's summat here." He began to pull his find out slowly. It looked like a long bundle of old rags, but on closer inspection it turned out to be tightly woven linen secured by flaking leather webbing. Drew carried it to the stairs leading up to the gallery and laid it down. Slowly and carefully he unwrapped it. Layer after layer of yellowing cloth came away in his hands until the last piece fell away. Together they stared down at what they had uncovered, their hearts hammering, tongues dry in their mouths.

"Holy Mother of God preserve us," whispered Drew, crossing himself with a reverent hand.

ELEVEN

Marcus Allsop was not pleased, He paced over the worn carpet biting his fingernails. Of the three men standing by the door two twisted their caps in nervous hands. When he was like this the boss was dangerous. Finally the tallest of the three stepped forward and cleared his throat.

"Er, Mr. Allsop, sir. Do you want us to go on looking or should we be doin' summat else?"

Marcus stopped pacing and glowered at him. "What's the use of giving you something to do when you don't seem to be able to do it properly?"

"Beggin' yer pardon sir", another of the men came forward. "We did what we could but the directions you gave us wuz pretty sparse. The only place you could hide a sword in that church is in one o' them tombs, an' I aint goin' ter open up one o' them, not fer a lot more money than we're getting."

"All right, all right. It has to be somewhere that is linked to the Carricks. If it's not in the church we have to look elsewhere. I know they have the Sceptre and are looking for the rest, but how do they know where to look? They must have a map or something similar." He stopped pacing and snapped his fingers. "That boy, Thomas, he'll know, I'll get Betty Jackson to sweet talk him." He turned.

"Meantime, Len, take Farrell with you and see if you can get into the old tithe barn, on the Barmsby road. It belongs to the National Trust but they've done nothing with it so far. But it's old enough for something like the sword to have been hidden there. It used to belong to the Carrick estate but the old man gave it to the Trust years ago. It's a likely place, and full of hidden corners. You should have no difficulty getting in there, the security is none existent. Now get out."

The two men left reluctantly muttering under their breath. As the door closed Marcus turned his attention to the third man who had remained silent throughout the exchange. Now he came forward, and made himself comfortable in one of the deep armchairs by the fire. His relaxed attitude was more that of an equal than a hired help. He stretched his legs out to the flames, the May weather could be uncertain in the Dales.

"You can't expect much from riff-raff," he said pouring himself a glass of wine. "They know little and care less. They are just as likely to make off with the sword, or anything else they find rather than bring it to you,"

Marcus turned on him fiercely, "They wouldn't dare. They have already had a taste of what would happen if they did." The man leaned forward, dark eyes glinting under heavy brows. "Threats won't get you loyalty Mordred, or what you seek." The other man turned and all but spat at him, his anger visible and threatening.

"Don't use that name here, or anywhere else in this village!" He ground his teeth. "You are the only one who knows, who has any idea who or what I am, and I don't want it known ... is that quite clear?" The man in the chair shrugged. "Perfectly, though there are some in this village you despise so much, who are capable of working it out, and doing something about it."

"We still have time, we only need one or two pieces and they will be unable to complete the sequence of the ceremony. We already have the Cadence that will open the chamber and with a bit more practice they'll be able to get it right first time."

"I wish I felt as sure as you do about that, Marcus." He gave a sarcastic emphasis to the name. "A bird's hearing is not the same as a man's so you could have got it wrong. Still it's not my place, as you have pointed out so frequently, to disagree with you. So I will take my leave." He drained the glass and got up to saunter to the door then turned to make an elaborate bow. "Until we meet again, my Prince." He closed the door behind him with a soft derisive snap.

Marcus threw himself into the vacated chair. "If I wanted to hide a sword where would I put it?" he asked himself and bit through another nail. "Where would I put it?" Agravaine was right, though he hated to admit it. On top of all that he was not really sure of the Cadence. "Damn, damn, damn." He stared into the flames of the fire and tried to run the sequence through his mind.

An idea struck him, it was brilliant, and so easy. All he had to do was to wait until the Guardians had found all the regalia then, take the Greystone boy hostage. With a knife at his throat they could hardly refuse to sing the correct notes, especially that damned priest. Then the boy would obligingly provide the last one, simple and yet so clever, a plan worthy of his mother's son. He got up and poured himself a glass of brandy. He deserved it. Outside, hidden in the flowering May tree, an owl peered through the window and took note of the pleased expression on his face. Then it flew silently into the darkening sky.

* * *

Drew Docker drove back through the quiet lanes, the evening clouds already gathering and the sun casting long shadows over the moors. Beside him Thomas sat silent and thoughtful. It had taken them some time to get over the shock. The sheer power and beauty of what they had found had left them awe-struck. Tucked into Drew's shirt pocket was the yellowed piece of parchment that was its cause.

"What now Drew?" asked Thomas quietly.

"I think we had better keep this quiet until Father John returns the day after tomorrow. "This is big Thomas. I knew the sword would be powerful, but I didn't understand what would be the source of its power. That was never explained in the tales passed down to the Guardians. First I'm going to get you back home. Then I'm going to get my old shotgun and a few supplies and I'm going to camp out in the Manor until Father John gets back. Then we'll come and get you and talk over what's to be done."

"Do you think we did the right thing putting it back where it was? I mean something that important ...." His voice tailed off.

"Tom lad, we are the first people to see it for five hundred years or more. Every time the ceremony has come round parts of the regalia have been missing, and the sword was always one of them. So it will be safe for another few hours. This time is all the more important because an 'Arthur' will stand with us, so we must find all the things that were left for us to guard. Something tells me this time will be the time we have all waited for." He swung into the driveway.

"Here we are, I'll go back to the Pub and get someone to cover for me for a couple of days, then I'll head back to the Manor. Don't you fret now Tom, I'll guard that Sword with my life, it was placed in the hands of my ancestor to protect, and protected it will be, so help me."

"I know that Drew. Here are the keys. Call me if anything happens.." He took his bike out of the back and watched as the van reversed and drove away.

"Do you know what time it is young man? The least you could have done was phone and let me know what time you'd be home." Thomas spun round. Mrs. Jackson stood in the kitchen doorway, hands on her hips and breathing fire.

Thomas swallowed hard and looked at his watch, it said six thirty-two. "Oops, I'm really sorry Mrs. Jackson I was so interested in what I was doing I forgot to watch the time. Then I met Drew, I mean Mr. Docker and he offered me a lift and we got talking and, well I guess the time went out of my head. I really am sorry."

Mrs. Jackson sniffed. "Well get washed up and then have your dinner, though it 'll be dried up by now. What on earth you'd have to talk about with Drew Docker I'm sure I don't know." She disappeared into the kitchen while Thomas put away his bike and went to wash his hands and face. When he came back to the kitchen his dinner, looking the worse for its incarceration in the oven, was on the table. Frank Jackson gave him a commiserating look over the top of his paper, while his wife banged saucepans and china around.

As soon as he could he escaped upstairs and switched on his computer, there were things he needed to check on. For the next hour he searched the internet and finally, satisfied that he had enough to work on he printed out his notes and settled down to read them.

At nine the phone rang and Mrs. Jackson's voice floated up the stairs. "Thomas, it's for you, its that Drew Docker from the pub." Her tone was not encouraging. Thomas ran down and picked up the phone. Drew Docker's voice was bland and held none of the excitement of the afternoon.

"Tom lad, just wanted to let you know that I got hold of that Hunter Hawk information we talked about and it'll be here early on Monday morning. Until then, just you be patient."

"Thank you Mr. Docker, I understand perfectly." Thomas put the phone down and was not surprised to see Mrs. Jackson standing behind him, her eyes bright with curiosity

"Now what's all this about then," she asked frowning.

"Oh, Mr. Docker is getting me some information on a Hunter Hawk for my school essay. It's a type of aircraft. It's very kind of him isn't it?"

"Oh aye, very kind."

Her baffled expression made him smile. "It's alright Mrs. Jackson, I'm not going to start going to the pub every night." She sniffed and went back to the kitchen.

Thomas turned to go back upstairs when he caught the faintest whisper of a thought and quietly opened the front door. Grim sat on the doorstep, head on one side with his red tongue hanging out. Making sure Mrs. Jackson was still in the kitchen Thomas grabbed him and took him upstairs.

Once in his bedroom he rummaged in his emergency snack biscuit tin and came up with a rather old custard cream. Grim accepted it and crunched happily until only the crumbs were left. Then he sat with his ears up and alert. Thomas carefully folded the note he had written and was going to tie it to the dog's collar when a thought occurred to him. He sat down beside him and said softly, "I don't need to write a note do I Barney? I can tell you and you will tell Bessie." The dog gave a soft woof and licked his hand.

"Okay. Tell Bessie that Drew and I have found the Sword, and that Father John will be back on Monday morning. Drew, Mr. Docker, is going to ring me on Monday after school. Until then he'll be camping in the Manor House to guard it. But I think Mrs. Jackson is beginning to be suspicious. Can you remember all that?" Grim woofed again and jumped down from the bed and ran to the door.

Thomas crept down the stairs and let him out the front door. He just managed to close it when Mrs. Jackson appeared again. "What on earth are you up to, there's a terrible draught coming through."

"I thought I heard something in the driveway Mrs. Jackson, but it was only Mr. Sumpter's old dog, I shooed it off. Oh, will you tell Mr. Jackson he won't need to drive me to school on Monday. I'll go on my bike, I have to stay behind for some fencing practice. I should be home about six fifteen."

"Now you know your parents don't like you riding so far Thomas. Near enough to 8 miles is a fair way when you've done a day's schooling, 'specially over them hills."

"I know, but I really need to practice, and the days are lighter now. I'll be very careful, and I'll miss the rush hour coming home."

"Alright then, but just you make sure you're home by six fifteen, I won't have another dinner spoiled. By quarter past six mind, or no dinner at all. Now you get off to bed and I'll bring you up some hot chocolate." She stalked off to the kitchen.

Much later he lay in the dark thinking over the events of the day. Why, he wondered, did extraordinary things happen to ordinary people. Things like this should happen to important grown up people not schoolboys who wanted to be archaeologists and write books. He thought about Amicus who had been his age when it happened to him. Had he felt lost and lonely too. Had he lain awake at night and wondered why? He turned over in bed and punched his pillow into another shape.

He knew Amicus had grown up and got married and had children of his own: if he hadn't, he, Thomas would not be here now. He wondered what it would be like to be grown up, to be married and have a son of his own. It had never seemed important to think about such things until now. He would have to marry and have a family if the Carrick name was to go on. The thought of the lovely old manor being lived in by strangers was not an option.

It was strange to think that somewhere on the earth there was a girl growing up who would one day be his wife. What was she like? Where was she living now? What was her name? Would he like her? Would he like being married? His parents seemed to like it, he'd often seen them kissing, holding hands, and talking quietly together. Once, when he was little, he had woken from a bad dream and wandered into their bedroom. He remembered seeing his mother curled up in the circle of his father's arms, both of them sleeping deeply. The cosy sight had comforted him and he had gone back to his own bed. Lots of people got married he thought sleepily, so it couldn't be all that bad, and he would be able to tell his children about the Singing Stones. His eyes closed, he slept and dreamed.

He was walking along a lonely beach looking out over the sea to the misty islands beyond. The sunlight danced on the water's edge where two Jack Russell terriers gambolled among the waves. The sight reminded him of the day Grim had chased an otter along the riverbank and fallen in. The surprised look on his furry face had made it a memory to be treasured.

The body Grim had worn now lay buried in the circle of the Singing Stones. But Barney, walked with Arthur and Guenevere in Avalon. Since then he had never been without a 'Grim'. He turned to look at the cottage over-

looking the inlet.

He'd bought it three years ago drawn to the quietness and grandeur of the Western Isles and the rich heritage of its people. It was a place to rest from the world and re-live his memories. It was then he heard the singing.

> *Bheir me o haro van o,*
> *Bheir me o haro van ee,*
> *Bheir me hoor oho*
> *Sad am I without thee.*
> *Thou'rt the music of my heart,*
> *Harp of joy, o cruit mo chruidh,*
> *Moon of guidance by night,*
> *strength and light thou'rt to me*
> *In the morning when I go*
> *To the white and shining sea.*
> *In the calling of the seal kin*
> *Thy soft voice calls to me*
> *When I'm lonely dear white heart*
> *Black the night and wild the sea*
> *By love's light my foot finds*
> *The old pathway to thee.*

The voice was clear and sweet and matched the beauty of the girl who sat on the rocky outcrop. The red gold of her hair gleamed in the sun and Thomas knew, in those first few seconds of meeting Mara Macleod, that she was the one he had been waiting for, the one who would complete his life. She opened eyes the colour of emeralds, saw him, and smiled. "Thomas mo ghra, I'll be here waiting for you when the time is right. Go back now, and have patience."

Thomas woke to a sun-filled room rested and light hearted. He vaguely remembered dreaming about being in a place of mountains and sea, but dismissed it as merely a dream. It was Sunday and he had the whole day to fill. First things first, a shower and breakfast, then he planned on going to the Manor to see if Drew and he could solve some more of the clues in the window. He clattered down the stairs singing a song that seemed to have got stuck into his head.

"Bheir me o haro van o, Bheir me o haro van ee. Bheir me o hoor oho, sad am I without thee."

"What on earth is that you're warbling?" Asked Mrs. Jackson. "Sounds foreign." She ladled scrambled eggs and bacon on to his plate and filled a mug with tea.

" I don't know, I woke up with it in my head. Must be something I heard the school choir rehearsing. Gosh this looks good, mmm, tastes good too. Can I have a packed lunch please I want to go exploring, I'll take care to be back by six. Cross my heart." He grinned at her forbidding expression.

"I'm sure I don't know why you spend so much time look-ing at these old places," she complained. "Most young'uns like to go to clubs and such like."

"I want to be an archaeologist when I grow up and that means finding out about those old places. Today I want to go and see the old tithe barn on the Barmsby road." He jumped as Mrs. Jackson dropped the handful of cutlery she had just polished. "I'll get it," he said bending down to gather them.

Mrs. Jackson stood white faced.

"I think you should give that place a miss Thomas," she said faintly. There's talk of the roof being unsafe. You wouldn't want to be there if it came down, would you." I think you should try someplace else to explore. What about going over to Hetton Gill. It's a fair ride but they'll be finishing the Well Dressings at this time. You'll be able to see them at their best. Or there's the Beer Race over at Bidston, no, you'd best not go to that. But the Whitsun Brass Band Festival's on today. They'll have reached Diggle-on-the-Moor by lunch time. There's plenty to see and do if you've the mind. I'll get your lunch packed." She hurried off and Thomas went to collect his things.

As he came down the stairs he heard her on the phone and paused, not intending to listen, but unwilling to make his presence obvious.

"I tried to put him off Marcus, but you how kids are it's more than likely he'll go to the barn anyway. I thought you could call off your men. No, no, you can't mean that, he's a boy, there's no harm in him." She paused and when she spoke again she sounded unsure, less forthright, even scared. "I can't agree, I won't be a party to anything that'll harm him, I don't care what you say."

She slammed the receiver down and ran into the kitchen. Thomas waited a few minutes then followed her. She was slicing bread with a fierce look on her face but as soon as she saw Thomas she put on a smile.

"Now then, what would you like? There's ham egg and cress, or I can do bacon, lettuce and tomato with some hard-boiled eggs. I made an apple and cinnamon pie last night and there's some left: I'll put in a couple of slices."

Thomas decided on two with bacon, lettuce and tomato and two with ham. When she went to get some apples he sneaked in some cold sausages for Grim, in case he turned up. A bottle of water completed his supplies and he headed for the door.

"Thomas, wait. I want you to take this with you." Mrs. Jackson held out a mobile phone. "I know your parents didn't want you to have one but, well, when you're cycling all over the place like this I'd feel happier if you'd take mine with you. At least then if you are going to be late you can let me know." She looked a little tearful as he took the phone from her hand.

"Thank you Mrs. Jackson, I appreciate it, I'll take care of it I promise." On a sudden impulse he kissed her cheek. "Bye for now." Bettina Jackson stood in the middle of the kitchen, her hand on her cheek. She went into the hall and picked up the phone and dialled a number. A muffled voice came down the line. "Len 'arris 'ere, oo's this?"

"Len, its Betty Jackson. I've got a message for you from Marcus, He said not to bother about the old tithe barn today, tomorrow will do."

Len Harris was not pleased. "Wot the 'ell does he think 'e's playing at. I'm halfway there already. 'e should make up 'is bleedin' mind."

The phone was cut off sharply. Mrs. Jackson put hers down more slowly. Marcus would be very, very angry, but Thomas would be safe. She sat down at the table and put her head in her hands. What did it matter if they didn't find all that old jewellery and stuff. She and Frank, had enough, a nice house, work, health and the boys were grown and about their own business. No, Marcus Allsop had deceived her, he just wanted the treasure and didn't care if people got hurt. Truth was, she was fond of Thomas and was prepared to defy Marcus' plans for him.

Thomas himself was well on the way to the Manor. The roads were clear, everyone was celebrating Whitsun either at the Brass Band competitions or in the numerous pubs that dotted the Dales. He loved the feeling of the wind in his face as he raced down the Hills. Even the hard slog up the other side was almost enjoyable. He had hoped to see Grim somewhere along the way, but the little dog didn't put in an appearance. But Drew Docker was waiting at the gates as he slid to a stop.

"How did you know I was coming." he asked. Drew gave a wide grin.

"Stan Simonite was drinkin' outside the pub with friends when you went streaking through the village like a bat out of hell. He figured you were heading this way and called me. Wonderful things these mobiles. Come on, Marge Atkinson's here as well and we've got summat to show you." He led the way up the drive.

Marjory Atkinson was Deepdale born and bred and Stan Simonite's younger sister. She had the reputation of being a bit of an ogre, but in reality was always ready to help a neighbour in need. Her sharp tongue was reserved for those who took advantage of her good natured husband and called him out in the middle of the night for an upset stomach. She met them at the front door with a smile.

"Thomas, it's good to see you lad. Drew and I have been

busy and we think we've found another piece isn't that wonderful. You seeing the window was a map of hiding places was a Godsend."

"That's great news Mrs. Atkinson, has Drew shown you the Sword yet? What about the paper that was with it?" Thomas's words tumbled out in his excitement.

"No Tom, I'm keeping that bit of news until Father John gets back. But come and look at the window and see what we've found." Leaving his bike on the front step Thomas followed them inside and up the stairs to the window. Drew pointed to a golden rectangle edging the main picture. It showed three men on camels riding under a star.

One point of the star had been elongated and touched the crown of the middle rider. The Crown was a triple circle of gold linked together with what looked like a ruby. Thomas looked at it, then at the two people standing on either side of him. " What am looking for," he asked.

Mrs. Atkinson smiled and sat down on a handy stair tread. "Well now, three years ago Father John had the window restored, because there were a few pieces missing, and some of the leading needed re-doing. Before it was taken away he had a professional photographer take photos of it, for the insurance people. He gave copies to each of the Guardians. I framed ours and hung it in the sitting room. Well, when you found the Sceptre and Father John told us how it was all mapped out in the picture I began to think. I got Ian's magnifying glass and went over the photo bit by bit. When I saw that picture I thought to myself, I've seen that before. It's a strange way to draw a crown, looks more like a ring than anything else. It had me thinking for nigh on a week."

"Then yesterday I was in the church with Mrs. Arkwright doing the flowers for Whit Sunday and we ran out of vases. I went to the vestry cupboard where we keep the spares and on the top shelf was the box with the Nativity figures in it. Suddenly I remembered where I had seen that strange crown. I was so excited I nearly fell off the steps. But I went back and finished off the flowers, then made an excuse to stay behind when Mrs. Arkwright had gone. As soon as I was alone I got the box down and this is what I found." She opened her handbag and took out a carved figure.

"This," said Mrs. Atkinson in hushed tones," is Melchior."

The ten inch figure had been carved by the hand of a master. Every detail had been lovingly depicted, from the folds of his cloak to the curled beard. The painting was equally skilful, but when one looked at the crown it was evident that this was not a part of the original figure, but had been added. A triple circle of gold centered by a deep red stone enclosed the carved head which had been carefully shaped to hold it firmly with a tiny rivet of gold securing it.

"Look," said Drew, taking out his penknife. He gently levered the rivet from its place. With equal care he tugged the ring from the figure's head and held it out to Thomas.

Holding his breath the boy turned it in his hand. Once Merlin had placed this ring on the finger of Arthur, High King of Britain. If all went as it should, in a short while it would be placed on the finger of the one who would be the once and future king come again. The one who would bind the land together and renew it.

Marjory wiped away a tear, "Its silly I know, but it means

so much to me just to touch it, to know it is mine to protect until I hand it over to the one entitled to wear it. The three of them stood close together, bound by their love of an ancient land and the line of kingship that had been maintained for over a thousand years.

Thomas held the Ring high above his head so that the sun shining through the window fell on the ruby and made it blaze blood red. Still a boy in years, but a man in the making, his voice rang out clear and strong.

"By this symbol of the High King, I, Sir Thomas Greystone-Carrick of Carrick Manor pledge myself to the protection of Britain for as long as my life shall last."

"Amen" came the voices of his witnesses.

TWELVE

John Foxton gripped the phone tightly. His voice was level and controlled, but his eyes gleamed with excitement. "Yes, thank you Drew, sorry I was not with you at the moment of discovery, but as you know, my time is not entirely my own. Thomas and I will be with you as soon as we can. Goodbye." He replaced the receiver and turned to Thomas with a broad smile. "The Lord be praised Thomas, this is a great day for us." Thomas met his smile with one of his own.

"You don't know all of it yet Father, there's more to come. I came to school on my bike today so Frank wouldn't have to collect me. I'm leaving now and with luck I'll be at the Manor just before you. See you there." He ran out leaving the priest with his mouth open.

"But Thomas I really think ...." But the boy had gone. A tap on the door made him turn. "Ah, Brother Benedict, can I help you?" A thin earnest face peered round the door followed by an equally thin and lanky body. "Yes Father, I want to draw your attention to Thursday's history lesson, you will see that I have changed the direction of the lesson towards the more moral effect of the Industrial Revolution. The change from craft work is very significant I feel, and should be given more emphasis." The Brother droned on oblivious to the fact that his superior was miles away in his own thoughts.

Thomas was now on the Barmsby road and pedalling hard. He had been waiting for this moment since early morning and was determined to be there when Father John arrived. Five miles down the road he turned off and was passing the old tithe barn when he noticed an old Ford van in the yard. Two men were approaching the barn itself carrying an assortment of tools, among them an axe. Thomas stopped to watch as they struck the lock off the door and entered, closing it after them.

Thomas got off his bike and ran across the road. Cautiously he opened the door and peered in. The men were making a systematic search of the barn. One was sounding the walls while the other was attempting to pull away sections of panelling.

"What if we don't find nuffin' Len?" Marcus'll 'ave our guts fer garters."

"Then we'll 'ave ter find sumfink then won't we," snarled his companion.

Wood splintered as another panel was ripped off the wall and something snapped in Thomas as well. "Just what do you think you are doing? This is National Trust property and private. You have no right to damage an ancient monument!".

The two men swung round. "Well, if it 'aint young master Greystone. The little Lord 'o the Manor. We're very honoured Fred, 'is lordship's come ter give us an 'and." He advanced towards Thomas who backed away, only to find Fred behind him. Len pounced forward and grabbed him by the scruff of the neck.

"Nah then, Master Thomas wot do yer know 'bout this here National Monument? We knows there's sumfink hidden in 'ere and we'd like ter know where it is, see. Now, you can tell us quick like, and we'll fink about letting you go, in a couple of hours or so. Or, if you don't tell us, then we'll 'ave ter try a little persuasion. 'Ang on ter 'im Fred while I find sumfink ter tie 'im up wiv."

"There's nothing here to find," Thomas told them, wriggling in Fred's grip. "Nothing at all. What are you looking for anyway?"

"Well now, somefink like an old sword mebbe."

Thomas went still. "You're working for Mr. Allsop aren't you? Well you won't find any swords here. This place has been gone over by experts."

"Well seein''as 'ow you know 'oo we are, mebbe you know where we ought ter be lookin.' Care to tell us lad?"

"Why not look in the museum at Shipton, there's plenty of old swords there." A back-hander across his face was the only answer Thomas got. The force of it made him dizzy and he began to understand the danger he was in. Len would have no trouble beating up a boy, he would enjoy it. The Carrick blood rose hot inside him.

"There are no swords in the Barn," he repeated stubbornly. "Who would keep weapons in a place like this?"

"But you might know where ter look fer one, mightn't you, yer little rat. Well I'll get it outa yer, see if I don't." He raised his hand again, but Farrell intervened.

"Quit it Len, you could get us all in serious trouble beating up a kid. Marcus'll have yer over the coals fer this. Mebbe the kid really don't know where it is."

Len began to pace over the dusty floor of the barn. Then he came back and stood in front of Thomas. "Let's try it agin. You know, and I know, that somewhere in this village there's a sword that Mr. Allsop wants very badly. I know, that you know where it is. I want it and I want it now. Kids like you disappear everyday so don't think it can't 'appen ter you sonny boy. Now, 'ow abaht it? Are yer goin' ter play ball or not. I'm not fussed abaht leaving you trussed up like a chicken out on the moors. What I don't want is ter go back to Allsop wiv aht the sword, see. 'E 'as ways of making you see fings as would freeze the blood of any man."

Thomas looked up at him. He thought about the sword they had found and the secret it held. He thought of his parents and Father John and the disgrace that lay before him if he gave in to Len's demands. He made his decision.

"No," he said quietly.

* * *

Father John turned into the Barmsby road and changed gear. He wondered if Thomas was already at the manor. He had expected to catch him up on the road but so far there was no sign of him.

A blur of white and back shot past him and almost vanished under his wheels. He turned the car frantically into the spin and came to a stop with the front wheels almost in the hedge. As he opened the door a frantic bundle of fur jumped up at him barking hysterically.

"Grim? What on earth are you doing! I almost killed you! What is it? What do you want?" The dog ran up the road still barking, then came back again. Father John grabbed him and picked him up.

"Calm down Grim, I know you want to tell me something. Listen to me, Barney, take some of my energy, use it to shift for a moment."

The dog stopped barking and rested its head on his arm. The man drew in a deep breath and let his strength flow out to the animal form. The inside of the car grew misty and cool and out of the mist came the indistinct form of the Jester. His voice was thin and weak but enough for Father John to hear.

"Tythe barn, two men, Allsop's ... have Thomas, danger, danger! Quickly. Thomas in danger." The form grew misty again dissolving back into a small agitated dog.

Father John slammed the car into reverse and backed away from the hedge. With Grim in the front seat, paws on the dashboard, he roared down the road. As he drove he reached into his pocket for his mobile mentally asking for forgiveness for breaking the law and punched out Drew's number. He gave a few terse instructions and rang off.

A mile further on he saw the Barn and Thomas's bike lying by the side of the road. Sweating with fear at what he might find, he drew up before the entrance. As he did so a man ran out of the barn and headed for the Ford. He saw Father John and the furious terrier and backed away holding up his hands.

"I didn't do nuffin.' I don't want ter hurt the kid. Honest. Oh Gawd." Grim set his teeth into his leg and hung on growling. "Mister, please get 'im orf me leg." The priest offered up another prayer for forgiveness and felled him with an upper cut made more savage by his fear for Thomas.

"Grim, on guard!" he shouted and ran for the open door of the barn. Grim pounced on the fallen man and set his teeth a bare half inch from his throat and growled.

Inside the barn, Len looked up from his victim. Thomas was tied with his arms outstretched to the front end of a rusting tractor. His face was streaked with tears a dark bruise discoloured one side of his face and his nose was bleeding. His attacker had hold of a tire iron and was about to bring it down on his hand when Father John cannoned into him. The two men fought, rolling over and over in the dust of the barn floor. Hampered by a cassock and his age, the priest was at a disadvantage and was getting the worst of the battle when a large hand ripped Len off him.

Drew Docker took one look at Thomas's bruised face and Father John's bloody nose and split lip and went berserk. By the time the priest had untied the boy, Len Thorpe had lost all interest in his surroundings and was a crumpled heap on the floor.

Drew blew on his knuckles. "That felt very, very, good," he said. "Now, let's look at you two."

Several hours later things had calmed down considerably. Thorpe and Farrell were in custody charged with abducting a minor and causing grievous bodily harm to said minor. A secondary charge of assault and battery to a priest had been made, plus a third charge of breaking and entering and causing damage to a listed building. Throughout the proceedings both men had resolutely maintained that the whole thing was their own idea. No mention was made by either side of any involvement of another person. No bail was sought or offered Thomas and Father John had both been seen by Dr. Atkinson, who had earlier treated Len Harris for a black eye, a broken nose, and the loss of two teeth. Wisely Len refrained from a counter claim of assault and battery by a respected local publican.

An hysterical Mrs. Jackson with Frank in tow had arrived to collect Thomas. The drive home was punctuated by self-recriminations for letting Thomas go to school by himself, anger at Thomas for rushing into the situation without thinking, and tearful promises that she would never let him out of her sight again. Promises that Thomas had hastily told her would not be needed now that the men were in jail.

Drew, took Father John back to the school and delivered him into the hands of an astounded Father Abbot. "What on earth were you thinking of Father John," he kept saying, "Fighting is hardly becoming to a man of the cloth."

Weary but elated, the unrepentant priest complete with a black eye and several stitches had pleaded a temporary mental black out and gone to bed with two aspirin. Drew took Grim back to Bessie and filled her in on what had been happening.

During the next few days Deepdale was awash with variations on the theme of the "Fight at the Old Tythe Barn."

Thomas, Drew and Father John were the heros of the hour. Marcus Allsop was conspicuous by his absence, and Len and Fred were charged on all three counts and remanded without bail for their appearance in court in August. It was assumed that Thomas had been the target of a kidnap plan because of his father's fame and wealth.

It had been a mammoth task for Thomas to persuade his parents not to come home on the next plane. Mrs. Jackson had scared the life out of them claiming that he was now in danger 24 hours a day Thomas himself had laughed it off as an adventure and a talk with Father John and Les Finch from the police station had finally calmed their fears. They planned now on being back for the end of term concert.

The most irritating result was the tendency of the Jacksons to follow Thomas around like guard dogs. He complained about it so much that Dr. and Mrs. Atkinson offered to have him until his parents returned, in order, they said, to give Mrs. Jackson a chance to get over the stress and excitement. Thomas accepted with enthusiasm though Mrs. Jackson took longer to convince. Eventually she and Frank went off to stay with their eldest son in Hartlepool, and Thomas settled into the large, rambling house that served as both surgery and home and began to revise for his exams.

For the next few weeks he was wholly occupied with school and the Guardians formed a tight ring of protection around him, allowing him to concentrate on the everyday world. But the Atkinsons insisted the weekends were for relaxation which took the form of informal garden lunches with the other Guardians.

Edna Pugh the school teacher and local historian filled

him in on the history of Deepdale and the Carrick family, one of the oldest continuous lines in England. From Edna he learned about some of the local estates he would soon own.

"With properties such as farms, houses, fields, livestock etc, comes responsibility Thomas," she told him quietly. "For centuries these people have looked to your family for protection, help, advice, and justice. The old idea of Noblesse Oblige is and always will be part of your family's way of life."

Petronella Anderton, called Posy by everyone, walked with him round the grounds of the Manor and drew up a plan for the reconstruction of the gardens, orchards and woodlands.

Bessie usually popped in for a while with Grim by her side and Thomas always greeted her with a little bow and a kiss on the hand. The others observed this courtesy with quiet approval. Bessie herself shed quiet tears of joy, for by now everyone realized that if all went well this would be the last time the King's Chamber would be opened. On Lammas day Thomas would take up his title, the once and future king would be crowned and Bessie would rejoin Arthur in Avalon.

One of the high spots of the first meeting was the revealing of the Sword. Drew brought it from its hiding place and reverently unwrapped it before the awed eyes of the Guardians. It was truly the weapon of a king. Two handed, and made from what had once been known as star metal, it had been lovingly cleaned, sharpened and polished by Drew, as its protector.

On the top of the hilt shone a magnificent ruby, held in by a ring of Welsh gold.

But it was not the elegant blade, or the gemstone that held their attention, it was what had been set into the hilt. An ancient handmade iron nail, rusted and discoloured was embedded into the English oak. Drew took from his pocket an envelope containing the frail yellowed parchment that had been wrapped around the hilt. He handed it to Father John who translated the Latin script.

Candlemas day in the year of Our Lord 465.

This day there came to my hermitage a lady of great beauty and grace dressed all in green .She gave into my hands a pouch of gold pieces and bade me use them for the poor, but to keep enough for the making of a sword. The blade and hilt were to be of the finest star metal and the grip of mature oak. She took from her neck a chain on which hung the finest ruby I ever did see and said it was to be set into the top of the hilt. All this I did write to help my memory. Then she gave to me a silken scarf and told me it concealed a relic of great import that was to be embedded into the oaken grip for this was a sword destined to be used by a great and powerful king who would never die like other men. Within the scarf lay a nail that had once held the hand of the White Christ to his cross. As I uncovered it my small dwelling was filled with light and I heard a voice naming me as its guardian for the time it would take to make the sword.. The lady left saying she would return in a year and a day for the sword. I sought out an honest smith and spoke with him of the lady's wishes. For a full year he laboured and the sword took shape as a thing of strength and beauty. He melted down a gold piece and used it to frame the ruby, a second piece he used to frame the relic and hold it in place. Then he polished and edged the metal As the last touch was made on the last day the lady appeared. She smiled and blessed the smith and his work and wrapped the sword in her mantle. She gave to me another pouch of gold for the poor and vanished before our eyes.

This day by my hand;

Albinus of Tremaris.+

His voice faltered as he came to the end. As one, the Guardians knelt and bowed their heads. The power of the relic came softly at first then more strongly. It reached out to touch each one in turn, asked a question, and received an answer. To some it gave a vision, to others it spoke of love, to two of them it gave strength and courage. To Thomas it granted a wish. For a time they remained bathed in its light and grace, then slowly it faded and became simply a sword … for the moment. They woke to find an hour had passed.

A few days before Mid-summers Eve Marcus Allsop re-appeared in Deepdale. He brought with him some men, friends, he claimed, who booked in to The Carrick Arms. All looked young and strong. They strolled around the village, drank in the bar, smiled at the villagers and spent money in the small shops, but their eyes were cold and they held themselves like warriors. All of them wore about their necks a chain carrying a small black sphere of onyx.

At the same time there were reports that Farrell and Thorpe had escaped from jail and were on the run. Thomas was immersed in his exams, and the circle of protection around him tightened. The Vicar complained of an attempted break into the church. News that made Drew and Ben Warrener take to camping in the manor and the local police kept a round the clock watch on the church.

By mid June the exams were over and Thomas surfaced to find preparations for the midsummer festival in full swing. Father John now set Thomas to practising his Mage note to open the King's chamber. It was a race against time as his voice showed signs of breaking. The pieces of the regalia that had not been lost were taken from their hiding places to be cleaned and polished, and Nurse Pym and Thomas began looking for the Shield.

Father John as the main trustee of Thomas's great grand father's will had begun to get the manor house in order. Large vans continuously rolled up the drive to be emptied of their contents by willing hands. Thomas had the time of his life running from room to room as pictures and curtains were hung, carpets were laid and furniture returned. It was while the movers were carrying a large oval mirror up the stairs to one of the bedrooms that Stan Simonite grabbed Thomas by the shoulder and shook him.

"What is it Stan?" he asked, rubbing his shoulder. "That hurt."

"Sorry lad," whispered Stan, who'd been repairing worn treads on the stairs. "But just look at the carved frame round that there mirror and then look at the picture o' the shield and the mantling on the Carrick Coat of Arms in the window. See, that be the same pattern. What's more, a mirror that size shouldn't need four hefty men to carry it up a flight of stairs."

Thomas's eyes grew round as he looked, first at the picture and then at the mirror as it disappeared into the main bedroom. Stan closed one eye in a wink, and they went to find Father John.

The priest was in scruffy jeans and a sweat stained tee shirt carrying a clipboard of lists showing where each piece should go. On the pretext of needing some advice they dragged him to the main bedroom to look at the mirror. It seemed far too thick a frame for a piece of glass. But on turning it round they found eight wooden pegs holding the backing in place. John sent Stan off to get his box of tools.

"They didn't have screws back then, so I'll need to tap them out gently, forcing might crack the framing." said Stan. They laid the mirror flat on the massive four poster bed that dominated the master bedroom, and Stan went to work on the first peg. He tapped it from side to side, gently easing it forward until it could be gripped with pliers and pulled out of its ancient socket. It took a long time before each peg reluctantly gave up the fight and was parted from its place.

When the last one yielded they paused to close the door. Stan took hold of the stout wooden backing and heaved it from the frame. Hundreds of years of dust billowed out, choking them as it swirled around coating them in a grimy mist. A gleam of silver peeped from beneath a piece of ancient sacking and Stan lifted it away to reveal Arthur's Shield. Half as tall as a man, more Roman in shape than the medieval type Thomas had expected. Nor did it display the Lion or the Dragon. Instead they saw a Black Bear on a white field standing *en garde*, wearing a golden crown as a necklet.

Stan lifted it from its hiding place and turned it round. The back had once been covered with leather but that was now just mouldering strips. The metal arm and handgrips were rusted as was the edge of the shield itself. It bore signs of its use in the form of dents, scratches, and a hole that could have been made by an arrow. Its whole history was displayed on its surface.

Stan was the first to speak. "I'll take it back to the workshop and get Jim Lovell to give me a hand. We'll fix up that backing good and proper and repair the dents. Arthur'll get it back in good shape I promise. Best tell Nurse Pym we've found her piece." He picked up a hanging for the four poster bed not yet in place. "I'll use this to cover it and bring it back tomorrow." He carried his precious burden downstairs and they heard him drive off.

Thomas turned to his companion. "How many pieces have we got now Father?" he asked, counting off on his fingers. "The Crown, the Sword, the Shield, the Ring, the Sceptre, what else?"

"Bessie has the Cup, Posy has the Royal Seal safe. The Sword Belt and Scabbard we know where to find, and I have the Ampulla of Oil with which the King is anointed. We need to find the Orb, The Spurs, and the King's Horn."

"What about the Chain of Office" asked Thomas. "That's the last piece."

Father John laughed, "That's easy Thomas, it has never left this house. Come down stairs and I'll show you." In the hallway Father John unwound the central candle sconce. It was similar to many in other castles and manor houses, a circle of wood braced by cross bars, with metal candle holders and drip pans. Four short chains were attached to each cross bar and all fastened to a main chain which in turn was attached to the rope that lowered it. Father John let it down to waist height and fastened off the rope.

"Look at the centre chain," he told Thomas. It was different from the others and more ornate, discoloured and dusty. But Thomas could see that the chain consisted of medallions separated from each other by engraved links. Each one was a triumph of the jewellers art, a bears head holding a ruby in its mouth. The dirt and dust of over four hundred years had hidden it from view.

"It is time to get it cleaned and ready," he said, and released it from the other chains, attaching them directly to the rope.

Thomas took the chain in his hands, amazed at the weight. " How will we get it cleaned, something like this must be worth thousands of pounds."

"One of the things you learn in archaeology is how to clean ancient artefacts", Father John told him. "I'll clean this myself. "

"I can't wait to get to university and study archaeology," said Thomas, falling into step as they made for the door.

His companion stopped and looked down at him. "Thomas," he said gently, "You many not be able to do what you would like to do. You will have a lot of responsibility on your shoulders. You will have to learn to manage the estates for a start, and not only in Deepdale. There are others in Scotland and down south, as well as a small castle in Ireland. Even your grandmother did not know how much wealth your great grandfather controlled. I am afraid it will not be possible for you to disappear for months on end."

Thomas stood still, shocked, as his dreams came tumbling round his ears. " What will I have to learn then?" he asked.

"Business Studies for one thing. Possibly Agriculture or Law. You are going to have to study hard and for a long time." Thomas was silent, then he said quietly and a little sadly." You told me once to be careful about wishing for things, because you might get them."

"I remember," said Father John, "You thought it was a funny thing to say."

"The Sword offered me a wish, and I wished to be as good a Lord of the Manor as my great grandfather. I think I've learned an important lesson. We can have anything we wish for, but we have to earn it because even wishes don't come free. The Sword didn't really grant me a wish, it made me choose a path and now I have to make it come true by my own hard work." He turned and looked back at the man who had become so close to him. " Father, is it always so hard to grow up?"

"Only if you figure out the difference between knowing what you want, and what you need to do."

The boy thought about that for a while then he turned to the priest with a smile. "Well, at least I'll have you to give me advice," and ran down the steps to the car.

Father John felt the sting of tears as he followed him.

"Oh Thomas, Thomas," he thought. "You have become very dear to me. But you will need all your courage to face the days ahead. I'll be at your side for a while longer but how can I tell you that I won't be there as you grow up. That I won't survive the battle that lies before us."

THIRTEEN

It was Thomas's first Mid-summer Day in Deepdale and he was up early to make the most of it. The whole village was involved and the little square in front of the church was filled with stalls, games, and things to do and see. In the very centre of the square stood a raised platform on which the local Morris dancers were to perform in the afternoon and in the early evening a medieval Mummer's play was going to be the high spot of the day.

The local girls had woven long garlands of flowers and ribbons and were wandering around trying to lasso the boys with them. The fee for release was a kiss for each girl and a coin for the charity box and they were doing a roaring trade. The stalls were loaded with food and drink of every kind and Dr. Atkinson warned Thomas that the local Elderberry wine was a lethal brew guaranteed to bring the unwary to their knees and not to be tempted to try it.

He perched himself on the church wall, with a 'ragamuffin' pie, a local delicacy filled with an assortment of different meats topped with homemade chutney, and surveyed the milling crowd. What would they think, he thought to himself, if they knew what was going on in their midst. What if they knew Drew Docker could change into a stallion, or Posy, selling floral coronets and hat bands from her stall, was sometimes a black and white cat? Or for that matter that their highly respected local doctor was perfectly capable of becoming a sleek, swift greyhound? He laughed out loud at the absurdity of it all.

"One would never guess such deep dark secrets could lie at the heart of a charming little English village like Deepdale, would one Thomas?" The voice was smooth, elegant, with a hint of an accent he couldn't quite place. But he knew who it was. He turned his head and looked into the eyes of Marcus Allsop and an imp of mischief rose in him. He jumped off the wall and bowed low.

"A bright midsummer morning to you Prince Mordred. The Fete goes well does it not? It will not be long now until Lammas-tide comes round again, it will be a memorable one I think, for both of us, though perhaps better for me than for you." The surprise on the other's face at his easy recognition made him smile.

"You remember your Camelot manners well young Greystone, or should I call you Sir Amicus?" He took in the straight back, steady eyes and self confidence and for one mind whirling moment saw himself as he could have been long ago. "You have the look of the Carricks, lad, they were always a proud line."

"They had something of which to be proud my Lord. Loyalty to their king and his cause." Thomas was aware he was on rocky ground, but it didn't stop him. He rushed on, suddenly needing to test Mordred's resolve. " How could you treat him so Mordred, just one word and it would all have been so different."

"It will be different, this time. Once the crown is mine, the sword is mine, once the sword is mine, the seal is mine, once the seal is mine the kingdom will be mine, if not actually, then as the Prime Minister. This time nothing will stand in my way."

"I will stand in your way Prince Mordred, I and the Guardians of the Singing Stones. You cannot stand against us."

"Not only can I stand against you, I will, young Greystone. I will destroy you all and take the revenge I have desired for so long. Enjoy your Midsummer Day boy, it may be your last." He turned and strode away, pushing blindly through the crowds. As if from nowhere, six men dressed in black surrounded and walked with him towards the High Street.

"That was dangerous Thomas, courageous, chivalrous, and well meant, but it was dangerous," said Father John behind him. "He will not rest easy now you have named him. You must be very careful from now on. Do not go out alone, take Drew or one of the others with you at all times." He smiled and put his hand on the boy's shoulder. "Now how about we try our hand at the coconut shy?"

* * *

Mordred was badly shaken, he'd been very careful to keep up his persona as Marcus Allsop in the village, yet there had been no hesitation in young Greystone. No hesitation and no surprise, and a complete acceptance of his obvious longevity. The boy was a natural and very powerful seer. He had seen into the deeply hidden corners of his [Mordred's] heart in that first searing glance and hit on the one moment in his life when he and Arthur had been close.

Back at the house he leaned against the stone mantelpiece and rested his head on his arm. The centuries rolled back and he was 15, newly come to Camelot, and an angry teenager. It was an afternoon in May and as he was walking in the woods he had come upon a solitary fisherman sitting beside a flowing river. Not until the man turned, hearing someone behind him, did he realized it was his father and turned to leave. Arthur called to him.

"Mordred, don't go, sit with me and we'll catch some supper and eat it here, just the two of us."

The desperate need in him for love and recognition responded to the quiet words and for a few hours they had sat, sometimes silent, sometimes talking of fishing, archery, horses and finally of themselves. As they ate the fish they had caught together Arthur spoke.

"Son, I know you are angry, with me, with life, with everything. But give it time and things will come right. Stay with me here in Camelot and when you have proven yourself to me and to the Round Table, we will talk about your inheritance. If I had known of your birth I would have brought you here sooner than this. Because your mother is my half sister, Church law forbids that you inherit the throne, but I give my word that you will not want for land, wealth, title or power."

For one stark moment Mordred had wanted to accept, just to be a part of his life, to be his son. Then his mother's voice sounded in his ear.

"You are the rightful heir, had your father not been born Gorlois your grandfather would have ruled Britain, and I would have been queen after him. You are my sword, my arrow, my vengeance for my father's death. You will be king after Arthur."

The moment was broken and Arthur knew it. Mordred had stood up and flung the words in his face. " The crown and the throne are mine by blood and by right, and I will have it, have it all. You are the usurper, my father by accident, through a moment of lust. You are as illegitimate as I, yet you sit upon the throne of Britain. I will do the same and I will kill you if I have to, Sire." The last word was shouted with vicious spite, then he turned and ran leaving Arthur in tears by a dying fire.

Mordred returned from the past to find the small room filled with his men, his warriors. They stood, sat and leaned against the walls watching him silently. He straightened up and took a deep breath.

"I have had news from the Lady Morgana, they have found the Shield and the Sword. Only three remain to be found, the Orb, the Spurs, and the Horn. They have over a month in which to find them and I have no doubt they will. My plan is to wait and allow them to think they have won, to wait until the last possible moment before we strike. By the way Gervaise, back in the cave you will find Harris and

Thorpe hiding out, take food and supplies to them, and tell them to stay hidden until I give permission for them to surface. Garth, take a message to my Lady Mother and tell her that we can no longer count on the support of Bettina Jackson. It appears she has become too fond of Master Thomas Greystone and has changed her allegiance. Go now."

Gervaise lifted away from the door where he had been leaning and walked through the house and into the small back garden followed by Garth. There they took hold of the ebony spheres about their necks and closed their eyes. Moments later two black crows lifted into the air and headed for Ragnock Tor. In the house Mordred briefed the rest.

"The Guardians, such as they are, are no match for trained fighting men, and several of them are women who no doubt, will run screaming at the first attack. The men are untrained, except for the publican, he is big and he was in the army for some years. He and the policeman should be your first targets. Morgana will see to the most dangerous, the priest. He has knowledge of the old ways and the training to use it. Also, he will have the protection of his faith. I will go for the boy." Agravaine strolled over to the table and negligently hitched a hip on to it.

"You have forgotten something of great importance Mordred, and, I think, the most dangerous. The one who is there to be crowned. Think you he will come alone and unguarded? If so you are a bigger fool than I thought".

Mordred turned on him snarling. "No, I had not forgotten, but he will not arrive until the last moment, as always. Everything concerning him will be timed to the second. The Guardians will be ready at least half an hour before. That is when we will strike. I cannot be seen by the main participant, after all, I plan to become very close to him over the next decade or so." He laughed harshly. "Now go, leave me all of you, I have things to do."

Thomas slept late the day after the Fete. It had been a long day, filled with laughter and good companionship. Late in the evening all the Guardians had gathered at the Manor for a celebration of their own. There was still a lot to be done, but most of the furniture was back, carpets were down and the kitchen had been completely re-modelled.

The Great Hall had been the first room to be completed on John Foxton's orders with Thomas's birthday in mind. The panelled walls and oak floor shone with a new coat of varnish, and ancient, threadbare banners now fluttered gently and proudly from their poles around the ceiling. A long table had been brought in and filled with food, wine, and soft drinks for Thomas. Comfortable sofas and chairs had been set around the room, with smaller tables now piled with empty plates and glasses in front of them.

Everyone had dressed for the occasion, Thomas was sporting his new school uniform, even Grim wore a red silk bow round his neck. To mark the occasion each Guardian had brought with them a gift which they now prepared to present to the new Lord of the Manor.

Father John called for silence and the Guardians rose to their feet and surrounded their young host. Thomas stood in the centre bright pink with embarrassment but at the same time filled with loving respect for these men and women who had given so much of their time, energy, dedication and friendship to him. Dr. and Mrs. Atkinson were the first to step forward. The doctor cleared his throat and gave a little bow.

"Master Thomas, or Sir Thomas as you will soon become, this is a momentous year for all of us, and indeed for you also. So we wanted to mark the occasion with an appropriate gift that we hope you will accept for they are given with love." He took from his pocket a silk handkerchief and opened it.

Nestling in the silk were two silver greyhounds. Five inches from nose to tail each with a collar of gold. " These will remind you when we are no longer here, of a magical summer when we joined together to fight for the land we all love." He pressed them into the boy's hand and kissed his forehead in blessing. Marjory did the same and hugged him. Then they stepped back and Nurse Pym came forward to offer him a silver Roe deer with tiny golden horns.

"Dear Thomas," she said gently. "We know how hard this has been for you, and we know still more is needed from you, but with these representations of our powers we wanted you to know that we will give you all our strength and, if need be, our lives to help you in your task." She kissed his cheek and made way for Drew.

"I'm not much good with words Thomas, but I want you to know that if I'd had a son, I would have wanted him to be like you." He pressed a silver Stallion into the boy's hand. Thomas flung his arms round him and held him tightly, tears stinging his eyes.

So they came, each one of them to fill his hands with their power forms. A silver Cat, back arched and ready to spring, a Ram with ebony horns and face. A sleek Ferret with eyes of tiny rubies. A Boar with tusks of ivory, and a Badger with a cub at its feet. A Hare standing on its hind legs, paws resting on its belly. All crafted in silver.

From Bessie came an owl with eyes of Topaz and sitting on a tree stump with a small terrier looking up at its mistress. Finally came Father John offering a silver Hawk with eyes of emerald, wings outstretched to take to the air. With each gift came the greater gift of loving words and the promise of support.

Overcome with it all Thomas would have wept, had he not felt the presence of his great grandfather beside him. Instead he went to the able and poured his first ever glass of champagne then turned to the company of Guardians. The child had all but gone, the young man he would soon be stood on the brink.

"There was a time I wished my father had never written a best seller, and that we had never come to Deepdale. When I felt so lonely that I thought of running away. Then I met the Guardians and one by one you changed my life and my way of seeing things. These figures will always stand on the mantelpiece in this Great Hall, and I will tell my children and my children's children about this magical summer when we all fought for something we believed in with all our hearts." He raised his glass. "To the Once and Future King."

'To The Once and Future King!'

The words rang out like a clarion call so clear and strong, that it reached far and wide over the land and sea to misty Avalon. Arthur, walking beside the foam edged sea, raised his head to listen and smiled. It would soon be Lammas-Tide.

FOURTEEN

The village church of Deepdale had its beginnings in Saxon times. Both the crypt and the tower showed their lineage quite clearly. But it had suffered change over the centuries and was now a hodgepodge of styles that somehow still managed to blend in with the rest of the village. It had been used as a stable for Cromwell's horses but later, under the direct instructions of Charles the Second had been re-consecrated as the church of The Three Apostles, the only one so named in England.

The three saints stood in effigy over the West Door. Carved by a skilled hand they had often featured in books on ecclesiastical architecture. Grouped together, eyes lifted upwards, each held a sphere surmounted by a symbol of their office. Peter's bore an ashlar, the squared foundation stone of the Master Builder. John's supported a triple flame symbolising the Word of Creation. That of James held an equal armed cross set with stones, all were grimed by centuries of dust and smoke.

Posy, Deepdales one and only Florist, arrived loaded down with two baskets of flowers and hurried into the cool dimness of the church. "Sorry I'm late ladies, the deliveries have only just arrived and I had to get them all into water. Now I have sweet peas, white roses, some Antirrhinums, Lupins and Agapanthus and Gypsophila." The Church's regular flower ladies swiftly divided the fragrant blooms between them and set about the decorations, chattering among themselves.

"I heard as 'ow Betty Jackson's been taken poorly at 'er son's place," Lily Barker offered, filling the vases with water.

"Poor Betty, she were lookin' forrard ter thet holiday," commiserated Flo Darnely. "She were reet upset over young Thomas getting beaten up."

" 'Appen she'll need some cheering up, I'll send her the local paper so's she can see what's goin' on like, she hates not knowing the gossip." Chuckled Norma Blake deftly arranging a spray of roses against a background of ferns, They gossiped on happily leaving Posy to gather up the baskets and get back to the shop. As she left a young man loaded with elaborate camera equipment came hastening up the path. She paused as he hailed her and walked over to him.

He spoke with a slight stutter, "I s-s-say, d-d-do you live here?"

"Born and bred" She told him cheerfully. "Can I help you?"

"Oh, P-p-please, if you would. This is the Church with the c-c-carving of the Three Apostles isn't it?"

"Yes, it is, you can see them right there over the door. We're very proud of them in Deepdale."

"G-g-great, do you think I could ask you t-t-to just stand in the door there, it's to get an idea of p-p-perspective and size." Always ready to help Posy put down the baskets and trotted over to stand in the doorway. The photographer set up a tripod and screwed his camera into the top, then bent down to adjust the settings. He took several shots and then stood up.

"I s-s-say, did you know that w-w-one of those spheres l-l-looks as if it was ready to fall off. It's listing to one side. C-c-come and see for yourself."

Posy hurried over and bent down to squint through the lens. The three figures came into sharp relief and she could see the sphere of James leaning precariously to one side. Then she saw something else. The third sphere was not made of wood, it had been painted to look like it, but the paint had peeled in places and underneath was a gleam of gold. She knew instantly what she was looking at. The Orb. She turned and grabbed the young man by the shoulders and planted a smacking kiss on his cheek.

"Thank you, thank you," she babbled, "We would never have known without your help." She grabbed the baskets and was halfway down the path before the astonished young man could blink.

"Drew, Drew, where are you ... Drew." Posy flew into The Carrick Arms like a whirlwind. " Oh, there you are ... come on. I have something to show you. You too Stan Simonite, and you'd better get one your long ladders and bring it with you." She dragged Drew through the door and hustled him along the road towards the church. Drew, in his shirtsleeves and with the bar cloth still over his shoulder tried to keep up with her.

"Er, Posy, where the Hell are you taking us?" He looked back to see Stan puffing along behind him. "What is it?"

Without letting go of his arm Posy turned and hissed, "The Orb, I've found the Orb," and doubled her speed.

The three of them were breathless when they arrived, and found the photographer still taking pictures. Posy unceremoniously pushed him away from his camera and instructed Drew to look through the lens.

"Do you see it?" she asked triumphantly, as he peered through the lens.

"Aye, I do that. Come here, Stan, and take a look at this." Belatedly Posy realised she owed the bemused photographer some kind of explanation.

"I'm so sorry, but you see, we are very proud of the Three Apostles and anything like this must be seen to and repaired as soon as possible. We are most obliged to you … Mr. … Mr?"

"Oh er, Cawley, Pete Cawley." He offered a card. "I'm h-h-appy to have been of service. Things like this are v-very rare, so its g-good to see such care taken of them."

Drew turned from his conversation with Stan, and held out a hand. "I'm Drew Docker, I own The Carrick Arms. We are all obliged to you Mr. Cawley, when you've finished here please call in to the pub and have lunch and a drink on me. Now if you'll excuse us, we'll go and see about getting this repaired at once."

The young man stammered his thanks and returned to

his work and Drew and Posy made their way back to the pub. Stan went off to see the vicar and get a tall ladder. Drew lost no time in getting in touch with the other Guardians and left a text message for Father John. Then he got two cups of coffee and took them into the kitchen at the back.

" You know, I think we're getting a lot of help from them upstairs," he said, rolling his eyes heavenwards. "Talk about miracles."

"Well, I'll wait until we are quite sure it IS the Orb before I start counting my blessings, but if it is, then we are only short of the Spurs and the Horn." She sipped her coffee. Maybe I'll take a trip out to the Manor this afternoon and have a look at the window again. John and Thomas are bound to be out there doing something. I swear those two spend 18 hours out of the 24 there … at least John does, I'm off, thanks for the coffee Drew dear, see you later"

The before lunch crowd began to fill up the bar and it was not until 3:00 that Drew looked up to see Stan Simonite with a wide grin on his face coming through the door. He patted his coat pocket and winked at the landlord and passed through to the private room at the back.

Drew closed the door behind them and turned to see on his table a sphere of gold. It was badly tarnished and still had bits of paint adhering to it, but it was without any doubt The Orb.

"I told the vicar not to worry and I'd see to it and get it back up there by the day after tomorrow. I have something similar in the workshop and I'll carve out a cross and stick some coloured glass on it. He's so short sighted he'll never know the difference once it's up. Isn't it a beauty." He handed it to Drew who took it in hand reverently. Just the size to fit into a man's hand it was encompassed with a thin braid of engraved gold of a different colour.

"That be Welsh gold," Stan told him "Tis more reddish than modern gold, the wedding rings of the Royal family are always made from Welsh gold. The cross is inlaid with four different stones, emerald, sapphire, ruby and topaz." 'Tis a rare piece of craftsmanship I'm thinking."

Drew handed it back to him," Well see that it gets to its proper Guardian when you've cleaned it up. Now to find the Spurs and the Horn, tho' there's not much time." He added gloomily.

* * *

At the Manor the last of the furniture had been delivered and was now in place. Apart from things like new household linen, china and cutlery, which Thomas hoped his mother would see to, everything was as it had been in his great grand fathers time. He and Father John were sitting in the kitchen talking when the bombshell was dropped.

Leaning back casually in his chair John Foxton steepled his fingers and said calmly, "Thomas, have you any idea how much money you will come into on your birthday?"

The boy looked at him, surprised by the sudden question, then said slowly, "Well no, not really. I know you have control over some of it, and you have used it to pay for the storage and new bits and pieces, but apart from that no I don't. I suppose it must be a lot because this kind of house needs a lot to run." He shrugged his shoulders, not really interested. Father

John was amused at his off handedness.

"On your fourteenth birthday you will have limited access, under the joint authority of your solicitor and myself, to just over two million pounds. At eighteen greater control of that will come to you. At twenty-one another five million will be added and at twenty five you come into control of the entire estate.

This comprises the manor, several farms around Deepdale, in Devon, and over the border in Scotland. There are several multiplex companies in which you have a leading stake in North and South America, England, New Zealand and South Africa. You have substantial shares in several Merchant banks, a coffee estate in Brazil, a tea plantation in India, and large areas under cultivation in Hawaii. There are Art Galleries in London, New York and California, and a chain of ten hotels around the world.

Apart from all that there's a house in Barbados as well as apartments in New York, London and Rome. You own over a million acres of farmland in various parts of the world, and an art collection valued at one hundred million. In total when you are twenty-five you will be worth an estimated two billion pounds. I rather think that looking after all that puts paid to the career in archaeology you had thought of planning Thomas.

Thomas was silent for a long time, struck dumb by what he had just been told. He looked across at his companion. "I can't even imagine what a sum like that would be in terms of money. If he had so much money, why did my mum and dad have to struggle so hard all those years? Why didn't he help them? Why did he let my grandma live in that awful home?"

"He was very bitter when your grandmother left. He had been the Mage of Spheres since the age of thirty and did not marry until his forties. By the time your grandmother was born he was set in his ways. There were two boys before her, but neither lived very long. She was his last hope to pass on the leadership of the Guardians.

"Then she fell in love with Thomas Greystone. He was not from these parts and had no idea of the importance of The Singing Stones or any interest in them. She left with him without even saying goodbye. The hurt was so deep he could not forgive her and they never spoke again. He flung himself into the world of business to forget and was very successful. But he kept an eye on the family from afar.

"Then your father was born. He was a bright lad and his grandfather saw to it that he was offered a scholarship to Grammar School. Then through his solicitors he sent him on to Cambridge and as her husband was dead by then your grandmother accepted his help, but nothing more than the fees and essential books. When Steven married your mother he bought the small flat you used to live in and gave it to them as a wedding present. He would have helped more but your father would not accept it. They met occasionally and he paid the fees for grandmother's nursing home ... though she never knew that. He helped as much as he was allowed to do so.

"When you were born your great grandfather took on a new lease of life. By then your grandmother had realised the Guardianship would very likely be brought to a close in your lifetime and told your father as much as she could.

Your father found it hard to take in, besides, all his energies went into his writing. Nor would he accept the title or the Guardianship. He did not have the dedication it needed, but you do. Your Great Grand father died very suddenly, without warning, but he had left explicit instructions for your education, the appointing of the title and the estate. Then Fate intervened and your father wrote a highly successful book. The rest you know."

"Father John what is it that I have that makes me so important to all this?"

"You are a Seer and a very powerful one. That is why you and Drew get on so well. He has the same ability, but yours will be stronger when it is trained."

"I don't think I know what a Seer really is or does" said Thomas.

A Seer is a visionary. He or she can see ahead of time, and sometimes back into the past. They are mentioned in the Bible. Ezekiel, and Isaiah, and Samuel were all seers. You don't need to do anything about it Thomas, it will rise up inside you as and when the time is right. It is nothing evil or dark in power, it is a special gift of God and meant to be used as an instrument for good. Drew will help you to understand it when it appears."

He got to his feet and took their cups over to the sink. "Now there is something you can help me with, something important and it needs to be done quickly, so there's no time like the present. I take it that you will want to move into the Manor when your parents return." Thomas nodded and grinned.

"I think mum will get a kick out of living in a real Manor House."

" In the run up to Lammas-tide there are likely to be some attempts to make life uncomfortable for all the Guardians. Drew, Stan and Les will be living here, with your permission of course…" He raised an eyebrow in Thomas's direction. "As the owner you have the last word of course." Thomas crossed his arms over his chest and frowned.

" Well, that's a pretty hard decision to make, I'll have to have your word there'll be no wild parties, and gambling on the premises. Us owners have to be careful of our good name you know." He grinned and gave a thumbs up. "Of course its alright, the bedrooms and bathrooms are finished and the kitchen's done so they'll be fairly comfortable. Do you think the Carrick account can lash out on supplies and stuff. I don't want them to have to provide their own food. We'll need bed linen as well. Perhaps Mrs. Atkinson could see to that for us."

"All that can be taken care of, but there's something else that must be done. The house and grounds must be warded against attack." Thomas's eyes grew round.

"You mean Mordred would try to harm anyone living here?"

"I think we can take that as a certainty. In ancient times all places of importance were warded. That means the Powers of Light were asked to stand guard over them and repel any attempt to strike by the Dark Side." Thomas shivered, suddenly it didn't seem exciting anymore, but cold and creepy.

"Is that what you're going to do now? Will it be frightening?" He asked quietly.

"Are you afraid Thomas?"

"Yes Sir, I don't know what to expect, or if I can be brave enough, though I'll try."

"That is all any of us can do lad, try our best. But I don't think you will find this frightening. Wonderful, uplifting, awesome perhaps, but not frightening. Did you know that the Manor House has its own Chapel?"

"Yes Sir, it's in the little wood behind the main house, but its locked, I've never been able to see inside."

"I've kept it locked because it's a consecrated place and once a week since your great grandfather died I have said Mass there for him and later for your grandmother. I know the question you are going to ask, the answer is no, they were not Catholic. But as you will learn, all faiths founded on the Light lead to the same thing, The Mystery that created all things. That includes religions that were old before the coming of Christ. If it acknowledges the Light, then it is of God. I say Mass for those I loved in life to ensure they know my love is still there even though they are not. Come."

They walked through the small wood silently, both lost in their own thoughts. The little chapel was bathed in sunlight as Father John opened the door and stood back to let Thomas enter. It was small with room for maybe twenty people, but beautifully decorated with carved seats and an altar of Blue veined marble. It had obviously been cared for on a regular basis and was spotless. The front pew was cushioned in blue velvet, its back and arm rests embellished with birds and animals. A small brass plaque read. *Carrick Family Pew.* Thomas went and sat down.

Father John disappeared into the vestry and emerged a few minutes later with a crisp white surplice over his usual black cassock. He turned to Thomas and said " No matter what happens do not interrupt, or call out. Can you do that?"

"Yes Sir"

The priest turned to the altar and genuflected and made the sign of the cross, then raised his right hand.

"In the east where the Light is born I summon the presence of Raphael, the Healing Hand of God." He turned to the right. "In the south, where the sun stands high at noon I summon the presence of Michael the Sword Bearer of God." He turned right again." In the west where the Light sinks to its rest I summon Gabriel, the Messenger of God." He turned. " In the north where the blessing of rest and sleep is given I summon the presence of Uriel the Guiding Hand of God." Facing east again he bent his head in reverence.

"I ask with a humble and grateful heart that the wards of protection be raised about this house, this chapel, and the grounds that surround it. Make it strong against the Darkness and confound those who would destroy its peace. Guard those who sleep and work within that they may fulfil the work ordained for them. Let life flourish within its boundaries and be made fruitful. Let this place of worship be like a flame against evil and a point of gathering for the Light. Let that Light live and grow within the hearts of those who dwell here." He knelt, covering his face with his hands.

Thomas held his breath sensing that something was happening. He could feel the approach of something enormous, powerful, and wonderful with a feeling of joyousness about it. As if the whole of the manor, the land, the birds and animals, trees and plants, down to the last blade of grass and the very stones deep in the earth were singing with happiness and welcoming what was hurrying towards them. A shaft of light that was more than sunlight flowed through the stained glass window behind the altar and down the steps illuminating the whole chapel. Thomas watched, his eyes filled with wonder, as the Light divided into four different colours, gold, scarlet, blue and green that became in turn four pillars of swirling brilliance that moved to stand in each quarter.

John Foxton rose to his feet and beckoned to Thomas. He came slowly looking at each pillar of light in turn, not afraid, but without words to describe the emotions within him. Each pillar seemed to be filled with eyes, eyes that looked right into him and understood everything, and loved him for being himself. John took his hand and turned him to face the east.

"Raphael, Son of the Morning, Lord of the Eastern Gate I present Thomas, the Mage of Spheres and ask for your blessing upon him." With his child's innocence Thomas politely held out his hand. Beside him Father John drew in his breath sharply. There was a moment of silence, then golden light extended and encompassed the hand.

"Be thou among those blessed by the Most High Thomas, Healer of Minds."

"Thank you Raphael" said Thomas politely, I hope He blesses you as well".

The Pillar flashed through a mind blowing series of colours and there was a sound like a Shout from a thousand voices that rang through the chapel. Trembling John turned him to the south.

"Michael, Son of the Morning, Lord of the Southern Gate, I present Thomas, the Mage of Spheres and ask for your blessing upon him." Again Thomas held out his hand. The scarlet light wrapped around it like a strong handshake and a deeper voice spoke from the pillar.

"Thou art Blessed by the Lord of Hosts Thomas, Wielder of the Sword of Sacrifice."

"Thank you Michael, may you be blessed also."

The Scarlet Light grew and expanded and a filament reached out and touched his forehead as a chord of music crashed and thundered through their minds.

He was now turned to the west, and the voice of his mentor was shaking with the power building in the chapel.

"Gabriel, Son of the Morning, Lord of the Western Gate, I present Thomas, Mage of Spheres and ask for your blessing upon him." Thomas held out his hand and the blue light touched, extended up the arm and finally encompassed the whole boy within itself. Beside him Father John moaned and grasped the altar to hold himself upright.

"The Blessing of the Word be upon you Thomas." The voice was like liquid silver filling his mind and body with its power.

"Thank you Gabriel, may you be blessed as well ... er, Gabriel do you really have a Silver Trumpet?"

The sound of angelic laughter filled the air. it rang around the chapel and was echoed through dimension after dimension. Happiness radiated through Thomas and he knew he would never forget the sound.

"Thank you for your blessing, and yes, I do have a silver

Trumpet, and one day, when your work here is done, you will hear it calling you home Thomas. I give you my word." The Light withdrew and Thomas turned of his own accord to the north.

"Uriel Son of the Morning, Lord of the Northern Gate. I present Thomas, Mage of the Spheres and ask your blessing upon him." The priest's voice was just a whisper.

"The Blessing of the Lord of the World be upon you Thomas, use it to guard those placed in your care, a great responsibility has been placed upon you and it will last throughout your life," the voice this time was musical and motherly, and a tendril of green light caressed his face.

"I will do my best Uriel, thank you for your blessing, may you be blessed as well." He turned to Father John who stood with tears running down his face. You were right Sir, it isn't frightening at all."

The combined lights converged on them briefly enclosing them, then it was gone. There was just the two of them, alone in the chapel with the sun coming through the door that had opened of its own accord and the power within was flowing out in the grounds, racing up the pathways, lingering in the woods and flower beds, filling the house and grounds enclosing everything in an invisible net of light, and protection.

FIFTEEN

Betty Jackson finished her cup of tea and the last of the buttered scone. I really must stop eating so much, she told herself as she paid her bill and went out into the sunshine. There was a cool wind blowing, but Hartlepool was supposed to be 'bracing' rather than tropical. She walked along the esplanade enjoying the feel of the sea wind on her face.

Taking a break had been the right thing to do after all, she had felt so poorly those last few weeks in Deepdale. The shock of the attack on Thomas and Father John had been the last straw. She hadn't realised how fond of Thomas she had become. Come to that she didn't want Father John hurt either. Though a staunch Methodist in her beliefs, harming a 'man of the cloth' went against everything she had been brought up to believe in .

She knew as soon as she had warned off Thorpe and Harris that she would never be allowed back into Marcus's group but that didn't bother her. She had saved Thomas from being hurt. The money Marcus had promised her and with which she had planned to buy a little bungalow in Hartlepool was lost now, but she had a clear conscience which was worth much more. She paused to look out over the sea to where a tanker was making its way southwards, and shivered as she felt someone behind her. She turned.

"Excuse me madam, could you tell me the way to Moreland Avenue?"

The speaker was a tall, slimly built man in his thirties, with dark brown hair and brown eyes and an elegant moustache. Neatly dressed in a dark suit with a leather jacket over it, he looked harmless, but a prickle of fear went up Betty's spine. He reminded her of someone, someone she had met briefly.

"I'm afraid I am a visitor here myself," she said, instinctively drawing away from him. "Perhaps you should ask at one of the shops, or the post office over there, they'd be sure to know, it's not a big town and everyone seems to know everyone else here."

"That is so in many small towns and villages in England. So comforting I always think," he said and thanked her and turned away crossing the road as if going to the post office she had indicated. She watched him, still trying to place him in her memory, then turned to head back to the bus stop.

Gervaise watched her from the window of the shop and noted the number of the bus she took, then slipped hurriedly from the shop and down a deserted cul de sac. As he ran towards the high wall at the back his form changed flowing into that of a crow. He lifted into the air above the rooftops and turned into the wind, seeking and finding the bus carrying his prey. A street beggar who had followed him into the alleyway stood frowning, puzzled. He was sure his mark had gone down here .... He was a toff and had looked good for a pound or even two. Shaking his head he retraced his steps and forgot about it.

The crow kept pace with the bus, following it as it made a leisurely round of the town centre then headed out into the suburbs. A few miles further on the crow was joined by another of its kind, and then a third. Morgana's thoughts reached out to touch those of Gervaise and Garth.

"Wait until she leaves the bus and follow her into the front garden. Attack her then, there is shelter in the trees around. Go for the eyes first, then the throat. I will summon the wild ones to help." She soared away. Minutes later a flock of wild crows with Morgana in their midst joined them as they followed the bus, a silent and menacing cloud of darkness.

* * *

Thomas rode up to the Manor house and stopped to look at the newly restored shields displayed in the centre of each gate and the larger central shield on the archway that rose above them. He never tired of looking at them and was still in awe of the title that awaited him. He opened the gates and rode on up to the house.

Posy and the two gardeners who had been taken on were working in the walled garden. It looked like a disaster area at the moment, but knowing Posy it would soon be different, a place in which to sit, think, and enjoy the riot of colour and scent she had planned. He waved as he passed and went on to the house.

Drew, and Les Lovell had been busy, the brass on the front door had been polished to perfection and the door handles gleamed like gold. Inside, the two men were hanging curtains and listening to the cricket scores on the radio. Thomas handed over the basket of food and bottles of beer he'd brought from the pub and wandered off to explore. It was one of his favourite occupations and he was gradually getting to know every inch of the elegant building that would soon be his home.

As usual he made for the attics where he was gradually sorting things out into piles. Books, pictures, toys, chests of clothing, ornaments and even swords and guns. A few days before he had come across a gun case containing two guns that had sent Drew into frenzy of excitement. They were, he explained in a hushed voice, a pair of matched Purdeys. Guns made by the most famous Gunsmith in England. Each one was made by hand to fit the length of arm, width of shoulder and preferences of the client. Drew took one in his hands with the kind of reverence accorded to Holy Relics and lovingly pointed out the engraved lock plates, hammer and trigger guard. The case came with a complete set of tools that bore the Carrick escutcheon which was repeated on the stocks of the guns themselves.

It had given Thomas one of the most satisfying moments in his life to say to him, "Take them Drew, let them be a present from me." Drew's reaction had been one of complete shock.

"Thomas, I can't do that. Do you have any idea of what a pair of guns like this would cost to buy, seventy thousand pounds at the very least, probably more with the original tools and their provenance. Put them up for auction and they will buy you a Porsche when you are old enough." But Thomas insisted and enlisted Father John's help in persuading him to accept them. Finally a speechless Drew had hugged Thomas and thanked him profusely over and over again.

Today he was going over the third of the four attics which contained mostly furniture. As he rummaged around he came across a small handmade desk in a rich walnut wood and thought it would look nice in the bedroom he had chosen for his own. He dusted it off and started to go through the drawers. He found pens, postcards, and yellowed writing paper with the Carrick Coat of Arms on the top, old bills, used stamps, and dried up bottles of ink. Then in one of the drawers he found some bundles of letters each tied with a different coloured ribbon. One was a bundle of letters from his great grand mother Jessica Louise to her husband before their marriage. He set them aside to read when he had more time.

The second lot were letters from many famous people, friends of his great grandfather during Word War 11. A third and smaller bundle were letters written by Sir Piers Carrick to his runaway daughter, but never posted. The last contained just four letters, all from his grandmother. One telling him of the birth of her son, Steven, the second written on the birth of Thomas himself, the last two were written just before the old man's death, letters of love asking for his forgiveness. In one she wrote that she was returning something she'd stolen the night she ran away. Thomas sat down and began to read.

> *"It was wrong but I was so angry with you. I wanted to hurt you as you had hurt me and the best way was to steal something you valued. Not money, I had the money Mama had left me, but by taking Arthur's Horn I knew you would not be able to complete the opening of the King's Chamber. I hoped to bargain with you to make you accept Tom into the family. But you wouldn't and I was too proud to send it back. I am so sorry Papa, please, please forgive me. It was wrong of me to take something so important not just to you but to England.*
>
> *I know Steven will never be The Mage of Spheres, he does not have the power for that, but Thomas does and you will need the Horn to call up Arthur. I am returning it with this letter and in the hope that you can find it in your heart to forgive me. I have never stopped loving you Papa, even when I was angry. Now you have made arrangements for Thomas to take on the Title and the estates I feel I can at last hope for your forgiveness. Your errant but loving daughter, Jennet."*

Scrawled across the bottom of the letter in a shaky hand Sir Piers had written:

'Horn now with solicitors'

Thomas sat quietly for a long time thinking about his grandma then put the letter into his pocket and went downstairs. He borrowed Drew's mobile and phoned Father John to tell him the Horn was safe. Things were slowly falling into place.

* * *

John Foxton walked back through the school grounds to his rooms. A feeling of apprehension hung over him and he couldn't think why it should. He had received Thomas's call concerning the Horn and that was good news, he had just attended confession and received absolution and should have been feeling at peace. But something was nagging at him. He turned aside and walked into the sun filled cloisters hoping to still the agitation inside and sat down on a bench to meditate.

As he closed his eyes he felt a wave of fear pass over him, but it was not his own fear, it was someone else's. A soundless call for help. He could see a cloud of black wings, feel pain, heard the voice of Betty Jackson and knew she was in danger.

Using the Angelic Wards of the schools chapel as a focal point he sent a call for Michael winging through the air. At the same time he rose and headed for the chapel his rosary already in his hand.

"Holy Michael, Guardian of Souls, Protector of the Weak and the Defenceless, answer her call for the love of Mary's Son."

At the Manor Drew had also heard the mental call for

help and headed for the chapel meeting a frantic Thomas along the way.

"Drew I could hear Mrs. Jackson's voice in my head what is happening?"

"I don't know Tom lad, but I think she is in trouble. Since the protection wards for the manor were put up in the chapel that's the best place to start."

* * *

They had chosen their time well. Just as Betty Jackson opened the garden gate, the crows struck. At first she thought there were just one or two but as she turned she saw the dense flock swooping down on her and panicked. She dropped her purse and raised her hands to protect her face. Her hat went flying and hard sharp beaks tugged at her hair. When she tried to brush them away they went for her face and her eyes.

Screaming she fell to the ground and curled into a ball. They were trying to kill her. She knew what they were, Mordred had sent them, this was her punishment for helping Thomas. As she tried desperately to protect herself she reverted to her childhood prayers, "Gentle Jesus meek and mild" she prayed and with the words she remembered Father John and from the heart sent out a call for help.

She heard people calling her name, felt them trying to fend off the birds but felt herself beginning to lose consciousness. As she did a bright light surrounded her and she knew her call for help had been heard. As suddenly as they had attacked the birds lifted off into the air and fled westward croaking as they went. All but three of the largest birds who circled overhead dodging the stones thrown at them by Betty's frantic son. The sound of an ambulance siren brought her momentarily to her senses.

"Gary," she whispered, have they gone?"

"Yes, Ma. They've gone and the ambulance is here, let's get you to hospital, you're bleeding badly. God alone knows why they went mad like that. I've never seen anything like it." He stood aside as the medics took over and began to examine her.

"Gary, please, before they take me off, please, ring Father John at St. Edwards Priory School in Deepdale, if you can't get him call Drew Docker at the Carrick Arms and tell them what has happened. Promise me you'll do that."

"Okay, Ma, I'll get on to them right away. I'll follow the ambulance on the car and call them on the mobile as soon as we get to the hospital. Now rest easy. Let them make you comfortable." But she had lost consciousness again.

At the hospital they began to assess the damage. Claws and beaks had torn her face and hands badly and there was damage to one eye. A slashing beak had caught her throat dangerously close to an artery and she had lost a lot of blood. She remained only semi -conscious for almost an hour and on coming round more fully asked for her son.

"I'm here Ma. I did what you asked and rang the school but Father John wasn't there, so I got hold of someone at the Carrick Arms. They said they'd get a message to Drew Docker right away. Don't fret, everything's under control. The eye specialist will see you tomorrow and Dad's here, he's talking to the doctor now. You were very lucky old dear, somebody was passing and grabbed one bird who was trying to stab your eye out, he wrung its neck. He said his name was Michael and seemed think you'd know who he was, but he disappeared before I could thank him".

Betty sank back on her pillow, her head, face and hands were bandaged and there was a patch over her right eye. She felt bruised and shaken and very frightened, but deep down she knew her call for help had been heard. She managed a shaky smile.

"Yes dear, I know him, I'll thank him when I see him again." The sedatives began to work and she drifted into sleep.

* * *

"I don't care," said Thomas stubbornly, "I'm going to see Betty and I'll go alone if I have to." Drew threw up his hands and shook his head. Father John, worried though he was, could not help but smile. There was more of old Sir Piers Carrick in his great grandson than they had thought.

He stood up, "All right, we will all go, you and Drew and I, but I will make the arrangements if you don't mind. Also, we will go there and back in the one day. I will not risk any more than that. Do you understand Thomas?"

"Yes Sir, when are we going"?

"Tomorrow, it needs to be as soon as possible. Oh, and Thomas, I rang the solicitors this morning. The Horn was put in their care, though they don't know what it is, they just received a sealed box to keep for you. The terms of the will mean they need to see you in person, with your parents and me, in order to hand over the documents etcetera, and you will have to sign for them. Since your parents will be home shortly I made an appointment for us all to meet at their chambers on the twenty-sixth of July. That will give us time to get things ready for Lammas Eve .

Now I suggest we go home and get some sleep. Mordred will have spent a lot of energy on that attack, so he won't be doing much for the next few days." He drove Thomas back to the Atkinson's and gave instructions for him to sleep late in the morning.

Back at the hospital in Hartlepool Betty Jackson was dreaming. She was watching herself being attacked by the crows, she saw herself beaten to the ground by their wings, claws and snapping beaks and heard herself screaming for help and people running towards her.

"Father John, Thomas … help me, help me. Oh God, help me please."

A shaft of light hit the middle of the flock and spread outwards momentarily scattering them. It thickened and dimmed becoming the figure of a young man who reached out and plucked a crow from her head and with a swift motion wrung its neck and tossed it away. Light flowed from the hand he laid across her eyes as the crows re-formed and struck again. The man remained by her side bending over her protectively until others reached them and began beating off the birds. Then he just melted away.

She could feel his presence now beside her as she lay dreaming. A soft, warm, feeling stole over her and she relaxed. "Thank you Michael," she murmured. "Thank you."

When she next opened her eyes the first thing she saw

was Thomas's face as he bent to kiss her cheek. Behind him stood Father John and Drew Docker, both holding large bouquets of flowers.

"Oh Thomas, how lovely to see you. You too Father and Drew. Oh dear, I seem to have been sleeping on and off all morning." She struggled to sit up and Drew put down his flowers to help her. "Thank you, thank you and what lovely flowers, it's so kind of you to come all that way." She began to cry and Thomas handed her a clean hanky to use.

"It isn't very far Mrs. Jackson and as soon as we heard we decided to come and see you," said Thomas settling himself on the bed.

Father John sat down and took her bandaged hands in his. "You are not to worry about anything Mrs. Jackson. I have spoken to the doctors here and you will not lose the sight of your injured eye, though it was a near thing. You have extensive facial injuries but as soon as you are stronger you'll be transferred to a Manchester hospital specialising in micro surgery. All you have to do is rest and get strong."

"Father, there was a young man, he helped me, protected my eyes but he disappeared before I could thank him." The priest smiled. "Yes, I heard about that, I am sure he considers himself thanked enough by your prayers. You were very lucky Mrs. Jackson."

They stayed for several hours then said their goodbyes, leaving her bright-eyed and smiling and surrounded by flowers and cards. On the way home Thomas leaned over from the back seat.

" It was Michael wasn't it, I mean our Michael from the Gate of the South? I got the same kind of shivery feeling in the chapel with Drew as I did when you and I .... Well when you did what you did to protect the manor."

"Yes Thomas, it was 'our' Michael. It means the warding is doing its job so we can feel safe when we are inside the wards. I have been thinking things over and I now suspect the attack on Mrs. Jackson was planned by Morgana rather than by Mordred. The use of the wild crows carried her signature. Also, for all his deviousness and hatred of Arthur, Mordred has never attacked women before. I like to think that some of his father's training still hides within him."

"What now Father," asked Drew after they had driven some miles in silence. He looked over at Thomas who had fallen asleep on the back seat. "It seems to me there's still a fair bit to do before we can say we are ready." The priest nodded.

"Indeed. The first task is to find the spurs, then we have all the regalia. Thomas has the Magus note in his head now, so that part is ready. I want to call a meeting at the Stones in the next few days to set up the Calling of the Knights. The spheres have not been used for a hundred years and may need psychically re-tuning. Weekends are difficult for you but could you manage this Friday?"

"I can do whatever I need to do," replied the publican. That's one of the better things about being your own boss. As soon as we get back to Deepdale I'll call the others and set things up. What else is on the cards?"

The School concert is next Thursday, the twenty-first, after that Thomas and I are free from School. I have to spend a day in Manchester on private business and I need to go and see my children in London. There are things I need to arrange." Drew looked over at him and felt the tension coiling inside him. "I understand" he said quietly.

John Foxton smiled. "Yes Drew, I know you do. Thomas's parents were due back tomorrow but have been delayed, Mrs. Greystone has Bronchitis and the doctors say she cannot fly until it has cleared up. They are now coming on Monday the twenty-fifth. On Wednesday twenty-seventh we all have to be at the solicitors. On the twenty-eighth I'd like to have another gathering of the Guardians with the Regalia just to make sure we all know our place in the ceremony in case … well … if what we expect to happen, does happen. Then I would like to have a couple of days to myself, to prepare for my part and to build up my strength. I think we should all take time off then to relax and ease the strain we've all been under these past weeks. Can you see to everything Drew?"

"Aye, I'll see to it, never fear."

They drove on in companionable silence, each wrapped in their own thoughts of the coming event and the part each of them were destined to play in it.

SIXTEEN

"But you told Gervaise yourself that she could no longer be trusted, what was I to think?"

"What you wanted to think ... as usual my dear mother, you have always done exactly what you wanted to do and never given a thought to what I might want." Mordred paced back and forth across the cave floor. " It would have been punishment enough for her to lose the money she was going to get from me. Now she is badly injured, may lose an eye, and is firmly on their side of the fence. What is even more important she called for help and got it ... from the Guardians Foxton set up round the manor. So the angelic realm is now alerted."

Morgana sulked in the corner. "I was trying to help."

"Well you didn't. Just keep out of the way from now on. I will not have you risking all I have worked for centuries because you want to indulge your taste for inflicting pain. In case you hadn't noticed mother dear, I am no longer a boy. I can think things out for myself. In fact I'm beginning to wonder if I should have listened to you in the first place. A thousand years gives you a lot of time to think things over." He flung himself down on one of the couches and put his head in his hands.

Morgana sat frozen with fear and fury. Was Mordred beginning to waver? Would he ... could he ... forget all she had taught him? She rose to her feet and went to kneel beside him.

"You are tired dear, it is only natural. You have come so far and achieved so much. Now it is all within your grasp. A few more days and you will have Britain in the palm of your hand. I should have told you about the Jackson woman I know, but I was so anxious to help. Rest your head on my shoulder dear, my sweet little boy, my winsome lad. It will be over soon and we can both rest for a while. Remember how you used to sit by me while I sat at my loom? You would pick out the threads for me and recite your lessons".

"I also remember the beatings, the long hours spent struggling to wield a sword meant for a man not a boy. I remember the nights sleeping on the battlements because you said the cold would make me stronger. I remember you killing my dogs because you said I must concentrate on my destiny and not play with them. I remember seeing other boys with warm loving mothers, and fathers, and envying them. Oh yes, I remember all those things and many more." Mordred rose, and sent Morgana tumbling to the floor.

"Take wing mother, being a crow suits you more than the shape of a woman. You were never womanly, a real woman has a heart, and you have none, just a stone." Morgana rose from the floor, her eyes blazing. "Maybe I should have made Agravaine my chosen knight. He at least accords me the respect due to me."

Mordred turned to her, holding her eyes with his. "I have just remembered something my father told me long ago. "Respect must be earned it does not come of its own accord. I suggest you leave me Madam, before I forget the very little respect that is your due."

When she had finally gone he sat lay down on a couch and closed his eyes. She was right, he was tired. Tired of plotting, of waiting, of moving from place to place, of hoping and watching. He was tired of living. He cast his mind back trying to remember one time, just one, when his mother had held him, comforted him, told him a story that did not include his duty to kill his father. But there was nothing, not one word or gesture to recall.

On the other hand he well remembered that day in the woods with Arthur, the taste of the fish they had caught together, the laughter, and the feeling of closeness. Then there was the day Arthur had given him a horse from his stables. A wonderful chestnut bay with a mouth like silk and the heart of a lion. If he tried hard he could feel the warmth of his hand on his shoulder, and the hope in his voice.

"Do you like him Mordred? He was sired by my own stallion and is the best in my stables. He is yours son, treat him well and he will carry you through hellfire."

Hogar, he had named him; that and his sword, another gift from his father, had been the two things he had taken with him when he fled from Camelot. He wondered how different things might have been if he had not made an enemy of Arthur. Eventually he slept curled on his side like a child, with tears stains on his face.

* * *

It was a beautiful day and Thomas was enjoying it to the full. He had worked all morning in the Herb garden with Posy and over lunch had discussed with her and Drew the best place to install a swimming pool. He wanted it attached to the house so it could be used the year round, but Drew pointed out that it was a listed building and permission to add to the existing house would probably be refused. He suggested a separate building complete with changing rooms and maybe a small gym, beyond the back lawns and away from the main house.

Now they had both gone and he found himself alone in the Manor for the first time in weeks. He wandered through the house absorbing its atmosphere, touching the ancient furniture and wondering which of his ancestors had bought each piece. He thought ahead to his first Christmas here with his parents and friends. A big log fire, he thought and chestnuts, and a tree from his own wood. There would have to be two parties, one just for mum and dad, me and the Guardians, and another for the village with fairy lights in the trees and torches lining the drive. It was exciting to look ahead and plan things. Now if the school concert went well and he had got through the exams with reasonable marks life would be perfect.

The sunshine called him out through the front door to sit on the steps and feel the warmth on his face. There was no wind, the trees were still and the scent of the wildflowers that lined the driveway filled the air. To the man standing by the closed gates the boy personified the image of youth, contentment and stability. He put out a hand and touched the gate feeling the faint vibration that told him it was warded, and by an expert. He knew he could not pass through those gates. He was not sure he wanted to do so, even if he could. It was peaceful in there and he knew his presence could destroy that peace. But he longed to be a part of it, to know what it felt like. His emotions flowed out and alerted the boy sitting on the steps, and he looked up.

Thomas held his breath feeling a flare of panic that subsided almost as soon as it came. He looked down the length of the drive and saw Mordred standing at the gate. He knew the wards would keep him out, but he could also feel the desperate longing of the man for what lay within those wards. All at once Thomas knew with a wisdom far beyond his years what Mordred's boyhood had been like. He could understand his longing for peace and the forlorn hope of being loved. He understood, sympathised and longed to help.

He made a decision that would colour the rest of his life, rose slowly to his feet and began to walk towards the gate, keeping his eyes on the man who waited. The Angelic Wards also waited and watched for much would depend on this meeting.

As Thomas approached the gate there was a sense of being outside time, as if somewhere, someone or something, was holding its breath. He came right up to the gate and stopped looking his opponent in the eyes.

"I bid you good day Sir Mordred," he said, falling easily into the court speech of Camelot." To what do I owe the pleasure of your company?"

Mordred leaned against the gate pillar and lit a cigarette. "In the old days before a battle took place it was the custom for both sides to meet and talk. I …felt a need to apply the old rules. Back then a table with a sword laid lengthwise along it was set up with a chair either side for the leaders to sit, drink and talk. It was considered civilised. These gates," he indicated them with a wave of his hand, "constitute the equivalent of that table. I cannot pass them and you will not leave the safety they provide. We can however talk for this space of time before the battle begins."

Thomas considered his words. "You are certain there will be a battle then?"

Mordred laughed. "Oh yes, there will be a battle Sir Thomas, you may be certain of that. After a thousand years of waiting I am not disposed to lose my dream."

"Is it your dream or the dream of the Lady Morgana?" asked Thomas quietly. Mordred stiffened and flung away his half smoked cigarette.

"My dream," he said savagely. " My claim to Arthur's crown is real."

"But your time has passed Mordred, it belongs to another Arthur now, another line, another lineage, another dynasty has a rightful claim to it. Why not let it pass and find the peace you seek?"

"You are wise beyond your years Thomas. We are very alike you and I. Both of us born to a destiny and a position, both are torn between duty and our own desires."

Thomas moved forward and took hold of the railings and said quietly, "But there is one vital difference. You were trained with hate and I have been trained with love."

Mordred dismissed his argument. "Like me, your father left you," he said.

"No!" Thomas shouted in his face. "He left for a purpose and I let him go to do what he wanted most in the world. I let him go and he is coming back. You let your father go because you didn't have the courage to defy your mother." Mordred opened his mouth to say something, then turned and began to walk back to his car. Thomas called to him.

"Mordred, don't go I'm sorry, I didn't mean to hurt you. Please come back and talk, I want to ask you something." Mordred stopped and turned almost eagerly. He couldn't remember the last time somebody had apologised for hurting him. He came close to the railings again.

"What do you want to know?" Thomas sat down cross legged on the ground and gestured to Mordred to do the same. He tugged a bottle of water from his back pocket and offered it through the gate.

"It's not wine or mead or whatever you used to drink back then, but it'll quench your thirst." Mordred hesitated a second, then accepted the bottle, drank and passed it back to Thomas who followed suit.

"What is it like to live for so long?" he asked. Mordred shrugged.

"Tiring, lonely, frustrating, and boring".

"How do you do it?" persisted Thomas.

We need to sleep for long periods of time, both I, and the woman you know as Bessie. You might call it a sort of hibernation. Every now and then we disappear for two or three weeks. We both have places where we are safe and can sleep as long as we need to."

Is that why Bessie lives in the cave?" asked Thomas

"Yes. Grim watches her while she sleeps, then she does the same for him".

"Where do you sleep?" Mordred was silent for a few minutes. Then decided since he would soon no longer need it he could safely disclose his hideaway.

"There is a cave, much larger than Bessie's near Ragnock's Tor. My mother found it and made it into a place where my knights and I could sleep undisturbed. They chose to sleep until I called them. I chose to stay awake. A few weeks ago I awakened them and now they wait with me for the Battle to come."

Thomas thought this information over for a few minutes then asked a different question. "What was it like when you were my age?" Mordred's laugh was suspiciously like a sob. He got to his feet and paced back and forth in front of the gates.

"It was bad. I was often cold, mostly hungry and always tired. Other boys kept away from me because they were afraid of my mother's powers. My half brothers were sent away by my step-father to Camelot to train for knighthood. I was kept at home to be trained by my mother's uncles and their men at arms. Several times I ran away, but I was always caught. It is difficult to escape from an island and she beat me so badly I decided it was better to stay."

Thomas was horrified. "Your mother beat you. How could she do that?"

"Because I was Arthur's son and every time she hurt me or beat me or made me go hungry she was punishing him for her father's death. She called me her 'Arrow of Justice.' She seldom even called me by name".

"Oh Mordred, that's awful." A thought struck him. "How old are you?"

"Actually or when I fought my father?" Asked Mordred with a grim smile.

"When you fought your father."

"I was twenty years of age when I struck my father down."

"You were only six years older than I am now. You could be my older brother." He sprang back as Mordred smashed his fist against the gate. The skin split and blood flowed from the cuts and splashed on the ground.

Thomas stood aghast as Arthur's son flung back his head and howled like a dog. Then sank down on his knees and wept, his face in his hands.

"I would have given anything, anything to have had a brother, someone to love, to talk to, to look up to. She killed my hounds in front of me to make me understand that I must think only of defeating Arthur. I was allowed to speak only to those she chose as my companions. All of them men and much older than me. She ... never ... even... held ... me ... when I got sick. Shouts, quarrels, beatings are all the memories I have. I envy you Thomas Greystone. Envy you the love and support of your parents, I envy you your friends. I should hate you for having what I was denied, but I can't.

Thomas came to the gate again and took out his handkerchief. With water from the bottle he washed the blood from Mordred's hand and bound it up, then held the wounded hand in his own and spoke gently to the distraught man.

"Mordred, do you really hate your father?"

"Yes! No! I don't know anymore. I'm tired Thomas, so very, very tired. I just want it to end, one way or another."

"Where is Morgana now," asked Thomas.

"I don't know and I don't care. We quarrelled over her attack on Mrs. Jackson. That was none of my doing I swear."

"Father John said it wasn't you. He said you had remembered what Arthur taught you, and you would never have attacked a woman."

"He said that ... about me?"

"Yes." Mordred brushed his hands across his eyes.

"Thomas, do you hate me"?

"No Mordred. I don't hate you. I just wish I could help you."

The man and the boy stood either side of the gates. Mordred pressed his wounded hand against the railings. Thomas put his against it, and they stood together for a long time. Then Mordred turned and went back to his car and drove away.

* * *

The following day was the last day of term and the school concert. Betty Jackson had insisted on attending so the hospital allowed her out for a few hours. Drew arranged a car and driver to pick her up and to take her back. Her face was still heavily bandaged but she was determined to keep her promise to attend.

The school's main hall had been decorated with flowers and banners and pictures the boys had drawn and photographs from the senior classes. All the Guardians who could turned up and Drew with his newly purchased camera was going to video it all. The result would be shown to Thomas' parents and those who couldn't attend.

First the students processed into the hall led by the staff. The school anthem was sung and an address was given by the Abbot. The prize giving was always popular and each recipient was given a hearty round of applause as they came up to get their prizes. Thomas received two awards, the first, a forty pound Book token, for his essay on The Historical History of the Dales, and the second, much to his surprise was the Class Math prize, a silver cup to be held for a year. Then came the concert.

The one act play, a comedy, was well received, then came a rather shaky performance of an excerpt from Vivaldi's Four Season's by the school orchestra followed by various instrumental solos. Thomas's vocal solo of *Panis Angelicus* was loudly applauded, making him blush with pleasure.

This was followed by a Martial Arts display and a choral selection from the juniors. The last offering was an exhibition of fencing in which Thomas again took part. As he lined up with the others dressed in his 'whites' he saw Mordred standing at the back of the hall. As his name was called he stepped forward and saluted with his foil, then, deliberately turned towards the back of the hall and repeated the salute. Mordred smiled broadly, and bowed in acknowledgement. Father John and Drew turned to see who had been so recognised and honoured and turned back again with their mouths open.

Thomas won his bout with ease and saluted the audience's applause. Mordred clapped along with them, then turned and left. The afternoon came to an end with the singing of the school hymn.

Let Me Bring Light.

Let me bring Light to this day O Lord.
Make me a beacon of your love.
Help me to lighten the shadows that threaten
And bring down the Light from above.

Let me bring peace to this day O Lord
And make me a message of Hope.
No matter what comes let me face it and win
As I learn how to live and to cope.

Let me bring Faith to this day O Lord
Make me both faithful and strong.
Help me to conquer all my fears and my foes
And help me choose right over wrong.

Let me bring Love to this day O Lord.
Make me a symbol of your Life
Make me strong, make me true, make me just like You
And rise above hatred and strife.

After that everyone gave three hearty cheers to herald the summer holidays and streamed out into the grounds. Mayhem reigned as the students and their families stood and talked, laughed and discussed holiday plans. The car park became chaos as cars and people jostled for room.

Thomas was alone in the changing room getting back into his uniform when he heard his name called. Mordred stood by the door.

"May I come in," he asked.

"Of course Sir Mordred," was the instant response. A wide grin changed the usually severe face into something closely approaching a normal expression.

"I think we can dispense with the formal address Thomas. I have a gift for you, if you will accept it. I will understand if you do not wish to do so." He held out a leather pouch. "I think this is something you will need."

Thomas took the pouch and opened it. Inside lay a pair of spurs inlaid with silver and engraved with the initials *AR*. "Arturus Rex," he murmured and looked up at Mordred. "Where on earth did you get these, and why are you giving them to me. You must know they are the last piece we have been looking for and that now we have them all."

"I acquired them from the son of one of the Guardians several hundred years ago. He had no idea what they were. The Battle will happen Thomas, that cannot be stopped now, but I want you to know that I wish it could have been different. If I could have had a brother, I would have wanted it to be you. Whatever the outcome of the Battle I have decided not to go on. If I lose, I will sleep for eternity. If I win ... well, I do not think I can change after so long a time, I was born to be a weapon against a man I did not know. I was and am a vessel filled with my mother's hatred. But Lammas Eve will decide it for all of us. Goodbye Thomas of Deepdale." He turned and left.

Later that evening over dinner with the Atkinsons Thomas told Father John and Drew what had happened between Mordred and himself and handed over the spurs. At first they were concerned such a confrontation had taken place. But as Thomas explained further Father John became silent. Finally he said.

"I am beginning to see the Divine Hand in all this. I hardly dare to hope for what seems to be unfolding but it maybe that we are all playing a part in something very wonderful," and would say no more.

As evening fell and lights began to come on in the village the Guardians began to make ready. Ian and Marjory slipped away first, flowing into their animal forms easily and disappearing into the shadows. Father John followed soon after lifting into the sunset sky with fluid grace. Drew and Thomas planned to travel together and last of all.

They waited for over an hour to give the others time to get to their destination then walked down the main road and into the lane leading to Deepdale House. They paused at the hidden entrance by the hedge and Drew told Thomas to go ahead and wait for him.

It was the first time Thomas had changed without feeling any pain, he flowed quickly and easily into his Stag form and waited by the pool for Drew to join him. The Second road was lit with its usual eerie light and as Drew came to meet him they turned their heads into the wind and set off for the Circle.

The exhilaration of the race filled them with joy in the freedom their other forms gave them. They encountered many others travelling the same road but on different errands. To all they accorded a courteous greeting and received them in return. At some point they were joined by Grim and as they travelled he conveyed to them the news that Bessie had woken from her sleep and would join them at the Stones. From his conversation with Mordred, Thomas now knew the reason for her absence over the last few weeks.

The last hill came into view and within minutes the Stallion and the Stag stepped into the circle, Grim remained outside and on guard. One by one the animal forms dropped away and the grey cloaked Guardians stood ready to receive their Mage.

Father John stepped forward to announce they now had the last piece of the regalia, but simply said it had been found, not how it had come to them. He spoke of preparations that still needed to be made and told them to clean and polish their Treasures and make them presentable. They then practised the Cadence all except Thomas, whose note could not be sounded until the very last moment. But he assured them he was note perfect, but added that he was glad it would be no later than Lammas, as any later and his clear A would possibly be a memory. Drew teased him saying that if his voice broke early he might have to open the Chamber with a Bass note.

Finally Father John told them to take their places and take out their spheres. Thomas went to stand by his Mage stone and took the chain from about his neck holding the little sphere in his hand. All stood silent listening to the instructions John Foxton read from an old parchment.

Each sphere contains a fragment of the spiritual essence of one of the Knights of the Round Table. When the time comes for the Once and Future King to be crowned they may be summoned from their sleep to surround and protect their King once more before departing into Avalon forever.

"You all know which knight has been assigned to you. Hold the sphere up shoulder high and mentally call the name, but softly, we do not wish to waken them fully, just to make certain the spheres can make the connection when needed."

Each Guardian concentrated quietly, long minutes passed and Thomas began to think the spheres had lost their powers over the centuries. Then he noticed the mist rolling up the Tor to cover the circle and its Guardians. Then it thinned out and separated and the dim outline of twelve tall mailed figures could be seen.

They stood in a ring beyond the circle and facing inwards, leaning on their reversed swords, heads bowed, shields at their backs, their eyes closed. Beyond the circle and behind each knight stood an armoured charger saddled and ready. Utter silence prevailed. Then beside Thomas there slowly formed the figure of Arthur. He alone stood with his eyes open, sword in hand, shield on his arm. Behind him a huge black stallion stood pawing the ground.

The Guardians began to name the Knights one by one.

Sir Bors,

Sir Gareth,

Sir Gaheris,

Sir Gawaine,

Sir Palomedes,

Sir Pellinore,

Sir Bedivere,

Sir Kai,

Sir Launcelot,

Sir Perceval,

Sir Tristram,

Sir Galahad,

Arthur, High King of Britain.

On the other side of Thomas another figure took shape as Merlin completed the roll call. His voice was faint but clear.

"You have done well. We will await your call on the eve of Lammas, when the two Arthurs will meet. Until then, accept our blessing."

As slowly as it has come the mist disappeared taking with it the Knights and their horses. Arthur and Merlin were the last. In silence the awestruck Guardians began to take their leave, disappearing one by one into the shadows and making their way back home.

SEVENTEEN

"The plane landed ages ago," said Thomas for the sixth time. "Where are they?"

Drew grinned down at him. "It's probably taking a long time to haul all the stuff they've brought for you up the walkway."

Thomas punched his arm in reprisal, then let out a yell. "They're here! It's them, look Drew, look! Hi mum! Hi dad! Gosh they look different. Come on let's get down to the exit." He raced off leaving Drew to follow which he did more slowly. He hoped things were going to be alright in the Greystone family. In his opinion it would have been better if the lads parents had stayed away until after his birthday. But that was the way of things.

Both Greystones were pushing trolleys loaded with cases and it took some time before they finally made it through Customs to their impatient son. Nora flung her arms round him, hugged him and cried over his four inches of new growth that made him taller than herself by a good two inches. Then his father shook hands and said with a wide smile;

"Sir Thomas, I'm so glad to meet you at last," Thomas blinked, then caught on as his father exploded into laughter and swept him up into his arms.

Drew was introduced and explained that he had a limo waiting for them. Thomas and his mother set off chattering and laughing in front, but Steven took Drew aside.

"I understand you have been of great help to Thomas, looking after him and the manor. Believe me we are very grateful to you. It's been a worrying time for us. I know what it is like now to be a bone between two dogs. But Hollywood producers regard family as expendable when there are million of pounds at stake."

"I've never been married or had a family of my own," said Drew," but looking after Thomas these past months has been a real joy for me. He's a great lad, you can be proud of him." They walked on in silence for a few minutes then Steven asked, "How are things going, with the ceremony?"

"Everything's in place now. But there's a very strong opposition, Father John is taking care of that. Thomas has taken most of it in his stride, the only thing that upset him was the title and the estate. He got it into his head that you'd be angry about being passed over."

Steven Greystone shook his head. "Drew, all I've ever wanted to do is write. I don't want to have to look after a large estate. I've signed a contract for three more books with an advance that has so many zeros after it, it makes me dizzy. Just this one film will make me a millionaire in my own right.

I don't want a title and I certainly don't need the money."

They reached the limo station and the chauffeur began to stow the luggage. Finally everybody was on board and they eased out into the traffic.

Mrs. Atkinson was waiting with lunch at Deepdale House as Betty Jackson was still in Hospital. She had made up beds, got in groceries, and had a hot-pot gently simmering in the slow burner. She waved away expressions of gratitude saying it had been a pleasure to help, and off she went, taking Drew with her and leaving Thomas alone with his parents for the first time in over four months.

The conversation ran at full tilt for hours, then gradually slowed until by the time they had finished dinner everyone was ready for bed. But Thomas had one more thing to say.

"Father John and Drew and lots of other people have helped me to bring the Manor House back to its original state. It looks lovely now and the gardens are getting back to how they used to be. We need things like bed linen and stuff, but it is almost ready to move into and I love it there. I'm hoping we can move, maybe in the middle of August. I've talked to Father John about having an indoor pool built in the back lawn, and if we start then it would be ready by the end of November and we can swim all the year round. Do you think you would like it there? I thought dad could have great grandfather's study to write in. His old desk is back in place and a HUGE chair. It will be a great place for Christmas parties too." He looked at them eagerly and added his trump card. "And just think, there's no mortgage to pay because I own it."

His parents laughed and his mother ruffled his hair.

"I'm sure we will like it," she said. "But can we just get used to being back in England first? Let's all get some sleep now."

Thomas lay awake for a while savouring the feeling of being a family again. He went over the last three months in his mind and tried to figure out how much he could or should share with his dad. His mother would go along with whatever offered the least resistance but his dad knew a lot more about the Singing Stones and grandma's family. Still it was pointless to worry over it. He turned over and fell into a deep sleep.

The following morning he was up bright and early with everything clear in his head and now feeling ready to deal with anything that came along. The first thing that did come along was Grim. He was sitting outside the backdoor when Thomas took in the milk, and was finishing off the last of the pot roast and a bowl of milky tea when his dad came down.

"What's this, a new addition?" he asked scratching behind Grim's ears.

"No, I wish he was, but he belongs to a friend of mine. He comes here sometimes for a bit of whatever is going. He's very intelligent. His name's Grim."

"Ah, that strikes a bell. There are several legends about dogs called Grim, but they are usually black," said his father pouring himself a cup of coffee.

"Yes, Father John told me." Thomas filled two bowls with cereal and put bread in the toaster. " Is mum still asleep?"

"Yes, she'll be a bit addled for a few days. It took her ages to recover when we went to LA. You know Thomas, America is a great place, especially when you have some success behind you. Next time we go you'll have to come with us."

Thomas took a spoonful of cornflakes and spoke round them. "Are you thinking of going back then? For how long?" His father hesitated then said quietly:

"Maybe for good."

Thomas choked on his cereal. "For good, but why? You don't need the money anymore."

"Your mother likes the sunshine all the year round. She's made a lot of new friends ... some of them very close, and has had offers to sit on committees and things. It's got everything Tom. Mountains, sea, valleys, forests, and the people are great when you get to know them. She's sort of ... well ... set her heart on it."

"I'm sure its great, but Dad, it isn't home. It isn't the Dales. I like four seasons, not just one. Besides I can't go, I'll have too much to do looking after the estate once I have finished university."

His father looked at him, for the first time seeing the man within the boy and realising that he had more of his great grandfather in him than he had reckoned on. He would see the responsibility of the estate as something he was born to and would not desert for someone else's whim. He felt the pull of the Dales as well, but knew that it might come to a choice between them or his marriage. A marriage that might or might not be saveable. He decided against telling Thomas anymore of what had gone on in America until a later time. He had enough to deal with.

"I know lad, and we're certainly not planning to go anytime soon. I have another three books to deliver and your schooling has priority. But maybe next year I thought we'd go over and look at the place in more depth. See just where we would like to live and what properties are on offer. Your mother was thinking of Miami, or New Mexico. But it is too early to think about it, and there are other things to consider. Father John has set up a meeting tomorrow with the solicitors. We'll all go into Manchester early and have lunch after the meeting. Has he told you much about what will happen?"

"I know on my birthday I take over the title and estate, but he and the solicitor control part of my money until I'm eighteen. Then I get more responsibility and money when I hit twenty one. Then at twenty five I'm on my own. I wanted to do archaeology at University but now it has to be Business Studies and Law. It sounds dull, but if I stick at it Drew says I can do archaeology as a hobby later."

"I have thought about it in the last few weeks and I've decided to cut back on a lot of the land and farms. They have been in the Carrick family for too long, it is time they were given to the farmers that work them. Did you know a lot of farms have been in the same family for hundreds of years? Jim Redfern's place on the Barmsby road has been theirs for three hundred years. His annual rent is due on Christmas Day. This year I'm going to give him the deeds for a present." His father stared at him.

"You're going to give away a farm?"

"Several of them over the years. It's too much money for one person dad, it needs to be shared."

Steven shook his head. "I'm not talking to my thirteen year old son, I'm talking to a forty year old CEO," he muttered. "Just don't tell this to your mother, she'll go potty."

Thomas laughed and finished up his toast and fruit juice.

"I'm off to the Post Office. I'm expecting a parcel of books today. Be back in half an hour. Get Mum out of bed, I want to see those presents you promised me. Come on Grim, let's go and stretch our legs."

His father sat at the table in silence staring into his coffee cup. Somewhere in the last three or four months he'd lost the last of his son's childhood. He may even have lost a wife. He wondered if the money and fame had been worth it.

Thomas loped down the lane with Grim trotting beside him. "Is Bessie alright now after her sleep," he asked the dog. Grim gave a soft woof and danced around his feet.

"Well when I've picked up the books you can go home and tell her that I'll be along later this afternoon. I'll bring something special for her and some sweet biscuits for you. How's that?" Grim barked his approval.

As they came up to the main road and began to cross over, a black BMW streaked down the High street and skidded to a halt beside them. Two men in black jumped out and grabbed Thomas by the arms. He was halfway into the car before he began to fight them. Posy and Nurse Pym, talking by the newsagent looked over at the commotion. They stood frozen for a second then started across the road.

The driver jumped out to help with Thomas who was wriggling like an eel and came up against a furious Jack Russell who latched on to his leg and bit hard. Agravaine reached down and grabbed the dog by his scruff and hauled him away, then landed a kick to the ribs that sent him flying across the road. He lay whimpering and half conscious. Thomas was in the car now and the driver slammed his foot down hard. Posy and Maggie Pym reached the scene as the car drove off in a cloud of dust.

Posy ran for Les Lovell at the police station and Maggie knelt beside the injured dog and tried to assess the damage. Passers by stopped to help as she rang for the vet on her mobile. Drew arrived with Posy and sent her on to Deepdale House to alert the family, then got his van and drove Maggie and Grim to the vet. Within thirty minutes the whole village was in an uproar.

The police had a description of the car and the men and were out looking for it. Thomas's parents were in a state of shock and being comforted by Dr. and Mrs. Atkinson. Drew drove from the vet to the Priory School to see Father John while Grim underwent surgery for broken ribs, and internal injuries sustained from Agravaine's vicious kick.

Bessie arrived in Drew's van with Father John close behind in his own car. Bessie was inconsolable and sat in Drew's back room with Posy. The incident had happened so quickly that few people realised just what had happened. Father John gathered as many of the Guardians as he could find and held an emergency meeting in the Carrick Arms.

"It's Mordred. He's trying to use Thomas as a bargaining point," said Stan shaking his head. "Without Thomas we can't open the chamber."

"No, I don't think this is the work of Mordred," said Father John. "In fact I'd stake my life on it. Mordred is changing and Thomas is the cause. Although I am not sure exactly what is happening, something at some point in time, has started to move in a different direction. We may think we know everything but there are greater minds than ours at work here. When I put up the Wards at the manor something happened that was more than the simple protection I had planned. Thomas made his own connection with the Angelic Forces, a very strong connection." He got up and began to pace about the room.

"There is a directness as well as an innocence about Thomas. He was born for a special purpose. You know angelic powers rarely if ever touch us physically, but," he placed his hands on the table and leaned forward to emphasise his words, "but, they actually touched him. He was being polite, as he usually is. He held out his hand and, every one of them took it. They touched him! Spiritual matter of an exceptionally high level touched him physically. That means there was an exchange of power and of intent."

"What do you think they want him to do?" asked Posy, her voice subdued by the intensity of the priest's words.

"I wish I knew, at least, I might have an idea, but it is so preposterous I don't want to voice an opinion, not yet."

"If it's not Mordred then it has to be Morgana," said Maggie Pym. "Thomas said Mordred had quarrelled with her over the attack on Betty. In fact," she went on as if talking to herself, "he seems to be ... well ... almost fond of Thomas ... in his way of course," she added hastily. Father John turned from the window where he had been standing.

"Exactly, I think you are right. I am going to propose something that will be very hard, but I am certain that it is the right thing. I say we do nothing. You can bet your life that Mordred will soon know about this. Let him deal with his mother's work. I think this is all part of the change. If we interfere we may cause more harm than good."

"What shall we do then" asked Bessie, raising a tear

streaked face from Maggie's shoulder. "Time is running short." Father John turned back to the window.

"I know, it is unfortunate that Thomas was taken today, tomorrow we were due to see the solicitor. Until he signs those papers he does not take full possession of the estate, and without that title he cannot truly claim to be the Mage even if he holds the sphere."

The door opened and Drew came into the crowded room. His face was drawn with worry. "Nothing," he reported. "I've tried with the crystal but it's as if a blanket had been dropped over it." He sat down and poured himself a cup of tea.

"That's Morgana's work," said Bessie bitterly. "She has cloaked your sight."

Drew's mobile trilled in the silence. "Hello," he said, "Drew Docker," He listened intently for a few minutes then said, " Okay, we'll come now." He closed the phone and turned to Bessie.

"That was the vet. Grim came through the operation well and has recovered consciousness. But the vet said he seems very agitated and felt it would calm him down if you went along and sat with him for a while. I'll take you down there Bessie and we'll see what's going on."

As soon as they had gone, the other Guardians left on their different errands. Maggie to begin her daily rounds and Posy to open the shop. Les Lovell went back to the station and Stan stayed with Father John.

"I was talking to Drew last night," said Stan fiddling with his watch strap. He said as 'ow you was goin' ter see your lawyer about your will." He searched around for the words he wanted, then finally decided to just say what he thought. "It seems ter me as you'll be thinking you'll not see this through ter the end. Be that true?"

The priest sighed and scrubbed his hands down his face. "Yes Stan, I think something as big as this will always need some sort of willing sacrifice."

"That may well be, but does it 'ave ter be you? Young Thomas is real attached to you and he'll need a lot of encouragement and help in the next few years. I be a fair bit older'n you and if anyone needs to go, it 'ad best be me. No need to beat round the bushes. You're needed far more than a carpenter that's seen better days. Well that's what I wanted ter say."

John Foxton took the gnarled hands in his own. "Dear friend, you humble me with your offer, and I will be blessed for whatever remains of my life for having known you. But this is my task and I must see it through. If it is to be, it will be. I will elect you, Drew and Maggie to take my place as his advisors for the next seven years. He will need old fashioned common sense and simple know how to guide him. Thank you for your offer, made as it is with love and faith." The two men sat together in silence.

* * *

Bessie sat beside Grim his paw in her hand. His breathing was rapid and shallow, but slowly, as if he realised she was there, the Barney within began to send her mental pictures. A rough track leading off the road between Deepdale and Hamley Naughton deep in the moors. Then, more slowly an image of a Tor with a triple head and ringed by scrub. A cave lit by a dim blue light and twelve couches set in a ring. The images faded as the little dog fought to remain conscious. Then with a last effort he sent an image of Morgana, Thomas and Agravaine.

Bessie stroked his head. "Sleep now little friend, I have your message, rest and heal. You have done well." The dog sighed deeply and let itself to fall into a warm darkness that held no pain. The vet reassured them that though he was very weak the little dog would pull through. Drew told him to send all bills to him at the pub and drove Bessie back to The Carrick Arms. There he took her in to the back room and poured her a brandy.

"Bessie I know you won't like it, but I'd be happier if you stayed here until Grim is well again, and until all this is over, one way or another. I've a nice quiet room at the back and you won't be disturbed. You'll be closer to him here, rather than up on the moor, and I'll take you to see him anytime you want." Bessie put her arms round him and wept on his shoulder with relief.

"That's a good girl, now come along and see the room and you can rest there as long as you need. Did you get anything from the little fellow?"

"Yes and I think I know the place. It looked like Ragnoks Tor. There seemed to be a cave. He showed me Morgana and Agravaine and from the look of the place it is where Mordred's knights were sleeping before he awakened them. If that's right, it is also where he sleeps when he needs to gather strength.

Drew, he has been very active these last few months and it may be that he has gone there to rest before the Battle.

Morgana might have taken Thomas there as well. In fact she may well be planning to take over the whole thing, the crown, the power, everything. I am sure she now sees Mordred as a hindrance rather than a help."

Drew gasped, "That would make a lot of sense Bessie, I'll get round to the others, at least we have a lead and can make some sort of plan. You get some sleep now." He settled her down and stayed with her until she slept then left on his errands.

* * *

Morgana was talking with Agravaine and Garth. The argument had been going on for several hours.

"Don't you see," she insisted. "He is going soft, he is far too fond of the boy and there is every possibility that he will lose the Battle for us. I will be able to use the power of the Crown far better than he. Besides I am my father's daughter, I have a right to it."

"Maybe by blood, but not by right." Agravaine pointed out." We have always followed the old law. We will follow a man, but not a woman. We are of the old ways and I for one will stay by them."

Morgana ground her teeth, and looked to Garth. He seemed more in agreement with her. He shrugged."Mordred promised us a share of his power. What assurance do I have that you would do the same?"

"I will have to consider all that, but first I must know I can rely on you and on the others." As the argument continued, Thomas lay bound hand and foot in a corner trying to catch what was being said.

He was sore from the rough handling and his wrists were rubbed raw by the rope. He looked around him at the cave and its fixtures and realised that this must be where Mordred slept when he was recovering his energies. If that was true he would be coming back. But when, and would it be before time ran out? This was all Morgana's doing and he would have bet all his pocket money for the rest of the year that Mordred knew nothing about it, which meant he would be furious when he did. But where was he?"

"Well now Sir Thomas of Deepdale. How is our little hero feeling now." Morgana's mocking voice pulled him back from his thoughts.

"I think Lady Morgana, that when Sir Mordred hears of this you will find yourself very unwelcome in his presence."

"Ah, but you see he will not find out, at least until it is too late. Agravaine, help him up will you and show him just why we hold the trump card."

Agravaine strode across to the couch and pulled Thomas roughly to an upright position. Morgana pointed an elegant finger to a couch set aside from all the others. It was set under a draped canopy that carried a Royal coat of arms. On the couch, in a deep sleep lay Mordred, his face more boyish in its relaxed state.

Thomas's heart sank, and then he grew angry. "What have you done to him, have you hurt him?"

"My, my, such concern for one who is your enemy. I am touched by your gallantry. But I have done nothing, he sleeps because he must, as we all must to survive."

Thomas knew how to hit back.

"All except you Lady Morgana. I know that you were punished by being turned into a crow, I also know that you cannot keep human form for very long. Soon you must go back to the form you despise so much."

Morgana's hand cracked across his face. "Upstart, you know nothing. Nothing. Soon the power will be mine and there is nothing you can do about it. The men will follow me because there will be no one else. I will see Arthur fall for the last time and he will rise no more."

"I think Lady, that your wits have left you," said Thomas, fighting back tears of pain. The gibe earned him another blow and he fell back on the couch.

She turned to the two men watching her. " Go and find the others, bring them back here to me. I will return tonight." She left the cave with a swirl of velvet skirts and a few minutes later there was the flap of wings. Agravaine and Garth followed and Thomas was alone with the sleeping Mordred.

How long had he been sleeping Thomas wondered. Probably since he had left the school after giving him the spurs. How long did he need? If he planned to lead his men into battle on Lammas Eve he would want time to get everything together. There were only four days left. Thomas struggled to sit upright and finally managed to sit on the edge of the couch. His arms had been bound securely and his ankles too. But there must be something in this cave he could use to cut himself free.

He moved to stand up and managed it after a few tries and looked around. At the head of each couch he saw the armour laid out. Where there was armour, there must be a sword. He hopped some paces and tried turning, and nearly fell, but could see the sword leaning against the armour at the head of the couch where he had lain. Taking it slowly, and judging his balance with each move, he hopped a pace at a time forcing himself to concentrate on keeping upright. If he fell he would never be able to get up unaided.

It seemed to take forever but finally he was there. Turning carefully he tried to place the cord against the edge of the word. He cut himself several times before he felt the cord loosening. Then the last knot gave way and he was free. He grasped the sword and cut through the ropes binding his legs. He rested for a few minutes, trying to get the feeling back into his arms and legs, then tore the sleeves off his shirt and bound up the worst of the cuts to his hands and wrists.

Now for Mordred.

He ran over to the couch and shook him, calling him by name but the man was deep in something more than a sleep. Again and again he tried, shouting, shaking, pouring cold water on his face. Nothing worked. He sat down on the couch and tried to think what else he could do. He didn't know where he was, and to try and get away without help across the moors at night would be foolish. Morgana and the others might be back at any moment.

Thomas got up and walked backwards and forwards trying desperately to think of anything that he could do to wake the sleeping Mordred. "What I need is something loud enough to wake the dead," he said to himself. "Gabriel's trumpet would be useful at this moment ...." He stood looking at the strange globe of blue light on the central pillar. Beside it lay a small hunting horn edged with intricate silver chasing.

A horn, a trumpet, something to wake the dead ...YES!

"Thank, you Gabriel," he shouted and grabbed the horn. He took a deep breath and blew it.

The sound rang around the cave, reverberating and echoing. It bounced off the walls and shivered down the narrow passageway. It erupted into the outside world and filled the moors with sound. Miles away it startled a group of men dressed in black and sent them scurrying towards cars, and motorbikes. It sent a large black crow flying into the air, screaming with rage and fear.

In the hidden cave Mordred stirred and opened his eyes.

EIGHTEEN

Mordred was dressed in full armour, his black and scarlet cloak swirling around him as he strode about the cave. He had been speaking for almost an hour to the twelve men who stood before him, eyes downcast, trembling from the power of his anger. Of Morgana there was no sign.

Agravaine, Garth and Gervaise had come in for his most blistering attacks, but none of the others had escaped entirely. Thomas sat on the couch and watched with fascination as Arthur's son showed his Blood Royal.

"We may go against Arthur, but we will fight as he taught us to fight. We do not make war on children. We do not instil fear in women. We are Knights, not animals. Which reminds me Agravaine, about the dog …." His tone dropped in volume and became soft and menacing. "Do you by any chance know the true identity of the old woman locally called Bald Bessie, the owner of the dog you almost killed?"

Agravaine shook his head. " She is a beggar, that is all I know. Morgana said …." He broke off as Mordred interrupted him.

"Ah, Morgana said that? A beggar, FOOL! DOLT! Beneath that form is Guenevere, Arthur's Queen. The dog is Barnaby the Queen's Fool, her protector and confidante, and you tried to kick it to death. I'm sure that will not endear you to the Lady of Camelot. Garth, change form. You will go to John Foxton at the Priory School and guide him here in his Hawk form and you will do it NOW! Do I make myself clear?"

Garth shook with fear at the savagery in his voice "Yes Prince Mordred … at once." He turned and left the cave. Mordred turned his gaze upon the rest. Take to your couches all of you" When all were lying down he walked to the central pillar, took up the globe and walked around the cave passing it over the heads of each man. One by one they fell asleep. Then he set the globe back on the pillar and turned to Thomas. He looked tired and suddenly lost.

"Father John will be here soon and you will go back with him. I regret this more than I can say. My knights will remain asleep until Lammas Eve. You will not be troubled by them, or by my mother." He sat down beside him. "I had thought to rest a while, but now I must remain awake, Morgana is still a force to be reckoned with. She will keep trying. I did not think to see her as a rival for the crown and its power. She must be very disappointed in me … and," he smiled. "She'll have been so angry that you blew the horn. Tell me Thomas, what made you do that, it is the only thing that can wake us once we rest."

"I tried everything then, I had this thought that if I had something as loud as Gabriel's horn it might do the trick, then I saw that one and decided to try it."

Mordred laughed outright. "You just happened to think of Gabriel's horn! Oh Thomas, when you are grown you will indeed be a force to be reckoned with. Morgana must have thought her time had come upon her unawares."

He laughed again and was still laughing when Father John walked into the cave with Garth. Thomas ran to him and hugged him. The priest put his hands on his shoulders and looked into his eyes.

"Thomas, are you alright?"

Mordred answered for him. "Yes, Father, he is safe and well and those who were the cause of his disappearance are now made harmless ... until of course Lammas Eve when we will all meet again. But you will need to beware of my mother. She has been thwarted twice now and is in no mood to be defeated again. Take him home. He will tell the police he escaped from his captors and got lost on the moors, wandering until he came across a main road and found a telephone box. There is no need to say more." He ruffled Thomas's hair. "Go home Thomas, and rest."

Father John took him outside and down the steep hillside until the reached level ground. In the far distance they saw the lights of a car blinking on and off to guide them.

"I called Drew to fetch you and take you home. I shall ... take wing ... and go back the way I came. I will see you tomorrow. He saw Thomas safely to the car then changed form to fly back to the priory.

Back in the cave Garth settled down on his couch and slept. But Mordred stayed awake and vigilant.

* * *

"Now Thomas, if you will just sign here, and here, and here we can conclude our business." The solicitor peered over the top of his glasses and beamed at everyone.

"I must congratulate you on your success Mr. Greystone, I have just finished reading your book, a fine piece of work, most enjoyable. I hear it is being made into a film."

Steven smiled. "Yes, it has been a fantastic year for me and my family. The film is finished now and the editing will take another two or three months. I think it is to be launched around Christmas. In fact, there is talk of a royal premiere."

"My, my, such an exciting time for you all."

"Thank you for all your help and advice Mr. Hawkins, I will see that you and your wife get invitations to the premiere."

"Most kind, most kind. Mrs. Hawkins will be so excited. So Thomas ... or rather Sir Thomas, as you are now legally Sir Thomas Greystone-Carrick of Deepdale. All the papers have now been changed into your new name. The bank will issue you with a cheque book, but for the moment you cannot make out a cheque for more than one hundred pounds on your own. More than that and you will have to have a second signature. Do you understand that?"

"Yes Sir," said Thomas quietly.

"Also you will be required to present yourself at the College of Heralds in London sometime within the next few months to secure your claim to the Coat of Arms and discuss any changes you might wish to have made. Messrs. Roper & Tyburn are your accountants and will see to all your financial affairs. If you have any questions you may call on me at any time. Now if you will excuse me I have another client to see." He bustled out leaving the four of them in the formal panelled room.

"Right," said Thomas. "What about lunch, I'm starving. I must have signed a hundred papers this morning." He seemed totally unfazed by the whole thing.

"I know just the place," said Father John, "How about Macdonalds." They all laughed and followed each other out into the sunshine.

In the event they lunched at a hotel in the city and Thomas was allowed his first glass of red wine to celebrate. Afterwards John excused himself saying that he had personal business to deal with, and he would see them the next day.

Thomas ran after him as he left and took his arm. "Father," he said, "Is there anything else about Lammas Eve I should know?"

"We are all in the hands of God Thomas. Whatever is to happen will happen and none of us can stop it. We can only do our best. Now go back and spend a nice day with your parents." He watched him out of sight and prayed for him to be given guidance when it would be needed, then turned away.

Thomas returned to his parents and they decided to go home and unpack and just have a quiet day at home. The excitement of his kidnap had quietened down, although his mother was still nervous about letting him out of her sight. The official take was that a couple of incompetent would be kidnappers had grabbed him and then panicked when he'd jumped out of the car as they were driving over Swarfedale moor. The police were still looking for the car but so far it had not been found.

The Guardians of course knew exactly what had happened and Les Lovell had managed to head off a bigger police inquiry. Steven Greystone had wanted to set up a state of the art security system at Deepdale House. But Thomas pointed out it would be a waste of money as they had the best system on the market already installed at the manor and hopefully, they would soon be living there.

On the way home they looked in at the vets and Thomas was overjoyed to be greeted by Grim with a little bark of affection. He was still weak but lapping up the attention. Thomas leaned close to him and whispered, " Bessie's is staying with Drew, and she is doing fine there." The little terrier licked his face and settled down again to rest. They also phoned Betty Jackson who told them she was due for an operation the next day, but that she would be coming home the following week.

Thomas made a mental note to ask Father John to arrange a holiday for her and Frank, somewhere warm and quiet. He thought he would like a nice quiet holiday himself when everything had quietened down. There were just two days until Lammas Eve.

The following day it rained and the forecast was for a week of bad weather. It was going to be a very wet ceremony, thought Thomas gloomily as he looked out at the leaden sky.

Drew had phoned to say Father John had been delayed and would arrive late and they were to go ahead without him at the displaying of the Regalia. Nora Greystone had gone down to London with two of her friends from the W.I. to buy bed linens and china and was safely out of the way until Lammas Day.

At four o'clock Thomas announced he was going to see the Atkinsons. To his dismay his father insisted on driving him there and waiting for him. He tried to tell his dad that he would ring him when he was ready to come home but Steven Greystone was adamant. Eventually Thomas spoke to the rest of the Guardians and asked their permission to let him sit in on the meeting.

After some discussion it was agreed. Steven knew most of them and sat down quite happily at what he thought was some kind of local history talk. But when Marjory Atkinson covered the table with a purple velvet cloth and laid on it the Ring of Arthur, his jaw dropped.

One by one the Guardians stepped forward and laid down their treasures. The Chain of Office, now gleaming and polished, the Great Seal, the Scabbard and Belt, the Spurs and the Orb. Stan produced the Sceptre with its gleaming sapphire, and Bessie a silver Chalice decorated with jewels. The Shield, burnished and with its leather lining replaced was laid down reverently by Maggie Pym. Next came the Kings Horn, which when blown would summon him and his knights. Then finally Drew produced the Sword, and the Ampulla containing the Holy Oil. Laid out on the table they sparkled and gleamed in the lamplight.

"Steven moved to the table and stood just looking. Then

he turned to Drew. "Somehow I thought it was just some kind of ancient folklore, you know, like Well dressing and the Padstow Hobby Hoss. But this ... this is for real isn't it?"

It was Thomas who answered.

"Yes Dad. But it isn't every year, just once in a hundred years. Until Arthur comes to claim the throne as the Once and Future King. This time will be the last time. The future King of England, who holds Arthur as one of his names, is coming and will be invested with the Regalia by the Guardians. Father John will anoint him and I will crown him with Arthur's ancient crown."

His father turned white-faced to look at him, at his son, someone he now felt he had never really known and whispered. *"The Prince of Wales is coming here, and you will be the one to crown him?"*

"Yes. He is the Future King as Arthur is the King who Once was. It has always been my task to place that crown upon his head. It was given into the keeping of Amicus Carrick by Arthur and it has been kept safe until now. But this opening of the Kings Chamber will be different. This time the Last Battle will be re-fought against Mordred and his knights, and for the last time. Each Guardian you see here will be represented by one of Arthur's knights in the battle. They will share their life force with them during that battle. Father, please understand that there may be casualties, and I may be among them. But we fight willingly because of our love for the Land and its King, for the two are bound together."

"No! No! No. "You can't do this Thomas, you don't have to do it ... he doesn't does he?" He appealed to the Guardians standing silent around them. "He's my son."

"He is The Mage of Spheres, Steven and he does what he was born to do, whatever the cost, as do we all!" Drew led the distraught man to a chair.

Marjory came with a tumbler of brandy. "Drink this Steven dear, it isn't quite as bad as it seems. We are all very strong and we have Arthur and the Knights with us. There is a possibility that some of us may be hurt. But it is not inevitable."

"What will I tell your mother, Thomas?"

"You can't tell her, Father. She must never know what will happen tomorrow night."

"Thomas, who, what, are you?"

"I am to be the Archmage of Britain, as was my great grandfather before me. As my son will be after me. Nothing can or will be changed. " He smiled suddenly and was once again a young boy just reaching manhood. "If it helps, I have a friend at court."

They broke up soon afterward having arranged that early the next morning Les, Drew, and Stan would collect the Regalia and take it to the circle where Stan would stay and guard it until the evening.

Back at Deepdale House. Steven left his bed and went down the corridor to Thomas's room where a light showed under the door. He knocked and Thomas opened it .

"I thought you'd come Dad sit down and be comfortable." He sat on the bed and waited for him to speak. Steven clasped his hands together to stop them shaking.

"I don't know what to say Tom lad. I'm too dazed by it all. I thought I knew all about it you see, I know what your grandma told me, but she made it seem like a sort of fancy dress thing. Now I know it's for real and I'm afraid I might lose you."

"Dad it's not certain that I will die, or any of us. It is just a possibility and the odds are with us. You've just written a book that has become a film, and it's possible you'll win an Oscar for it, so think of all this as a film plot. It might help."

"I write thrillers with a paranormal twist, Thomas. This is for real."

"I can make it a lot more unreal if you like," said his son with a grin. "If you didn't have Carrick blood in you, you couldn't write the kind of books you do." So why can't you believe in the same things when they really happen?"

"What kind of things are we talking about?" asked his father. Thomas got off the bed and took his hand leading him downstairs and into the back garden. "Please don't freak out dad. Just hold on and try to believe what you see."

Thomas stepped back and built up the image of the King Stag in his mind and let the change flow over him.

His father sank to his knees as the stag stepped delicately forward and touched his face with its tongue. Words formed in his head. "I love you dad, I'll always love you."

With the same ease the form flowed back into the boy he had been before. Then he led his silent father back into the house and they sat close together on the sofa. Finally they talked for a long time, then Thomas slept in his father's arms. Outside the sun rose slowly on Lammas Eve.

NINETEEN

Thomas woke to threatening skies and a rumble of thunder as a storm front closed in. He felt calm now the time had finally arrived and to his father's amazement chatted his way through breakfast as if it was a normal day.

The village seemed unusually quiet. There was a locum doctor at the surgery, both Ian and Margery had "gone away" for a few days. Posy's shop had an early closing notice in the window. Drew had two part-time bartenders in the pub, and Nurse Pym's relief had taken over her duties for a while. The rest of the Guardians had made various arrangements to cover their absence for the next twenty four hours.

Steven drove Thomas to the vet to pick up a weak but recovering Grim. The little dog was overjoyed to be out of the resting cage and they stopped twice on the way back to allow him the luxury of a short run and a convenient tree. Back at the house Steven provided him with some lightly cooked mince and a marrowbone for desert thereby making a friend for life.

"I'll look after him while ... well, while you are busy tonight," his father told Thomas.

I'm afraid he has to come with us Dad. If all goes well, tonight he'll return with his Queen to Avalon, as it was promised he would do. But thanks for the offer."

"How will you get him to the Stones, "asked his father. "It's too far for him to walk, he's too weak as yet. "

Thomas laughed. "He'll be riding a large horse, called Drew Docker. You see Grim isn't really a dog. His name is Barney and he's Guenevere's Jester. He wanted to stay with her so Merlin gave him a dog's form to protect her. If I give him enough energy he can take on Barney's form long enough to ride Drew to the Circle."

His father shook his head. "I can't seem to get it all straight in my head. The idea that magic is real and that these things can happen. God! Thomas, I'm so frightened. I'm afraid of losing you, and I love you so much. I feel I should be the one protecting you, and I know that against what you're facing, I'm powerless."

"This is old magic dad, and it's time is done. It rarely happens now, in our world. Our magic is electricity, computers, TV, spaceships going to the moon and back. When something can be understood and used every day by ordinary people, it stops being magic and becomes science. But there is something you can do, it will help us all and me in particular."

His father looked up eagerly. "Sure lad, anything. What do you need?"

"The energy Grim needs to use his human form long enough to ride Drew to the Circle will take a lot of strength from me, strength I could use during the Battle. If you're willing he could take it from you instead."

Grim whined, left his bone and came to Steven and placing a paw on his knee looked up at him. Steven gathered him up and buried his face in the clean smelling fur.

"Sure, we can do that can't we, Grim old lad?" The dog licked his cheek, hiding from Thomas the fact that he was licking away tears.

The day passed with Thomas and his father staying close to each other. They talked about ordinary things, holidays and what they would do together later in the year, as if planning was a talisman against anything terrible happening when the evening came.

But the evening came at last.

They had an early supper. Fluffy scrambled eggs and field mushrooms, with strawberries and ice-cream after. Then Steven went upstairs and returned with a small box tied with a lop sided bow. With it was a card. He placed it on the table and sat silent for a moment then said, " I thought I'd give this to you tonight, it's only a few hours and you'll be fourteen anyway. Just in case … you know …. His voice trailed off.

Thomas opened the card first. "To my son Thomas. With loving thanks for the joy he has given me over the last fourteen years, and will give me for the rest of my life." Inside the box was a gold watch. Engraved on the back was his name and the date, and beneath was a smaller card that said simply:

To my son, the Archmage of Britain
Given with pride on his fourteenth birthday.

Thomas threw his arms around him and they sat close together for a long time. No words were said, and none were needed.

The storm grew more threatening as evening shadows lengthened. Thunder circled the high moors and lightning flashed over the Tors. By 8 o'clock most of the Guardians were on the Second Road, where they experienced the same kind of weather but for very different reasons. The elemental world was re-acting to the mounting tension as the time for the Battle drew near.

Thomas left his father dozing and went upstairs to get ready. He showered and dressed in warm jeans and a sweater and over it threw a cape of dark blue, hooded and lined with silver grey. Round his neck he placed his grandmothers sphere and on his wrist was his father's gift.

When he went downstairs he found his father standing in the back garden feeding a grey stallion with pieces of apple. Grim sat beside him.

"Hello Drew," said Thomas, and the stallion danced forward to nuzzle his hand. He laughed and gently pushed him away and bent to pick up Grim. He held him close and pressed his face against him. "If all goes well, tonight you'll be with your Queen in Avalon, straight and strong. I'll miss you so much." Grim whined and licked his face

Thomas set him down and turned to his father. "Put your hand on Grim's back and just rest it there. He will do the rest, then afterwards you should go inside and lie down.

You'll feel weak and dizzy for a while."

Nervously his father obeyed. Grim gave a little woof and arched his spine against the caressing hand.

Steven could feel the energy leaving him, he was cold and shivery and suddenly very tired. He closed his eyes against a sudden feeling of nausea. When he opened them Grim had gone. In his place stood a small misshapen form. The contrast of the twisted body and the beautiful face with its large lustrous eyes clutched at his heart.

"You must be Barney?"

"Yes, and I thank you sir, for your gift of energy. I hope I will be able to repay you in some way. Could I trouble you to help me to mount?"

Steven lifted him gently on to the stallions back where he held on to the mane.

"Good sire Drew, go smoothly I beg you, I do not wish to find myself bedraggled before my Lady."

Steven turned to watch his son flow into his own change and drew a deep breath of admiration as the proud antlered head lifted to scent the wind. He opened the gate and the two animals cantered gently down the lane. He watched until they disappeared into the hidden opening of the Second Road then returned to the house. It was a long time since Steven Greystone had prayed, but he intended to do so tonight.

The Black Daimler sped silently along the deserted road. The small standard on the bonnet fluttering in the wind. The driver glanced into the mirror at the two men sitting in the back. The man sitting next to him turned and addressed the others.

"It's another twenty miles sir, then it will be on foot the rest of the way."

The man addressed nodded and went back to his silent contemplation of the darkening moorland. More than anyone he knew the importance of tonight's ceremony, its inner meaning and the way it would change the future of the land he'd been born to serve.

After tonight, those who sought to do away with the ancient traditions of Britain would be thwarted and driven into the dark where they belonged. He looked down at the signet ring on his little finger, at the triple feathered symbol and its motto. Ich Dien.*"*

"Yes," he thought," I will serve, as my mother has served and to the end of my life."

* * *

The Stallion and the King Stag raced across the land under the broken thunder clouds. The occasional hiss of lightning did not cause them to falter by a single heartbeat. The small figure atop the Stallion clung fiercely to his seat, head bent against the scattered flurries of rain. The moon was hidden every few minutes by dark scudding clouds that raced each other like hounds after a fox across the sky. Ahead lay the last dale, then the long steep climb to where The Singing Stones stood watching over the land they had guarded so long and the awaited end of over a thousand years of hope and loyalty.

As they thundered down the slope, flanks heaving, nostrils wide to catch their breath, the two magnificent beasts looked across at each other. Confident in their strength they rode the storm and breasted the Tor to stand like black statues against the skyline before stepping down into the hollow that sheltered the circle. The last of the Guardians had arrived and the ceremony could begin.

The Guardians turned to face the last two arrivals as Barney slid from the back of the stallion and took his usual form. He slipped around the stones to stand beside his mistress. The stallion took its place and became the burly figure of Drew Docker. The Stag moved to the Mage Stone and shook itself, flowing into the change with an ease that made John Foxton smile with quiet pride.

In a clear voice Thomas began the Calling of the Guardians.

"Ian Atkinson. Guardian of the King's Chain of Office."

"Both are present Mage of Spheres."

"Margery Atkinson. Guardian of the King's Ring."

"Both are present Mage of Spheres."

"Leslie Lovell. Guardian of the King's Belt and Scabbard."

"Both are present Mage of Spheres."

"Petronnella Anderton. Guardian of the King's Seal."

"Both are present Mage of Spheres."

"Edna Pugh. Guardian of the King's Spurs."

"Both are present Mage of Spheres."

"Guenevere, Wife to Arthur, Guardian of the King's Cup."

"Both are present Mage of Spheres."

"Stanley Simonite. Guardian of the King's Sceptre.".

"Both are present Mage of Spheres."

"Margaret Pym. Guardians of the King's Shield."

"Both are present Mage of Spheres."

"Drew Docker. Guardian of the King's Sword.".

"Both are present Mage of Spheres".

"Walter Meakin. Guardian of the King's Horn".

"Both are present Mage of Spheres."

"Ben Warrener. Guardian of the King's Orb.".

"Both are present Mage of Spheres."

"John Foxton. Guardian of the Holy Anointing Oil and Ampulla.".

"Both are present Mage of Spheres."

The last named stepped forward.

"Mage of Spheres. Guardian of the Crown of the Once and Future King."

"Both are present," said Thomas. "I am the Mage of Spheres. Let the Wards be raised."

Drew took two strides forward, the Sword in his hands. Opposite him Guenevere, her golden hair glimmering, stepped forward holding the Cup. Then came Stan Simonite bearing the Sceptre. Last came Posy holding in her hands the King's Seal. All turned outward to face the four directions, raising their Treasures on high.

Stan's richly accented voice came slow and steady. *"I do call upon the Powers of Air to guard and defend this place against all evil. I raise the Light of Raphael in the East."*

A bolt of lightning arched down and touched a torch driven into the earth outside the circle. It lit instantly.

Drew's baritone rang out above the storm. *"I do call upon the Powers of Fire to guard and defend this place against all evil. I raise the Light of Michael in the South."* A second torch flamed into being.

Guenevere's lighter tones followed quickly. *"I call upon the Powers of Water to guard and defend this place against all evil. I raise the Light of Gabriel in the West."* A third torch added its light to the others.

Posy's lilting soprano sang through the thunder. *"I call upon the Powers of the Earth to guard and defend this place against all evil. I raise the Light of Uriel in the North."* The last torch spluttered into flame. They all turned and looked to Thomas.

He came forward with the last torch and drove it into the centre of the circle. Holding the Mage sphere in his hand he spoke the last invocation. *"I call upon the Powers of the Spirit to guard and defend this place against all evil. I call the Light of the Archangel Metatron from the Above to the Below."* The torch blazed with a brilliant light that illuminated the whole circle as all returned to their places.

Each Guardian set their back firmly against their Stone and raised their spheres.

As they did so a clap of thunder split the air. Bolt after bolt of lightning speared the earth around the Stones, until it seemed that they stood in the centre of a battle between the elements themselves. But though the wind howled and the rain battered itself against the Stones, the torches never flickered, and the rain never touched those within the barrier.

From the heart of the storm came a flock of crows hurling themselves against the barrier again and again. One large bird separated itself from the rest and dived directly for

Grim who stood at the very edge of the barrier. Gathering every ounce of her power Morgana flung herself against the barrier and broke through. Guenevere screamed and grabbed hold of Grim. A hawk flung itself against the crow and the two climbed above the stones battling with wings, beaks and claws. For a split second Thomas stood frozen, then realised that the battle had begun.

"Wally," he yelled, "Blow the Horn! Everyone use their spheres now. Now!"

Wally Meakin grabbed the Horn hanging from his neck and raised it to his lips. The sound threw itself into the sky. Thunder could not dull it, Lightning could not stop it. It went ringing across the land, a clarion call that reached into the very heart of Britain and flowed into the four great warrior races that had bonded together. Old fears and old betrayals were forgotten as the land raised itself to do battle with The Dark. England, Ireland, Scotland, Wales, their long dead warriors rose from ancient and forgotten graves, and even older battlefields. Their bodies had long been dust but their spirits remembered and came to the call.

The storm clouds were ripped aside and through the rift they came, some walking, some mounted on armoured chargers, all with swords held aloft. Thomas felt his heart swell with pride as he watched them ride down the lightning paths in answer to the Horn. Wally sounded the Call a second time and Arthur's knights answered its summons. Man by man they came out of the mist and took their places in a ring about the Stones. Each knight paired with a Guardian: Gareth to Marjory, Palomedes to Ian. Gaheris to Les. Pellinore to Ben, Kay to Posy, Bedivere to Edna. Launcelot to Guenevere. Bors to Stan. Perceval to Maggie. Gawaine to Drew. Tristram to Wally, and as John Foxton returned to his stone, silver armoured Galahad took his place behind him. Back to back with the Stones between them, Knight and Guardian were linked by the willing sacrifice of energy and the Singing Stones became a triple circle of Light. Above the noise came a new sound ... the voices of the Stones themselves, deep, resonant and filled with ancient energy drawn from the very depths of the earth.

Thomas felt the presence of Arthur behind him and turned going down on one knee. Arthur lifted Excalibur and lightly touched him on both shoulders. Then froze as another Horn sounded. This had a darker tone and with it came a wrenching fear as out of the circling winds rode Mordred and his Knights. With them came grey shrouded figures that were less than human in form and feel. The Guardians shuddered to a man.

Morgana had raised the Undead.

"Sir Thomas Carrick of Deepdale. The Guardians have done well, now we will finish what was begun long ago." Arthur's deep voice held a note of pride.

"Indeed we will father." Mordred rode forward on a jet black stallion and offered a mocking salute to the King with his sword. "This night shall see the end of it."

Morgana emerged from the shadows dressed in flowing red, but with a breastplate of silver, and a spear in her hand. As the moon shone through a break in the clouds Thomas saw that each Knight of the Round Table faced an opponent Knight sworn to Mordred. Beyond the circle the opposing Forces of Light and Dark stood ready to do battle.

Morgana lifted her spear and cast it into the circle. It quivered at Arthur's feet. He smiled. "Morgana, impatient as always," he said and raised both sword arm and voice.

"TO BATTLE, FOR THE LIGHT."

To Thomas he said, "I will need your youthful strength and energy Sir Thomas."

"You have it to the last moment of my life Sire," answered Thomas.

There was no time to feel fear. It was a fight just to keep the energies going. Strong though they were the wards were soon breached and both sides fought in and around the circle. While outside it, the warrior spirits battled against the undead. As sword met sword, Thomas often saw a form, sometimes bright sometimes dark, falter and fall and crumble into dust. In and around the circle it was the same for Mordred's men were desperate, it was their last chance to take control of Britain.

In the thick of it both Mordred and Arthur fought with single minded purpose, and Morgana with stealth and cunning. More than once her spear treacherously claimed a victim from behind. As Thomas caught her eye he shouted at her.

"Coward."

She snarled and threw the spear straight at his heart. He braced himself for the pain, thinking of the sorrow his parents would know, then a black stallion appeared out of the melee and reared above him and a black shield was flung between him and the weapon. Thomas heard the thud as the spear head hit and remembered his dream.

"Beware young Thomas, my mother has a long memory and you have thwarted her once too often," said Mordred he grinned down at Thomas and turned back to the middle of the fight.

As the battle momentarily moved to the outside of the circle, Thomas caught sight of the other Guardians. They had come together in the centre forming a tight ring facing outwards to the fighting, some of them had been wounded, and Maggie Pym had her arm around the frail form of Edna literally holding her upright. Drew had acquired a sword from a fallen warrior and was using it, still holding his sphere aloft as he did so.

Thomas saw Guenevere holding Grim in her arms, his teeth no match for armoured ankles and feet. Here and there in the heaving mass he saw several figures that were not of either side. He recognised them as the Merlin, Nimue and the Lady of the Lake. For a moment Thomas wondered what they were doing there. Then he saw that they were gathering up the spirits of the fallen of both sides. Looking further he caught sight of other helpers and knew with a sudden clarity that all those who fell would be taken care of and helped, regardless of which side they fought for. Then the fighting grew fierce again and he found himself in the thick of it.

From time to time he caught sight of Arthur and the shining blade that was Excalibur rising and falling wherever the battle was at its height. Launcelot forced his way through a tight band of Mordred's men and hewed the head of Gervaise from his shoulders. He raised his sword with a triumphant cry of "A moi, a moi," and disappeared into the fray again. Kay was lying in heap at the feet of Stan Simonite who had produced a large hammer from somewhere and was battering the helmet of one of Mordred's henchmen with it.

Thomas looked for Father John but could not see him anywhere. There grew in him a certainty that new strength was needed from some other source. He tried to think of something more he could do. Then it came to him. In the middle of the fighting he began to sing the school hymn. Over the sound of metal on metal and the screams of wounded men his clear voice rose like a shaft of light.

> *Let me bring Light to this day O Lord.*
> *Make me a beacon of your love.*
> *Help me to lighten the shadows that threaten*
> *And bring down the Light from above.*

John's answering tenor took it up strengthening the underlying power of the words.

> *Let me bring Peace to this day O Lord.*
> *Pray make me a message of Hope.*
> *No matter what comes let me face it and win*
> *As I learn how to live and to cope.*

Drew, remembering his own past school days at the Priory added his baritone .

> *Let me bring Faith to this day O Lord*
> *Make me both faithful and strong.*
> *Help me to conquer my fears and my foes*

And help me choose right over wrong.

Thomas thought of his school friends who would be asleep now, but in that sleep they could be called on. He imagined them as they had been at the school concert and drew on the image.

Let me bring Love to this day O Lord.
Make me a symbol of your Life
Make me strong, make me true, make me just like You
And rise above hatred and strife.

As they sang the Singing Stones answered and added the strength of their ancient voices. Thomas sang with heart and soul, he thought he could sense his father back at the house and knew he was sending them what strength he could. The Power came back into the Defenders and here and there among them appeared new fighters who wore white armour and whose swords were tipped with flame. Above it all the elements raged as if they too were part of the fray.

Suddenly everything happened at once. Arthur was in front of him fighting two men at once. He had lost his helm and was bareheaded. He downed one opponent and turned to the other and found himself facing his son.

Mordred's face was filled with the madness of battle as he lifted his sword above his head. Thomas knew that everything hung upon the next few seconds. Abruptly everything stopped as if frozen in time and space.

Morgana appeared blood stained and ragged, a sword in her hand.

"Yes! Yes!" she exulted. "Now Mordred, strike him now and the day is ours. You will be King my son. Strike! Strike! Kill him…!"

Arthur stood frozen. The muscles of Mordred's arms bunched as he gathered his strength for the fatal blow. Silence fell over the battlefield.

Into that silence came the voice of the Mage of Spheres. Thomas spoke quietly and clearly "You are your father's son, not your mother's pawn."

For an instant Mordred froze, then dropped his sword to the ground.

Morgana screamed with rage. "Coward, Traitor. You failed me! " She picked up Mordred's sword and lunged forward intending to kill Arthur herself. But Mordred stepped between them and took the blade deep into his side. A moment later Morgana lay dead with Gawaine's sword in her throat.

Arthur gathered his son into his arms and held him close weeping. He wept as a soldier for a fallen comrade but even more so as a father for a son. Mordred sighed and opened his eyes.

"I've always wanted you to hold me like this," he said "Forgive me Father for what I did." Arthur kissed his forehead and whispered softly to him, smoothing the dark hair away from the pale skin. Merlin came and knelt beside the dying prince.

"This one act has set all to right," he said." Now the way lies open to Avalon for you and your father together."

Mordred smiled, then beckoned to Thomas who came and knelt beside him and took his hand.

"Thomas, little brother," he said, "You taught me so much, and because of you I now have a father too. Don't cry, you are a warrior now and there is work for you to do. I will wait to greet you in Avalon." He looked up at Arthur and said with his last breath, "That day in the forest with you … it … was … so … love," the words faded with the breath and Mordred lay still in his father's arms.

Galahad, Gareth, Palomedes and Pellinore came and lifted the body of the Prince on to their shoulders and carried him out of the circle. As they moved through the now quiet evening their forms became misty and dim and one with the shadows. Overhead the storm abated and the sky cleared.

"Where have they taken him?" Asked Thomas. "To Avalon," replied Arthur. "He will be healed, as I was healed, and where you will one day be welcomed, if that is your wish Thomas. But now there are more important things to attend to."

Thomas noticed that Mordred's Knights and the body of Morgana had gone. Of the Bright Warriors and the Undead there was no sign, only the now quiet Circle and the Guardians. Merlin and Nimue had returned to Avalon with the others.

Father John was pale and sweating and Edna Pugh no better. But they took their places by the Stones. Arthur stood in the centre with Gawaine and Launcelot on either side and waited.

Across the dark moorlands came three figures. Two on either side of a slightly smaller man who walked with an air of authority. They approached the circle and stood at its edge.

John Foxton went forward and knelt before the centre man.

"Your Royal Highness, Charles, Phillip, Arthur, George, the Future King of these Islands, we, the Guardians greet you. Be welcome." He rose and stepped back and the Prince entered the Circle alone. Arthur came forward now, Launcelot and Gawaine at his back. Smiling, the two men assessed each other, then Arthur Pendragon held out his hand and the new Arthur clasped it firmly. Thomas was summoned, came forward and knelt to give fealty to the man who would one day be his king. Then he returned to the Mage stone and the ceremony began.

The Guardians began the Cadence that would open the King's Chamber. Three base notes in the Baritone range boomed out, joined a few seconds later by three altos. This was repeated and then joined by three ascending Tenor notes. The next repeat began and was augmented by three soprano voices in a minor key. The last repeat was crowned by the pure A of the Magus Note from Thomas.

The Singing Stones answered with the same cadence but in tones as deep as the earth itself. They rumbled and vibrated with intense power, one note beating against the other, swelling and lifting and filling the night with a harmony heard only once every hundred years.

There was a grating sound as the Mage stone slid sideways to reveal an opening into which steps descended into total darkness. Thomas took one of the torches and disappeared into the subterranean chamber. There was silence among the onlookers. Then the light returned as Thomas emerged carrying the Crown. He come to the centre of the circle and took his place beside Arthur.

Around the outside of the circle a mist began to form, and in it dim figures in flowing robes slowly appeared. Soft voices began to chant the *Non Nobis*, its richness of tone underlined by a choral descant of great beauty. Guenevere and the women came forward and removed the jacket of the prince and placed over his head a tunic of red silk emblazoned with the three golden lions of the Royal Arms.

The two men in the centre faced each other with their supporters behind them as the Guardians brought forward their treasures and, introduced by Father John offered them to their rightful owner.

"Ian Atkinson, keeper of the King's Chain of Office."

Ian took the chain and placed it about the neck of the new Arthur and kissed his hand in fealty

"Marjory Atkinson, keeper of the King's Ring."

Margery placed it upon his finger and kissed his hand.

"Leslie Lovell, keeper of the King's Sword belt and Scabbard."

Les came forward and saluted then belted the scabbard about him, and paid fealty

"Ben Warrener, keeper of the King's Orb.

Ben knelt and offered the ancient symbol to the royal hand and paid fealty.

And so it went on, each Guardian delivered up the treasure that had been guarded by generation after generation to the new Pendragon of Britain. The Royal Seal, The Spurs, The Sceptre, The Sword was placed into its scabbard and the Shield on his arm. The Horn that had summoned Arthur joined them.

Then John Foxton came with the Ampulla of oil and anointed him to his great office on head, breast, and hands.

Then all stood back as Thomas came forward with the crown and offered it first to Arthur Pendragon. He blessed it and placed it briefly on his own head, then returned it to Thomas. He could feel the power that filled it and knew a great love and also pity for the man who would wear it. He felt he could understand a small part of the tremendous burden that came with its wearing.

The young man, no longer a boy, solemnly paced forward and stood before the one to be crowned. The Prince knelt before what that crown represented, and bowed his head. Thomas raised it on high and gently brought it down and settled it upon the head of its rightful wearer. The Future King rose and turned to face those who had kept faith with that crown for over a thousand years and as one voice they hailed him.

Viva!, Vivat! Vivat !Rex Britannicus. Vivat Arturus Caput Draconis!

That cry of acclamation was echoed by those who walk the Second Road, the Faerie, the Sidhe and the ones who came before them, and who had gathered to share this moment.

Vivat, Vivat, Vivat Rex Britannicus. Vivat Arturus Caput Draconis!

Lastly came a deep cry from the Singing Stones themselves as they acclaimed the rightful heir. As they had done throughout their long existence they hailed the Once and Future King.

Vivat, Vivat, Vivat Rex Britannicus. Vivat Arturus Caput

Draconis!

Arthur watched and listened smiling, then held out his hand to Guenevere. Together they passed into the dawn light with Barnaby following behind and as they went, the small form of the dwarf shifted and became straight and strong. He paused and looked back at Thomas and smiled, then followed his beloved Queen into the growing light of dawn.

The sun rose on Lammas Day, its rays bathing the new Pendragon, As it touched the gleaming regalia each piece melted into his body to become a living part of him and his sacred mission. Just the ring remained, and that would never leave him. After more than a thousand years the task of the Guardians had come to its appointed end. The Task of the new Archmage was just beginning.

EPILOGUE

The Dales Courier. August 2nd.

It is with great sadness that the Courier announces the death of two of Deepdale's best known and respected locals. Father John Foxton B.Sc. M.A. Ph.D. of the Priory School for Boys. Passed away peacefully in his sleep last night. A memorial service will be held at the School on the first day of the New Term.

Ms. Edna Pugh. Much loved teacher of the Deepdale Primary School passed away early this morning in Stockton Hospital. Cause of death was given as pneumonia. Funeral Details later.

In the chapel of the Manor House Drew comforted the distraught Thomas as best he could;

"He was willing to be the sacrifice Thomas. He had said

goodbye to his children days before. Edna was already frail in health and knew she would be at risk. I knew at least two would be taken and offered to be one of them, so did Stan but John refused. He said I had to look after you. Be glad for him Thomas."

They sat in silence for a while absorbing the healing atmosphere of the chapel, then rose to leave. At the door Thomas stopped and looked back at the altar, and for a fleeting moment saw Father John standing with the Four Guardians he had raised, he smiled and lifted a hand in farewell, then all faded into the sunlight coming through the stained glass window.

Outside in the sunlight Steven Greystone was waiting for them, a Jack Russell puppy wriggling and yipping in his arms.

"I thought you might like a bit of company Thomas," he said smiling.

This is not the end of the story. To become the Archmage of Britain Thomas must undergo a long and hard training, and there is one who would oppose him. Read that story in 'The Hill of Dreams.' Then if you want to know how he met with Arthur and Mordred again, you will have to wait for 'The Ring of Swords.'

LET ME BRING LIGHT

Words and music by Dolores Ashcroft-Nowicki
Musical notation by Peter Bengtson

Dolores Aschroft-Nowicki is a third generation psychic who has worked with magic since childhood. She studied under the late W. E. Butler and with him was a founding member of the Servants of the Light School of Occult Science. She travels the world lecturing on all aspects of the occult and is the author of many successful books, including *The Shining Paths, Inner Landscapes, Illuminations, The Ritual Magic Workbook and First Steps in Ritual.*

Future publications to watch out for:

Temples of the Zodiac (audio)
The Jeweled Body (audio)
Journey Through the Tarot (audio)
SOL Tarot (reprint of original deck)
The Turquoise Bridge (book)
Royal Road of the Tree (audio)
Illuminations (audio)
Living in the Light (autobiography)